LOVE, DEATH, AND OTHER INCONVENIENCES

HORROR STORIES OF LOVE AND LOSS

HAUNTED HOUSE
PUBLISHING

Love, Death, and Other Inconveniences
First Edition February 2018

CONTENTS

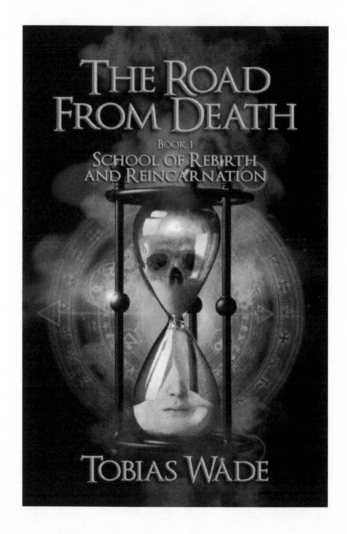

FORWARD

"The real problem here is that we're all dying. All of us. Every day the cells weaken and the fibers stretch and the heart gets closer to its last beat. The real cost of living is dying, and we're spending days like millionaires: a week here, a month there, casually spunked until all you have left are the two pennies on your eyes.

Personally, I like the fact we're going to die. There's nothing more exhilarating than waking up every morning and going 'WOW! THIS IS IT! THIS IS REALLY IT!' It focuses the mind wonderfully. It makes you love vividly, work intensely, and realize that, in the scheme of things, you really don't have time to sit on the sofa in your pants watching Homes Under the Hammer.

Death is not a release, but an incentive. The more focused you are on your death, the more righteously you live your life. Only when the majority of the people on this planet believe – absolutely – that they are dying, minute by minute, will we actually start behaving like fully sentient, rational and compassionate beings. For whilst the appeal of 'being good' is strong, the terror of hurtling, unstoppably, into unending nullity is a lot more effective. I'm really holding out for us all to get The Fear. The Fear is my Second Coming. When everyone in the world admits they're going to die, we'll really start getting some stuff done."

-Caitlin Moran

LET ME IN

Blair Daniels

I woke up to my daughter crying at 4 AM.

That's a horror story in itself, right?

Unfortunately, it gets worse.

Let me start from the beginning. My husband, Michael, and I live in the rural town of H____, Michigan. We have a 5-week-old daughter named Riley. She's doing well, but wakes up several times a night. Every. Single. Night.

Thankfully, on weekend nights Michael takes baby duty. He's amazing— he gives her a bath, reads her a story, rocks her, and puts her to sleep. And he sleeps right in the nursery with her. The only thing he's bad at? Singing lullabies—he's completely tone-deaf. (I usually shut the door when he gets to that part.)

So, last night when I heard the baby crying at the ungodly hour of 4 AM, I assumed Michael was on it. I rolled over, and tried to fall back asleep.

But she continued wailing.

Waaaaah. Waaaaah.

I pulled the covers over my head.

Waaaaaaaaaaaaaah.

I turned up my white noise to full blast.

Waaa—aaaaaa—aaaaahhhh!

I jolted up. Dammit, Michael, are you even trying to calm her down?! I heaved myself out of bed, threw on my robe, and opened the door.

Waaaaah. Waaaaah.

I froze in the doorway.

The cries weren't coming from her room.

They were coming from downstairs.

I peered down: dim, golden light shone across the floor, coming from the living room. "Michael?" I called.

No response, other than a blood-curdling waaaaaaaaaaaaaah.

"Is everything okay?" I shouted, louder this time. The shadows shifted across the floor, but no answer. I took a step down—footsteps, coming from her room.

I froze.

The doorknob turned—

Michael walked out of the bedroom, rubbing his eyes, his mouth wide with a yawn.

"You left Riley downstairs alone?! What's wrong with you?!" I began running down the stairs, my robe flying behind me—

He grabbed my arm.

"That isn't Riley."

"What are you talking about?!"

"Ssssshhh." He pushed his door open. I turned, and my heart began to pound. In the dim light I could see a little pink bundle, rising and falling with each breath.

I held my breath. Slowly, I backed up the stairs, careful to not make even the quietest creak.

He pulled me into the bedroom. Click—he shut the door. Click—he locked it, dragging a chair in front.

"Maybe it's just the baby next door," I said, trying to calm myself.

"The Johnsons live a quarter mile away."

I looked at him, my eyes wild. "Maybe it's—"

"It was coming from downstairs, Catie. You and I both heard it." He began pushing the dresser. It didn't budge. "There's someone down there."

"But—"

"Ssshhh!" Michael held a finger to his lips.

The wailing continued.

"Hear that?" he whispered.

"Yes, I hear the screaming baby."

"No. There's a pattern. Two short cries, then a long cry, then a raspy cry."

"So?"

He turned to me, his eyes wide. "It's a recording."

I felt the breath catch in my throat.

"Someone's down there, playing a recording of a baby crying?" I said, incredulously. "Why?"

"Isn't it obvious?" With a grunt, he pushed the dresser; it wobbled, and shifted maybe half an inch across the carpet. "To lure us out there."

Waaaaaah.

I jumped. But it was only Riley crying, woken by our loud whispers. Michael swooped her up, singing a terribly off-key rendition of Brahm's lullaby in her ear.

"We need to call 911," I said, feeling my pocket. "My phone. Where's my phone?! I must have left it in the other bedroom—"

In the soft moonlight, Michael was pale as a ghost. "And mine's out of battery..."

"Maybe we can get out the window," I said. Shaking, I wrenched it open. The cool breeze blew in, and the forest was black as ever. Our only neighbors —the Johnsons—were too far away, and the drop... just looking down made my stomach turn. The lawn bench looked like it belonged to dolls; the barren garden beds were like tiles on a checkerboard. "What do we do?"

"I'll get your phone."

"What? You just said yourself—someone is out there!"

"Your door is five feet across the hallway. I'll make it across before they can get upstairs."

"Michael—no—"

"The dresser's too heavy to move across the door. The chair isn't good enough. Sooner or later, they're going to come upstairs, kick down the door, and who knows what. I'm going." He handed Riley to me. "Wish me luck."

Before I could stop him, he opened the door.

And as soon as he did—

The cries stopped.

I froze, clinging to the crib. They know you're out there! I screamed, internally. I rushed to the door, gripping the knob, ready for Michael to rush back inside –

Thump.

A footstep, at the base of the stairs.

Thump. Thump.

Slow, heavy footsteps, growing louder and faster—the unmistakable sound of someone running up the stairs—

Thump! A crash, a yelp of pain—

Michael dashed back in. I slammed the door shut.

Thump.

The door rattled.

Thump. Thump.

The hinges groaned.

"Let me in!"

My eyes widened.

It was Michael's voice.

"Hey! Leave us alone!" Michael shouted, holding me close.

"Catie! It's me!" Thump, thump. "Let me in!"

I looked at Michael. "That sicko must've recorded my voice," he whispered, handing me the phone.

"Whoever that is – it's not me!" The voice cracked with desperation.

"Get out of our house!"

"Catie—please—it's me!"

Michael grabbed the dresser. Groaning, he dragged it across the door. The pounding grew louder, faster; the cries grew frenzied and shrill, becoming a blood-curdling scream—then silence.

By the time the police arrived, he seemed to be gone.

"We'll dust for fingerprints and run it through our database," one of the

officers told us, "but most people are smart enough to wear gloves these days." They gave us paperwork, phone numbers, and left.

After checking the locks for the hundredth time, we sat down on the bed. Riley, severely overtired like both of us, began to wail.

"Can you put her to sleep? I'm exhausted," I said, rubbing my eyes.

"Of course." He lay Riley across his chest, rocking her slowly. I stumbled across the hallway to my bedroom. The sun was just rising over the pine trees; bright golden rays shone through the window, lighting up the room. Sighing in relief, I collapsed onto the bed, and closed my eyes.

Across the hall, I could hear Michael's soft voice singing: "Lullaby, and good night... go to sleep now, little Riley..."

Perfectly on key.

MAGNUM OPUS

Jesse Clarke

"Shit, man. You headin' outta town, or something?"

"No."

"You sharin', then? Your buddies better be liftin' part of the cost."

"Nope. Not sharing."

"Okay… you ain't skippin' town an' you ain't sharin.' So what's the deal with you buyin' in bulk all've sudden?"

"Don't worry about it, Phil."

He handed me the bag with the Opus but he kept his hand on it.

"You ain't tryin' ta use this all at once, are ya?"

"I said don't worry about it."

"Look, man, I gots like, an obligation to make sure you ain't gonna try an' do that. So make me a promise. You know this stuff. You know what it does."

"Yeah, its the deadliest drug in the world, Phil, and you sell it for a living. Since when do you care about responsibility?"

"I dunno, man. I just… don't wanna lose a good customer, is all, you know? That's $600."

I handed him all the money I had left in the world, not like it mattered. Then I took the bag and walked the three blocks past the bakery and the bent lamp post and up to my apartment for the last time. There was another eviction notice on the door, not like it mattered, but I pushed past it.

I threw the haul onto the old table by the chair, took out the baggie of Opus, crushed the brick with a knife and set up the rig. It's a bit like heroin in how you fix up a dose. You melt it, then you tie off and stick the needle into whatever vein there was left to be found. Then you push it down and watch the drug swirl with your blood for a bit, which is beautiful in its own, sick way—and then you push it in the skin.

And that's where it differentiates from heroin. With heroin you feel a rush of warmth, but with Opus you just feel cold. If you ever see a scrawny son-of-a-bitch curled up and shivering on a park bench on a summer afternoon, you can bet with an appreciable degree of confidence that he's either got the shakes or he's gotten his hands on a bit of Opus.

And then after that passes? That's when you feel really, really good. Words can't describe it, to be thoroughly honest, although 'euphoria' is the one word people like to pick off the low hanging branch. All that can be said is that when it hits you in all its force and all it's momentum and all it's breathtaking might, you can't speak or move or even think. You just lay there and bathe in the majesty of it all, even as your organs scream, until you pass out. It's a basal pleasure that needs to be experienced to be believed. But stay the hell away from it, and all that. Blah blah blah…

Not like it matters. It's what comes after the euphoria that counts anyway.

So I did my business. And I felt the rush, I felt that old euphoria, and then I felt the black clouds swirl in. My vision tunneled, and soon I was floating away on a dead river, clinging to the last bit of flotsam adrift from a monumental shipwreck. And then I was gone.

Hang on, Jess. I'm coming.

∽

You know what's a funny expression? Being 'beside yourself.' I've always understood what it means, of course: you're beside yourself when you're heartbroken, or traumatized, or angry beyond what words can articulate. You haven't learned yet how to cope with spectacular pain. But until you're actually 'beside yourself,' hearing the expression doesn't make sense, even if you don't ruminate on its implications. Is there supposed to be another one of me who shares in pain that's too intense for either one of us to bear? Is that what it means to be beside yourself? I didn't know.

But I found out.

It turns out, interestingly, that being 'beside yourself' is what happens when your world comes crashing down, but you react not with rage or sorrow but with numbness. Its like you're watching yourself go through the motions of grieving but you can't actually feel anything because of this emotional firewall that your brain, in all its finite wisdom, erected. You're in shock: like its someone else whose life was just turned upside-down and not yours, an out-of-body experience, and you're just along for the ride.

Nothing feels real. The police telling you she's gone? Fake. It has to be, and therefore it is. Phone calls flooding in? Loved ones saying how sorry they are for your loss? Lies. But you go through the motions anyway. And you say 'thanks. Yeah, I'm doing okay. No, I don't need anything. I don't know when the funeral is. I'll let you know.' And all the affairs and the proceedings and the weeping and the disbelief that follow are just part of a weird, twisted dream.

Its not real. It can't be.

But deep down, of course, you know it's real. Deep down you know there's an avalanche of pain and anguish and hurt—more of it all than the human spirit was ever built to catalog—waiting like a dragon on the other side of that firewall. And eventually—maybe on the first night you crawl into bed alone, or maybe not until her favorite movie comes on and she's not there to share it with you, or when you hear that old song 'Firelight' on the radio that played when you first kissed her and you thought to yourself how did a guy like me get a girl like her?—maybe that dragon will find its way in. There's no going back from that. You're a new man now. And a lesser one than you once were.

That's when you truly learn what it means to be beside yourself; when the real you and the you that was just going through the motions of grief collide into one gigantic, shattered, sobbing mess. You don't care what you look like when it happens. You don't care where you are, or who's watching, or what they'll think, and that's because you can't. One minute you're doing okay, and the next all the power of your spirit and all your strength of arms are being spent on weathering a storm that can't be weathered. Enduring the unendurable. Accepting the unacceptable.

She's gone. And she's not coming back.

For me it happened at Jessie's funeral. Before that I'd been a robot, but as soon as everyone left (even her parents) and I was the only one standing there on the grass? I lost it. The finality of it all hit me like a storm of fists and the firewall broke down. The dragon swept in. And I just collapsed at the headstone and cried until it hurt, and then I cried some more. My best friend. My partner in crime. My girl. Gone, along with a piece of me.

It's an impossible and surreal experience to describe; its mutilating and unfair, and yet it is what it is. Life goes on without you, no matter how hard you scream at it: 'I'M HURTING HERE, GIVE ME A FUCKING SECOND, WILL YOU?!' And you're sinking, and drowning, and you're throwing your arms out for a life-line, and all bets are off. When that life-line comes, if it ever does, you take it. It doesn't matter what it is.

"It's called Magnum Opus," Ronnie had said, in the middle of the bar as if he were selling me car insurance and not a Schedule 1 felony.

"Magnum Opus?"

"Yeah. Got me through my break-up with Ash. Stuff is fucking phenomenal, Mark, I swear to God." I should have noted his emaciated physique, scraggly beard, and his unemployment and thought: well it sure doesn't look like you got through it in one piece, Buddy. But I didn't; the logical part of me had been on hiatus for twenty nine days at that point (yes, I counted), and I didn't know if it was ever coming back.

"What's it like?"

"You get this cold rush when you inject it. Then you just feel fuckin' awesome. Can't even really describe it to you, bro—you just gotta try it."

"Sounds kind of like heroin, except for the cold rush."

"Nah, man. Heroin's great, don't get me wrong, but its just physical. Opus was made for stuff like this."

"Stuff like what?"

"Loss."

I blinked.

"Yeah. Some hallucinogenic property, or somethin' or other. Its real attached to your emotions, so if you're going through some shit it plays on that and you get these like, visions."

"Visions, huh?"

"Yeah. For me, I saw Ash every time I hit it, and it was all healing and stuff. And I know a guy who lost his dad and when he took it, dude, he was like havin' catches and going to baseball games with his old man. I mean it was all in his head, but its so real you can't tell the difference."

I should have said: 'Not interested, thanks,' and left right then and there. But I didn't.

"How much is it?"

"It ain't cheap, bro. But I know a guy who slings it for fuckin' pennies on the dollar. C'mon, I'll take you there."

~

Phil is a weird looking son-of-a-bitch, to say the least. I think he has maybe twelve teeth left (all yellow), weighing in at a hundred and twenty pounds soaking wet. He's covered ankle to jawline in tribal tattoos. Also, he's at least fifty, balding on top yet still sporting a silver-streak pony tail with a road-map of wrinkles. As far as I can tell, the dude lives in the alley he sells from despite easily pulling in upper five figures doing the actual selling. Ronnie spoke up first.

"Yo, Phil! You got anything for me?"

Phil looked me over and took mental note of how out of place I was—no tattoos, no piercings, short haircut—and then said: "Who's you're friend? I ain't lookin' to git busted."

"Nah, Mark's cool, bro. Just lost his girl so he's all like, in pain an' stuff. Think you can hook him up?"

"Sure, man. Newbie special: one bag for $125. More where that came from."

I snorted. "Shit, $125?"

"Yeah, man! Told you Phil could hook you up. That's a fuckin' steal."

"I wouldn't pay that much for a used phone, Ronnie. I'm not paying it for this shit." I turned around and started walking away, but then Ronnie said: "You wanna see Jess again, right?"

I stopped. God dammit. I would pay $125 for that. I think I'd pay all the money in the world, in fact. I turned around.

"You promise me this'll work? Phil?"

"Yeah, it works, brother. Believe it; I'd be a fuckin' dead man if it didn't."

Ronnie took me back up to his place and got me a rig—a spoon, syringe, tourniquet, and a lighter—and he cooked up a shot and tied me off. I was fresh meat and my heart was pounding, so finding a vein to hit was as easy as it'd ever be.

"Its ready? Just like that?"

"Just like that, man."

"And its all melted, and everything?"

"Will you just trust me, bro? I got you. Been doin' this for a year and change. Make a fist."

"Okay, okay. Just nervous, is all."

"Make a fist, I said. Good."

He found the vein and cleaned the spot with a swab.

"What will it feel like?"

"Guess you're about to find out, ain'tcha?"

I didn't get a chance to respond before he stuck the needle in. Then the rush hit me in a tidal wave—frigid cold at first, and then a euphoric sensation the likes of which, like I said above, can not adequately be described. I said and thought and knew nothing anymore; I just curled up into a ball and rode the wave right into the emptiness.

~

"Firelight's on again, Markie."

"You know I hate it when you call me that."

"That's why I do it. To get a rise out of you. Markie."

I punched Jess lightly on the arm.

"Hey! You're gonna knock me off the hood."

"Better stop calling me 'Markie,' then, Big Red, or else you'll fall right off the cliff-side."

"Scrawny little bitch like you? I'm pretty sure I could take you down."

"Oh, yeah? Hundred bucks says I pin you in a minute flat."

She didn't even say 'you're on'—she just pounced on me and grabbed my wrists and tried to put me in a hold. It was adorably ineffective; I wriggled out with ease and got her by the waist and crawled on top of her.

"Say uncle!"

"Aunt."

"Alright! You asked for it. Ladies and gentlemen, the Crippler!" I made fake cheering noises, patted my elbow, and pretended to bring it down on her chest.

"Hahaha, the 'Crippler?!' That's the wrestler name you came up with?"

"You're just jealous I thought of it first. 'Crippler' is the shit and you know it."

"All I know is that you probably kiss like a girl, too, Mr. Crippler."

I leaned down and took the bet, and I kissed her. It only lasted a second. But the first kiss sticks with you the longest, after all, and when I pulled back we just stared at each other: her up at me in front of the whole night sky, with the band of the Milky Way reaching across it, and the cliffsides hit back by starlight, and me back down at her, lying there on the banged up, red-rusted hood of my car. I had the better view, by far, and I thought, 'how did a guy like me get a girl like her?'

I woke up on Ronnie's hardwood floor the next morning amidst an ocean of empty bottles and pizza boxes and vomit. It took me a second to piece back where I was and all that'd happened, and it utterly broke my heart when I remembered it wasn't more than a narcotic dream. But what a dream it was! In spite of the heartache and the headache, the dizziness and the thirst, I crawled over to Ronnie and shook him awake.

"Holy shit, man. Get me more of that stuff. Now."

"Mmmmph—what?"

"The Opus, man! I need more of it."

"Mmmmmph-you know where Phil is." His head fell back to the floor and he dozed off again. He was right. I knew exactly where Phil was, and after I called in sick to work I headed straight down to his alley, aching and groaning the whole way. I told my own broken heart she's real enough; she's back, even if it was just a dream. I was only one dose away from her. I got to the alley fifteen minutes later, and I don't think Phil had moved an inch.

"Back for more?"

"Yeah, that stuff was incredible, man. Give me another bag." I handed him $125 fresh from the ATM on 7th, but instead of taking it, he scoffed.

"Heh—like I said, man, $125 a bag was the newbie special.

Returnin' customers ain't eligible for that discount. Two hundred dollars."

"Two hundred dollars for a bag?! Are you fuckin' crazy?"

"Nope. An' it don't matter how mad y'are, either. You'll buy it anyway. Just you watch; this shit don't let go so easy."

He was right, dammit. Of course he was right. I sighed and shook my head, but I gave him the cash and I don't think there was even a fleeting second where I wasn't going to. There were very few things I wouldn't do, in fact, for another trip back into that dream. I got the little baggie and went the three blocks back to my apartment this time, past the bakery and the bent lamp-post, and when I got inside I cooked up the shot. I was in love all over again, and it was every bit as wonderful and every bit as terrible as love is supposed to be.

～

"So why do you love these old movies, again?"

"Because they're classics, Mark," Jessie said. "Show some respect when Jack Lemmon is on screen, will you? At least for me?"

"Okay, okay. It's not like I don't appreciate the stuff; It's just not for me, is all."

"How do you appreciate something that's not for you? That doesn't even make sense."

"Sure it does. I respect it. I admire it for its influence and all that."

"Ugh. People say that all the time, and its bullshit. Do you know what influence means? It means people looked at something and they said, 'hey, that's new and weird and beautiful, I think I'll try that next.' Nothing sets out to be that way. It just sets out to be the best version of itself, and every once in a while its best is enough to break down walls and barriers, sometimes completely by accident, and everyone else will try to get even a small piece of it so they can be great, too. But there's only ever one original. So all those movies you like, and all those TV shows and all the music? It can all be traced back to one moment in one person's head where a little bit of color first stood out amongst all the dull gray and they said, 'hey, that's new and weird and beautiful. I think I'll see where it goes.'"

"Oh, my God. Okay—we'll watch your stupid, 'new and weird and beautiful' Jack Lemmon movie."

"So I win?"

"You win."

She reached up and gave me a peck and then said, for the first time, "I love you."

And all of a sudden I was willing to watch whatever stupid, new and weird and beautiful movie she wanted.

I woke up in my bed. When the reality hit back—it was just a dream, fuck—my heart broke all over again. And she felt further away than ever. As she always did.

It'd been seven weeks of this. Every morning after I woke up and I realized that the adventure the night before was all in my head, it ripped me a fresh wound right in the heart of my spirit. Every day was like finding out she was gone all over again, but the solution to it all was, of course, another hit. Another dose. Another four hundred dollars a day (that bastard 'tolerance' necessitated a doubling down of the dose for the same effect).

Anything and everything that I could do to spend as much time in my fantasy world as possible, I would do. I would do it gladly and willingly. I paid what I had to. I hadn't been to work at all since Ronnie took me to Phil that night, and since then my savings had flown the coop. My credit card was maxed, and I'd ignored a combined sixty one missed calls from worried-sick friends and family. And yes, I counted.

But I didn't care about any of it. All I cared about was my Jessie, and our brief but precious moments together in a world that wasn't real but everything was okay, if only for a bit. I told myself, over and over until I truly believed it, that pain and suffering and poverty in one world was more than an acceptable enough price to pay for true joy in another one. So on and on I went.

KNOCK KNOCK KNOCK.

The sound of a rap on the door gave me a splitting headache, but I got up and opened it anyway and let the blinding sunlight hit me and my flat for the first time in days. The man on the other side, a mid-twenty something from the looks of it, gasped audibly when he saw my emaciated physique, scraggly beard, and obvious unemployment, as evidenced by the eviction notice on the door and the tracks on my arms. I spoke first.

"Yeah?"

"H-hey, uhm—hey. I saw the ad online about the flat-screen. That still for sale?"

"Yeah, it's here. Three hundred."

"Would you take two?"

"I'll take three. If I was willing to haggle I would've put 'OBO' in the ad. Take it or leave it."

I desperately hoped he'd take it and go. I needed the cash. But I needed three hundred, not two, since I'd only gotten a hundred when I pawned the phone.

"Okay, okay. I'll take it." He handed me a wad of bills and I helped him carry it out to his car. When he peeled off, I didn't even head back upstairs. I just pocketed the money and went straight past the bent lamp post and the bakery and down to you-know-where to get my next hit.

My head was spinning, but I didn't feel a damn thing. I just felt empty. And confused. It was dark in my room, and hot. Dark and hot. Rarely a good combination. Jessie was nowhere to be found, but then again that was the whole point, wasn't it? Fuck. I collapsed right down on the bed—queen-sized with a dip on the left that wouldn't ever be filled again.

I didn't sleep. Not tonight. I stayed up and tried to reconcile the fact that those officers were wrong with the fact that Jessie was now three hours late coming home. They'd told me why, but they were wrong. They had to be. My girl isn't dead. She isn't. She couldn't be, and therefore she isn't. She was just late getting home. She'd be here, right? Any second now, she'd walk through that door and everything would be okay. Everything would go back to normal. And I'd be waiting for her, right here on the bed.

It's gonna be okay. She's gonna be okay. I'm gonna be okay.

The door indeed opened a few minutes later, but instead of Jessie swirled in the darkness of the hallway. In an instant my heart rose and fell, and then the old familiar chill set in. There were a pair of eyes in there too. Red ones. Scowling ones. Ones I recognized; ones that visited me all too often and that got a little closer each time. I pulled the covers up over me, shut my eyes, and tried to ignore the voices, but they weren't dampened by my quilt.

"You haven't called," said my mother, right into my ear. "Why haven't you called? Your father and I are worried sick."

"Look at you," dad said. "Pathetic. Jobless. Starving. Unkempt. Penniless. Futureless. You've sold or abandoned everything of value. You should be fucking ashamed of yourself. Why can't you be more like your brother? He'd never do that to your mother and I."

Ronnie then said: "Dude, you're losin' yourself to this drug. You gotta be careful when you hit the needle. Doesn't matter what it is. You're not bein' careful. Not even I got down as deep as you."

I shuddered and cried and begged and prayed for it to stop. For it to go away. But of course it couldn't—not yet—because that's when Jessie showed up: three hours late, like she always was. When I heard her voice I burst into fresh tears and shuddered and squeezed my eyes shut so hard I thought they'd bleed.

"Look what you're becoming, Mark. I fell in love with a man with ambition. Intelligence. Humor. He loved life. But he died tonight, too."

I threw the covers off and screamed into the darkness: "FUCK YOU! GET OUT. GET OUT. GET OUT. GET OUT."

But the voice didn't stop, and soon the dragon stepped into my room. A step of confidence; then one of boldness, hot and snarling, to stand at the foot of my bed and say in Jessie's voice:

"Him I loved, Mark. But I don't love you. This is your fault. You could've saved me. This is your fault. This is your fault. This is your fault. This is your fault. This is—"

~

I bolted upright. It was morning, of course, and spread around me were liquor bottles and the rig. Of course. It was another dream, just a vision. It wasn't real. Dragons aren't real, either, but words are, regardless of where you hear them.

You should be fucking ashamed of yourself. Why can't you be more like your brother?

Him I loved, Mark. But I don't love you.

Pathetic. Jobless. Emaciated. Unkempt. Penniless. Futureless.

But I don't love you.

I don't love you.

The words played on a loop in my head. I took a swig, but they only got louder. I grabbed the baggie to see if even a little more Opus was in there. Enough at least to snort if not shoot, but it was gone. Of course it was gone; why wouldn't it be gone? I was good at one thing and one thing only, and that was getting every last molecule of this venom in my veins where it belonged. Why would I leave anything behind?

I don't love you.

I curled up again into a ball and cried a bit.

Futureless. Futureless. Futureless. Futureless.

They were right.

I don't love you.

Nobody did. I'd ruined everything. I'd burned every bridge. Fuck, I'd sold every bridge and etched them into tracks on my forearm. That's what I'd done. Fuck me. Fuck me.

Futureless.

I know.

I don't love you.

I know. I don't either.

I never did.

I guess I knew that, too.

Pathetic.

I stood up. Everything hurt. My head swam. My lips were so dry they cracked and bled. Not like it mattered. I looked down at the needle.

You're never gonna win, Mark. I've got you. Palm of my hand.

I know.

You're a dead man, Mark.

I know.

Do it. I know what you're thinking. Do it. Today. Just get it done. Do one right thing, just one, if you can manage it.

I will. I grabbed my jacket.

"Shit, man. You headin' outta town, or something?"

"No."

"You sharin', then? Your buddies better be liftin' part of the cost."

"Nope. Not sharing."

I went home and pushed past the eviction notice and threw the baggie on the old table by the chair. Then I cooked up my shot—a massive, lethal motherfucker of a dose. I tied off and found a vein after a good few minutes of hide-and-seek. And I stopped.

Am I really doing this?

I am. I was. So I did. I pushed the needle in and watched my blood swirl with it before being consumed by the blackness. I pushed it down into the skin. Freezing, aching cold. A rush of quantified, atomized pleasure, and then the black clouds swirled in. My vision tunneled, and soon I was floating away on a dead river, clinging to the last bit of flotsam adrift from a monumental shipwreck. And then I was gone.

Hang on, Jess. I'm coming.

∽

"Hey."

"Hey."

"Funny seeing you here so soon."

I blinked. I didn't remember this conversation.

"I don't remember this."

"Well it hasn't happened before."

"Huh. Big enough dose'll do that, I guess."

"Yeah. You can say that again." She looked around the swirling, endless clouds in which we stood, as if she, too, were new to this place. She looked back at me and said: "What are you doing here, Mark?"

"I don't know where here is, Jess. So how could I possibly answer that?"

"I think you do."

Maybe I did.

"I'll ask again. What are you doing here? What led you here?"

"You did."

"I did? You wanna explain that one to me?"

"I don't know. You were gone. So I followed you here, like I always do."

"You didn't always do that. You had a life of your own once, Mark. It was good. It was rich. You had a future. Why are you here?"

"I wanted to see you again. Is that such a crime?"

"Well. Here I am. Was it worth it?"

"Its always worth it."

"Not even you believe that."

She walked up a bit closer and looked at me with those big, ocean blue eyes that made my knees buckle, even now. She took my hand in hers and held it. It felt real. It felt warm. I wasn't used to that—warmth. I pulled back a bit, but she tightened her grip and then rolled my sleeve up to the elbow, exposing my forearm and all the cuts on it. All the bruises, all the tracks. Fuck. She stared at the mess for a second.

"I didn't want you to find out about that, Jess."

"Well its a little late for that. This isn't you, Mark. Why didn't you just say no?"

"Because I didn't, okay? It was offered to me, and I was still reeling from losing you, and I made an impulse decision. But this stuff is different! Its not just a physical high, Jess. It brought you back. It brought back everything I loved about you. One hit and fuck—we were right back on the road again with the windows down and the music blasting and the sunset coming up over the hilltops. We didn't know where we were going, and we didn't care as long as we were going there together. For a few hours every day everything was okay again. How could I say no to that?"

"It brought me back, did it?"

"Yes."

"Did it bring back the first fight?"

"What?"

"Our first fight. Remember that one? Do you remember me throwing your Econ textbook at the fridge and knocking down the magnet with the little dog on it? Or you just storming out while I sat on the couch and cried? Did it bring that back?"

"N-no. I don't think it did. Maybe."

"Did it bring back the time you hinted that you didn't like my new haircut, and how I gave you the cold shoulder for like, three days straight?"

"No."

"Did it bring back the time we had that stupid fucking fight about Jack Lemmon?"

"Yes! Yes. It did, and it wasn't a fight. That was the day you said you loved me, Jess. I remember. And I was so happy you said it that I allowed us to watch that movie even though I wanted to watch Mulholland."

"You said it first."

"What?"

"'I love you.' You said that first, not me, at the bakery by your apartment. You said it, and I was so nervous that I didn't say it back until the next day. I texted it to you. I said 'hey, I love you too,' and you wrote out this little novel about how scared you were that you'd said it too soon and that you almost wanted to take it back so you wouldn't scare me away. Remember?"

"...Yeah."

"And we watched Mulholland that night."

Shit. She was right. We did.

"...Yeah, we did, didn't we?"

"Yep. But your little drug didn't bring that up."

"I guess not."

"Did it bring back, say, my loud chewing? You always made a point to mention it. I never had a meal after that without being self-conscious about how loud I chewed. Did it bring that back from the dead, too?"

"No."

"Or how fidgety I was? I could never get comfortable, remember? 'Jessie, go to sleep. Stop moving so much.' If I had a fucking nickel."

"What's your point?"

"My point? Mark I'm a human. A fully fleshed out actual person, not just an idea. Me with all my flaws and all my imperfections and my quirks and hopes and dreams. You want me to believe a fucking drug fleshed me out like that? Its a drug, Mark. It's not magic."

"Well whatever it did, it was enough."

"Well It shouldn't have been! Don't you get it? You shouldn't be able to just bring someone back like that. I'm more than memories, Mark. You of all people should know the difference between loving me and loving the idea of me. I mean, fuck—what does it say about me, about us—that you could just conjure up one good rose-tinted memory and be satisfied? You said yourself 'it brought back every-thing I loved about you.' Not 'and everything I didn't.'"

"I said 'it brought you back.'"

"You said both, and then we found out it didn't even do that right."

"Don't do that, Jess."

"Do what?"

"That. Don't you fucking dare insult me by implying that I didn't love you the right way. I'm a sick, wrecked bastard, but if there's one thing I did right in all the time I knew you it was love you so much that it spilled over. I loved everything and everyone else more because of it. And when you died? When you died, Jessie, I destroyed myself just to catch a fleeting glimpse of a shade of you. I didn't run away from the pain. I owed it to you to stay; to learn that pain inside and out, to let it roll over me in waves and fucking ruin me as a man until I couldn't recognize myself anymore. I owed you that much. And if that's not love, then I don't know what is."

We sat down on the edge of a cloud and looked out over infinity together. She put her head on my shoulder, and then she said: "I loved you, too."

"...You loved me?"

"Yeah. I loved the man you were."

"The man I was?! I'm the one who's still here!"

"No, you're not. This isn't you, Mark. Its not. And you know that. I think a part of you died that night with me, out there on the road."

I looked at the tracks on my arm. She was right. I hated it when she was right.

"I know you hate it when I'm right, but I'm right all the same, aren't I? Do you recognize yourself?"

"No."

"Do you recognize your own thoughts anymore?"

You're a dead man, Mark. Palm of my hand.

"No."

"Do you think that's what I wanted for you when I was gone?"

"No."

"Is it what you'd want for me? To be tortured over your death? To think 'fuck, if I'd only done this or that, I could've saved him!'"

"No."

She took my hand, for real this time. I felt life again. It'd been so long since I'd felt alive.

Thump.

"How did you do that?"

"Do what?"

"That. After everything I did, it was you who brought me back to life. How did you do that?"

Thump.

"I don't know. It only ever worked with you."

"And that says something, doesn't it?"

"Maybe."

"Maybe it means I'm still down there somewhere."

"I hope so, Mark, Because I haven't fallen out of love either."

Thump.

"Really?"

"Really." We sat there for a while before she said, "Can you do something for me, Mark?"

"I'd do anything for you. You know that."

"Can you let me go?"

Thump.

"I thought you said—"

"I did. That's why I'm asking this of you. There might not be a happily ever after for us, Mark, but there's still one out there for you. And as your best friend, as your partner in crime, as your girl, I want more than anything for you to find it."

"I... I don't know if I can."

"Do it for me."

Thump.

She leaned in and kissed me, and it seemed like all the clouds and all the stars were falling into line one last time. I felt a rush, I felt a heartbeat, and then I was gone.

Thump. Thump. Thump. Thump.

"Hey, hey! We got a pulse!"

I bolted upright and gasped so loud the EMTs stumbled back.

"Welcome back to life, Mr. King," one of them said. "You over-dosed on Opus."

"H-how long was I out?"

"Out? You were dead. Blue in the face, no pulse, dead. For at least fifteen minutes. You're lucky your buddy Phil gave us a call to check up on you."

I fell back to the bed. I felt terrible. Headache. Iron taste in the mouth, parched and bleeding. But I was alive. For the first time in as long as I could remember.

I signed the paperwork and checked out of the hospital when I could, and I took the long way home. I had no car. I had no money.

No job. No savings. Nothing. And when I got back to my apartment, it was an absolute wreck. An empty one, too. Everything was gone. The furniture. The bed. The TV. All sold or pawned for drug money. But I was alive; I had a future, and maybe, just maybe, Jessie was right. Maybe there was a happily ever after waiting for me out there some-where, and all I needed was to run up and seize it. The idea was new and weird and beautiful, and I thought, you know? I think I'll see where that goes. I threw the needle in the trash.

A SILVER LINING, IN THE DEATH OF STARS

Jesse Clarke

Those red lights are only making the pain worse. It is an immense, earth-shattering pain; I try to move, but I can't; I try to speak, but I can't do that either. It hurts too much.

But still there's movement. I can feel myself being lifted up and placed on something—a bed, maybe, or—no.

A gurney.

"Alright!" one of the EMTs says, and several others then roll me into the back of an ambulance and they climb in behind me. But I'm already fading out, and feeling an inexplicable heat by the time those doors are shut.

One EMT, a blonde woman, gives me a look, just as I'm slipping away, and she says aloud, "Wait. Wait, I think I know...

~

"...we're made of that stuff, right?"

I turned around. There was a woman there, red-haired and about my age, give or take, and she was alarmingly beautiful. But how long she'd been staring at the exhibit alongside me I had no idea.

"I'm sorry?"

"I said 'you know we're made of that stuff, right'?" She nodded at the museum wall, which depicted in detail the births and life cycle and deaths of stars. I pursed my lips.

"We're... made of stars?"

"Yep. Isn't it awesome?" She stepped up beside me and moved her arm across the diagram as she spoke. "I just watched a documentary about it last night. Stars are just fusion factories held together by their own gravity. They start off fusing hydrogen to helium, and then they keep going on and on, fusing heavier and heavier elements until they're fusing the heaviest stuff. Then they exhaust their fuel and collapse under their own weight, and they blow off their outer layers and pretty much shower the galaxy with all these random elements, some of which are eventually used to create life."

"Huh."

"Yeah. I'm Robin, by the way." She extended her hand, and I shook it.

"Uh, hey. Brian. Nice to meet you." There was an awkward pause before I said, "Alright, I got one for you. If you replaced the sun with a black hole, what would happen?"

"Depends on its mass."

"Nope! The answer is—drumroll please—nothing. I mean everything would get dark and cold, but we wouldn't fall in. Earth's orbit would remain entirely unaffected."

"IF the black hole had the same mass as the sun."

"What?"

"What you said would only be true if the black hole in question happened to have the same mass as the sun. Which it wouldn't, because the sun isn't massive enough to collapse into a black hole."

"Oh. Crap."

"Yep. Me one, you zero. Sorry, pal."

"Alright." I said. "You're on. Whoever gets the most points by closing time buys drinks."

She smiled at that and punched me in the shoulder, just light enough not to sting. "Alright, loser. Come..."

～

"...on, Rachel." the paramedic says. He's looking me over, and then he looks to another colleague - the blonde woman - and he shakes his head. "This one's gone."

But Rachel continues right on running her tests, running her diagnostics, and she places a soft hand on my arm in case I'm awake enough to appreciate the comfort. I am, barely. But yet again I'm fading out, and that heat is coming right on back as I do.

"Not yet he's not," she says. There's pain in her voice that she does her best to conceal. "I lost one earlier, Todd. I'm not losing..."

～

"... another one!" Robin said, and I agreed and we rushed to the back of the line.

I said, "Told you you'd like the Ferris Wheels. Can't believe you've never been on one before today."

She shrugged. "Never thought they were as extreme as roller coasters. So I wasn't interested."

"Well they're not supposed to be 'extreme.' Ferris Wheels are for parents waiting on their kids and sick people trying to relax their stomachs."

"And adorable young couples, apparently."

And just then we were waved into the next seat. We sat ourselves down, and moments later the wheel began to turn; it dragged our cart around its underside and then lifted it up, to the top of its crest, where we could see the whole city at twilight, and the ships in the harbor that were back-lit red from the setting sun, and the clouds that were lined at their tops with just a little bit of starlight. Robin got up next to me and put her head on my shoulder, and I put my arm around her waist. For a moment I could've sworn the empty seat in front of us moved on its own, and was about to mention it. But Robin spoke first.

"Thank you for being here with me," she said. And I kissed her on the head, as the Wheel began taking us...

~

"...down on the eighteen hundred block of Gardersdale," one of the paramedic says. "Yeah, Another one. I know. Hell of a night."

As the EMTs work I try to remember what's happened, but God does it hurt, almost as much as that rushing heat. The effort is disrupted further when the ambulance hits a bump in the road and I nearly spill out of the gurney. But Rachel puts her hand on my chest before I do and she says, "Hang in there, Brian. Almost..."

~

"...there!" Robin pointed at the interstate ramp, and I took the turn and put St. Thomas Vineyard away in the rear-view.

"Still can't believe Mason got married," I said. "He's only known that girl for what, a year? Less?"

Robin shrugged. "They were in love."

"They hardly knew each other! They don't know if whatever they're feeling is genuine, life-long love, or just new relationship googley-eyes that hasn't worn off yet. I guarantee it—and I'll put money on this—they'll be done within a year. Just watch."

"You don't know that," she said. There was a brief pause, and then she added, "We've been dating for two years."

"So?"

"So... how far off do you think we are?"

I shrugged. "I don't know. Haven't really thought about it."

"You haven't thought about it? At all?"

"I mean of course I've *thought* about it. I just... I don't know if we're ready, you know?" I looked over at her, but she just stared out there at the rain with her chin in her palm. So I continued.

"Think about it like this: people prepare their whole lives for jobs, right? They start going to school as soon as they can talk, and they're not done till they're in their twenties, and it's all so they can get a piece of paper that says 'hey, hire me, I'm smart enough to work.' But marriage? Nobody trains for that. People just hook up and say, 'hey we're twenty five, or twenty eight, you're cute, I'm cute. Let's spend thirty thousand dollars on a giant ceremony and then be glorified roommates for five years until we're both fat and hate each other and get divorced because neither one of us knew or cared how much work this thing would require."

There was a longer pause then, before she said, with a degree of seriousness I wasn't in the least prepared for, "Is that where you think we're headed? 'Glorified roommates?'"

Quickly I calculated an avenue of retreat. But I calculated wrong. "No! Not you," I said. "Not us. I mean most people, you know? Most people just dive in and either get divorced or stick it out till someone gets heart disease. The divorce rate is more than fifty percent now in the US. But the 'I-don't-love-you-anymore' rate? Shit, that's probably close to ninety by the time everyone hits middle age. I just want to make sure you're the right person, you know?"

If ever there were words I wish I could've taken back, it were those twelve. She said nothing, but I saw her reflection in the window, and the little tear that welled up in the corner of her eye said more than words ever could.

"Listen, I… that came out wrong. I just meant—"

"Can you drop me off at my car, please?"

"I thought you wanted to come over—?"

"I don't feel good. Please?"

And we drove in silence for a while, as the rain picked up its pace and fell in sheets torrents. After another twenty minutes I made the turn onto my street and parked, and once I did she got out without so much as a glance and walked across the road to her own car. I ran to follow.

"Robin, wait!" I grabbed her lightly by the arm. It was slick with rainwater. "Talk to me. Please?"

"What do you want?"

I blinked. "I want you to talk to me. I just s—"

"No. I mean with us. Where do you want this to go?"

"Where do I want this to go? I want to be with you! Listen, I didn't mean to imply that—that I don't want that. I just want us to be smart about it. You know?"

"Well maybe love isn't something you can calculate on a spread-sheet, Brian!" She was shouting over the cacophony of the storm. "Maybe it's just this thing you feel, you know? And maybe it doesn't make any logical sense. Maybe it's not supposed to. But that's part of what makes it special; it's an adventure; it's a 'jump off a cliff with me' type of thing. And yeah, sure. Not everyone survives the fall, I guess. But if you find the right person, then—"

"A 'jump off the cliff with me' type of adventure? Come on, Robin! We're not writing up a dating website profile here; this is real life! There are kids involved, and finances, and house buying, and mort-gages and all that shit! Not every day is some cute little romance comedy. This is half your life we're talking about. Two-thirds, even. Okay? All I meant was that you have to be prepared for it. I just—"

"I thought we were prepared."

"What do you mean?"

She dug through her purse for a moment, and then held up a ring that was brilliant even when covered in the rain. I felt my heart skip at least a full beat.

"Is that, um—"

"It was my mom's," she said. "She gave it to me before she died. She said, 'find your partner in crime, Robin. Find someone who'll sweep you off your feet and jump off a cliff with you.'" There was a pause before she added, "And at the time she said it I thought I knew exactly who that person was."

I tried for a moment, but I knew, beyond the shadow of a doubt, that there was no combination of words in the English language that could be strung together to right this ship.

"Goodbye, Brian." She kissed me on the cheek, and rubbed the back of her hand on down it. And then she turned and got in her

Civic, and drove off until I couldn't see her tail-lights at all through the pouring of the...

∽

"...rain's comin' down hard," a paramedic says. "Careful going out."

The back of the ambulance flies open, then, and when it does the sound of the storm utterly explodes into it. I can feel the wind, and I can feel the rain, and they helped a bit with the oncoming heat. And then there are shouts, and lights, and running feet, and the hospital door...

∽

"Open?!" I shouted. The man at the counter of the place pretended not to hear me, so I shouted it again. "I said, are you open?!"

And he pointed at the sign saying the opposite, and went back to his reading. But I wasn't taking no for an answer; I pulled a twenty from my wallet and slapped it flat up against the glass. Within seconds the paper was soaked with rainwater, but it got his attention just fine, and once he saw me there he rolled his eyes and hit a button off to the side. The door clicked and whirred and slid open.

"Make it quick, man."

"I know, I know. I will. Thank you so much." I ran down the aisles and made it back to the counter in less than a minute. The man processed the sale.

"Date night?" he said. He bagged the card after the flowers.

"Something like that." And I thanked him and ran back out to my car, and I got inside, and I took out the card and scribbled on its inner sleeve the words: 'Jump off a cliff...

∽

"...with me, with me!" A doctor running alongside the cart motions to some nurses in the hall and they run along to follow. He turns to the EMTs. "He stable?"

"Uh, slipping. Heart rate's falling, breathing slowing. Not good. Mumbled something about being too hot earlier, but if anything his temperature's too low."

Someone shows the doctor a chart and when he reads it, his face is grim.

"Alright," he says. "Let's…"

~

"…move!" I shouted at the car as I passed it by. "Just a little rain, assholes." But it wasn't; it was a lot of rain—sheets and buckets and torrents of it, in fact. It'd long since turned the dirt to mud and it swept up against my windshield like ocean surf. I was going far, far too fast for such conditions. But at that moment I didn't…

~

"…care about that," the doctor says. "I just want to get his fluids up. Rachel!"

The woman from the ambulance runs up and she discusses my condition in harsh whispers with the doctor. It becomes impossible to hear what they're saying as I fade back out. But it's clear from the body language that she hasn't yet give up…

~

'…hope for a reunion with these guys?'

'Well, Bolan and Snake say they're against it, entirely. So that doesn't bode well for fans. But look what happened with Guns N'—'

I switched the radio off, and I wrapped both hands around the wheel with such force the knuckles turned white. The car hit seventy miles per hour. Seventy-five. Seventy-nine. The windshield wipers were flying, but they weren't going fast enough.

Suddenly I saw things in the middle of the road, and I slammed my foot on the brakes; The car jolted and shuddered and fought for traction, and I felt the tires squeal and the metal of the car grind in...

∿

"...protest."

"I don't care if he wants to protest!" the doctor snaps back. "You tell him to wait in the lobby like everyone else!"

The nurse accepts her orders and heads back out into the hallway. "I'm sorry, sir," she says. "You can't see him until—"

"Until what?! That's my son in there! That's my son! That's—"

There's a scuffle, and shouts as a security guard drags my father from the wing. Rachel pauses as she hears the shouts, and then her eyes well up a bit with tears. She looks at my face and appears to realize something. She doesn't say what. The shouts continue, but they fade. And so do I. And in comes the heat as I do.

"That's my son!" Dad says. "That's my boy! Let me see my son! Stop! Please...!"

∿

"...stop!" The police officer had both hands up as my car barreled towards him. "Stop! Stop the car!"

Finally there was a jolt and a shudder as the tires gained control at last. The car slammed to a halt. Both the officer and I sighed in relief, and then he approached my window and tapped the glass with his knuckle. I lowered it.

"I'm sorry, sir!" I shouted over the rain. "Roads are crazy out here. You okay?"

He ignored the question. "I'm gonna need you to sit here for a bit, okay?" he said. "Just until the accident's cleared up."

"Accident?"

"It's bad." He nodded in the direction of the wreckage, and then he said again, "Just sit tight! We'll wave you over when there's an open lane." And then he ran off into the storm."

I scanned the scene. There was a man on the side of the road sitting on the pavement with a poncho for the rainfall and his head in his hands. His SUV was totaled; the front end was bent and twisted and hideously mangled.

But the other car was in far, far worse shape than that. I squinted hard, and could only make out panels of white amidst charred black chunks of metal and the force of the rain. But it was enough.

It was a Civic.

Oh, God. Oh, God, no. No, no, no.

I got out of the car and left the door hanging open in the rain.

"ROBIN!!" I shouted. "ROBIN!"

And then I saw it; a fleeting glimpse of movement, a white sheet flipped over a face and a single strand of that red hair that fell out from it.

"ROBIN!" I screamed. "That's my girl! That's my girl!"

One of the EMTs, covered in blood from the waist up, turned to look at the spectacle I'd made. But then someone shouted her name.

"Rachel!" The doctor says. "You with us, or what? Let's go!"

She blinks as she stares at me, and then she says, "Yeah, yeah. Sorry. I just realized this guy was—"

"Just get the charcoal, please? We don't have time."

And she does; she runs off to fetch exactly that. And then I feel a hideously invasive sensation—a tube is being placed in my nose, and then I feel it falling down, into my throat. I clench my fist and begin to squirm. A nurse sees this movement, and he holds me down and says, "Whoa, whoa…"

"…Whoa, you okay, man?" My roommate stumbled back as I threw open the door. I charged past him. "You comin' in hot!" He said. "You good, bro?"

But I ignored him; I went into the bathroom and I leaned against the sink for a moment. I grabbed my temples and set my jaw and sobbed without a sound; aching, wracking, heaving sobs. I heard a knock.

"Hey, man," he said. "You good, dude? Anything I can like, get for you? Or—?"

"I'm fine," I managed. It wasn't convincing in the slightest, but I didn't care. I opened up my phone. There was a text from Robin there, from this morning.

It read, 'I love you,' and they were all at once the most beautiful and the most painful words I'd ever read. 'I love you.'

I love you, too. I'm coming. Hang on, baby. I'm coming.

Then I backed out and found my dad in the contacts list, and typed, 'I love you, Dad.'

Moments later I got a response: 'I love you too, son! You okay?'

But I ignored it, and then I threw open the cupboard, and I grabbed an old...

"...bottle of pills," a nurse says. "Swallowed the whole thing. Lucky his roommate called it in when he did."

But the doctor is incredulous. "Well. That remains to be seen, now, doesn't it?" Then he turns to the door. "Rach—"

But she pushes it open with her elbow before he finishes. "I got it, I got it. I'm here."

"Alright!" He says. "Let's get to work, folks!"

And then there is thick, wretched black stuff funneling down that tube and into my throat. I'm almost desperate enough, but not quite strong enough, to resist it. I can feel it sliding and pumping and pulsing; I struggle as much as I can against the restraints, but all my effort and all my strength of arms musters up not more than the faintest whimper. But Rachel hears it. She holds my hand, and she says, in soft enough a whisper that only I can hear, "Don't follow her, Brian. Don't follow her. Please, Jesus. I need this win."

But it's too late. One by one, as the spikes on the EKG slow to sporadic pulses, I see the nurses turn to each other and they shake their heads. One by one by one, that is, until there is only a trembling Rachel there, and she's holding on for me tight enough for everyone in the room.

"Call it," the doctor says, just as the darkness swirls in and I'm falling away. The conversation carries on as I pass.

"2:32 AM," one nurse says.

But I can hear Rachel screaming—"No! He's not gone! There's still time, there's still time to save him, there's still..."

But she's wrong. I am gone. Her voice is fading away into a darkness that's swallowing me whole, and throwing me to the winds. And just when the magnitude of the situation dawns on me, then comes that damned heat; monstrous amounts of it. It rips and it tears and it scorches and it scalds, and if I'd had the ability to scream out or even breathe I would've done so until my throat was raw. But then there's a new pain. A different pain.

A hand reaches out from the blackness, and it grabs my left forearm with such mighty force that the resulting pain eclipses that of the heat. The nails of that hand rip right through the flesh, and then I'm being pulled. There's a rushing wind; it is cool and refreshing and beautiful, and suddenly I'm somewhere else entirely.

I blinked. The darkness was gone, and the heat with it, and that sensation of being devoured. Instead there were starlit clouds as far off in every direction as the eye could see. I looked at my arm. There were nail-marks, I saw: four deep cuts beneath the inner wrist and a fifth on the side, in the shape of a hand. They bled a bit. And then I heard an all too familiar voice.

"You okay?"

I stood up, slowly, and I turned.

"Robin. What was that? That darkness? And the heat, and th—"

"Its where you would've spent your eternity, Brian, had I not pulled you out."

I had no words other than the weakest "Thanks."

"You know," she said, holding her own arm. "Suicide's not exactly what I meant by 'jumping off a cliff'."

I blinked again and took a long, deep breath. "Yeah. I guess I didn't think things through."

"Not sure you fully realize how much of an understatement that is."

"Well, maybe I don't. But you know what? I'd do it again, Robin. I'm serious."

She nearly rolled her eyes, but I doubled down on the sentiment.

"What I said? Out there on my street? I'm sorry. You were right. Love isn't about taxes or headaches or tolerating each other 'til we're seventy. It's like your mom said; it's about sweeping your girl off her feet. It's about jumping over cliffs with someone, and not knowing where you'll land, not even caring as long as you get there together. And if this is where we land, wherever this is, then I'm okay with that."

I leaned in for a kiss, but she stopped me with her hand before it landed, and I opened my eyes.

She said, "I can tell you've been working on that speech for a while."

"Over and over again in the car, until... until I got to the scene of the wreck." I looked at the ground, and then back up at her. "And I realized, right then, that if you left the earth itself then I would too. So here I am—"

"I was wrong, too," she cut me off.

"What?"

"About love. I was wrong. My mom was wrong. There was a pause before she added, "Can I show you something?"

"Uh, okay. Sure."

And then she took my hand, and Infinity rolled in and it faded back out, and all of a sudden we were somewhere else entirely.

"Are we—?"

"On the Ferris Wheel? Yep. Turn around."

I did, and there we were, past Robin and past Me, on the seat above and behind us. I remembered it like yesterday; we were staring out at the whole city at twilight, and the ships in the harbor that were backlit red with the setting sun, and the clouds that were lined at their tops with just a little bit of starlight. I rustled in my seat a bit and it moved, and Past Me furrowed his brow when he saw it. But then Past Robin said: "Thank you for being here with me," and she got a kiss on the head.

"What do you see?" Robin said.

"Us, about a year ago. I remember that day like it was yesterday. Your mom had just died, so I took you here. To get your mind off things."

"You did. That was the first day in months I'd felt truly safe and truly at peace. That was love."

"I know it was. And I still love you, just the sa—."

"It's a kind of love," she said, cutting me off again. "And it's beautiful when it lasts. But can I show you something else?"

"Uh… okay."

She took my hand again, and again Infinity itself rolled in and out like the tide, and then we were standing in the hallway of the hospital.

"What do you see?"

I looked around. "I don't know. A hospital."

She nodded in the direction of a particular room. "Look there."

So I did. There was a woman on the cot. She was emaciated and hairless and deathly frail, and the Doctors inside were shutting off the last of the machines.

"A dying woman," I said. "Looks like cancer."

"Yep. And there?"

I looked down. There was a nurse crouched down in front of the same door and talking to a girl—maybe eight or nine years old, if I had to guess—in silly voices. The girl had been crying, but the nurse managed to make her smile a bit, even as her mother died on the other side of the door.

"Looks like a nurse comforting a little girl."

"That's right," Robin said. "And that little girl will remember that nurse for the rest of her life—even if they never meet again or even exchange names—as the person who came to her in her darkest hour and made her smile." She turned to me. "That's love, too. Just as beautiful and just as precious as what we had."

"What's your point?"

She didn't answer; she just stuck out her hand with a sad smile, and I took it. Infinity faded in and back out a third time, and then we were in the waiting room.

"See that?" Robin said. She nodded towards the corner of the room, and I squinted.

"Oh hey!" I said. "That's Dylan! What's he doing here?"

"Called the ambulance when you didn't come out of the bathroom," she said. "He knew something was wrong, and when they drove you off he followed them here. Been standing there ever since, asking for information on you every time a nurse walks by. He's starting to annoy them."

I watched my roommate for a bit, and sure enough he grabbed a nurse as she walked by, and asked her a question that I couldn't hear. She said something pleasantly dismissive, and he nodded before leaning his head back up against the wall and closing his eyes.

"Wow. Had no idea he cared that much."

"That's love, too, Brian. Would you do the same for him?" But she held out her hand again before I could answer, and I took it. For a fourth time Infinity blinked.

And then I was in the emergency room, looking down on myself. I was covered in vomit from the charcoal and the pills, deathly still. Most of the nurses and the doctor were still walking out the door.

But Rachel wasn't; she was crying openly now, and making no effort to hide it. She reached for something. A needle, it looked like, or a syringe.

"What's she doing?"

"You'll see," Robin said. "But that there? That's also love." And she held out her hand once again and said, "One more." I took it, and then we were in the parking lot of the same place. The rain was coming down harder than ever.

"Turn around," Robin said. I did, and I stopped; there were no words.

It was my father in his car. He was holding a Bible up to his chest with both hands, and he was crying in a way no child should ever have to see their father cry.

"And that there?" Robin said. "That's the kind of love that can move mountains."

I put my hand up against his window. He didn't seem to notice.

"He can't see you, Brian. Not from there."

I wiped my eyes with the back of my hand. "Okay," I said. "I get it. I screwed up."

She released my hand, and all of a sudden we were back in the clouds again, under the stars. I wiped another tear before it fell.

"So now what? It's too late for me to go back down there. I'm already gone."

Robin took another step forward, and without another word she put her hand on my temple. My eyes rolled back.

Then I saw it.

Rachel and I are on a beach. Our child is playing out in the surf, and the sun hits her hair just right, and for a moment it is made of gold.

And then the image fades, and another one takes its place.

A birthday party. I have silver hair at my temples. Rachel does too. But it doesn't matter. Our little girl is turning ten.

And then that image fades too, and is replaced by another, and another, and another; each one yielding another moment where someone loved someone else enough for it to break through the clouds and be seen forever, even if the moment itself lasted only for a heartbeat.

Finally there is an image of Rachel and myself on a porch as old as we are, and she holds my hand and says: "I'm glad you didn't follow her."

I say back, "Me too," and I kiss her on the head.

Robin pulls back her hand, and again standing out there in the clouds together.

"How did you do that?" I asked.

She shrugged. "Time has no meaning in this place. I've been here a while, Brian, and the doctors haven't even left your operating room. Don't think too much about it. Just think about what you want."

"That," I said. "Was that my future?"

She shrugged again. "Could be. I don't know what you saw, and I don't need to know. Was it enough?"

I nodded, and she stepped forward again, saying: "Then go and get it."

"I'll miss you too much."

"Well there's nothing wrong with missing someone," she said. "That just means love lasted a little longer than what ignited it. So go ahead and miss me. You owe me that much. Feel the loss; stand up to the storm like a man, and memorize the pain, and learn it inside and out and let it roll over you in waves and run its course. Then one day you'll wake up and you'll have scar-tissue where the skin used to be, and you'll be stronger than the grief ever was."

"I can tell you've been working on that speech for a while."

She shrugged. "Like I said. I've been here for a while," And then she kissed me, one last time, and for the briefest moment all the little scars and cuts and nicks and scrapes in my heart were filled up and made whole. "You're made up of the stars, kid," she said. "Now go light up the world."

And then she was...

~

"...gone, Rachel. I'm not telling you agai—"

But I shot upright before the doctor could finish the thought. I gasped for air as I did and grabbed at my chest with more strength than I'd had in hours. There was a needle in it; a bolt of life to the heart, and Rachel broke down in tears when she saw me.

"Well," the doctor said. "Welcome back to the land of the living, son. And Rachel?"

She turned around.

"Good work, kid. Made me proud."

He left, and she turned back to me and tried to hide a smile as she did. "Hey there. How're you feeling?"

"Better than dead." There was a pause before I added, "Hey. I'm glad you got your win."

She took my hand and squeezed it. For a moment she paused when she saw a scar below the wrist that looked like the result of fingernails dragging through flesh. But then she dismissed it and said: "I am too. And you'll get yours. Okay? I promise you will."

I said, "I know." And with that she got up and left the room to go save someone else's life. I opened my father's text and hit reply:

'I will be.'

WORST DAY OF MY LIFE

David Maloney

The worst day of my life was on December 18th, 2007.

That was the day of my high-school talent show. I'd prepared all semester, and it was my time to shine. Every detail was just right.

I had practiced the song: Radiohead's Creep on my acoustic guitar until my fingers bled. Even today, the dark splotches on the rosewood fretboard remain. I'd recorded myself singing, enduring the embarrassment of listening back to my nasally adolescent voice, changing one thing and then another, until finally the sound was passable, if not pleasant.

I hadn't given any thought to the song. For me, it was a foregone conclusion. It was the song that summed me up, the one that summed up my pain. In my fantasy people would realize that I wasn't just a weird loner; I was an artist, capable of experiencing the most exquisite and sensitive feelings.

When I got on stage, my hands were shaking and my stomach was squirming. The eyes of my classmates sat heavy on my chest.

I played the first few bars, and as soon as I opened my mouth to sing, my voice cracked.

I stopped.

I heard someone snicker in the audience.

I tried again.

Another crack.

There were more snickers now. People tried to stifle them, but I could hear. One last time I strummed the opening bars and opened my voice to sing, but I couldn't. The sound just wouldn't come out.

People were laughing now. I wanted to run away, but I was paralyzed. My stomach sunk, my cheeks were hot, and tears began to sting my eyes.

"He's crying!" someone shouted.

The tears ran freely down my face, and I ran off the stage to jeers.

There was a side exit down the band hall corridor, and I shoved the heavy, metal doors open, bursting into the cool night air.

It smelled like wet grass and cigarette smoke. I turned to my right and saw Emily Ross leaning up against the wall with a cigarette.

Emily Ross was the prettiest girl in school. According to the rules of high-school as I understood them, that should have meant that she was popular, but for some reason that wasn't the case.

Years later I'd realize that the other girls were jealous of Emily, an outsider that had moved in from the big city and drawn the attention of every boy in school. The attention was unwanted by Emily, but that hardly mattered to the collective thought of insecure teenage girls.

For now though, Emily's unpopularity was a mystery to me.

"Hey kid," she said. "What's wrong?"

Emily was two years my senior, but it still stung when she called me 'kid.'

I shook my head and hurled my guitar into the bushes.

"That wasn't very nice," she said. "What did that guitar ever do to you?"

"N-nothing," I said.

Great, first the voice crack now the stutter. I heard Ms. Andrews announcing the next act through the door, and I realized with sudden horror that Emily must have heard me flub the song.

"I came out here to get away from the talent show," she said. "My ears aren't too good, so I can't hear it out here."

She was lying to make me feel better, and I was happy to pretend I didn't realize it.

"You want a cigarette, kid?" she said.

I'd never smoked before, but I slowly nodded.

She held one out and I took it. She tried lighting the end, but the flame guttered out in the wind.

"No, you've got to do it like this," she said. She grabbed my hand and pushed my fingers together, bending them as a shield against the wind. This time the cigarette stayed lit, and I coughed so powerfully I almost threw up.

She laughed, but it was a different kind of laugh than the ones I'd just endured from my classmates. It was a kind laugh.

"Take it slow, kid," she said. She took a long draw on the cigarette and the warm red glow of the cherry lit her face.

I'd never in my life seen someone look as beautiful as she did right then. She walked over and picked my guitar up out of the bushes.

"Let's go somewhere," she said. "I wanna hear that song."

Those were the days when a touch of the hand was an electric shock, a moment of eye contact a violent throb of the heart. The days when I still believed that if the right person loved me, all my problems would be solved.

And as far as I could tell, that person was sitting across from me now.

We sat Indian style on the carpet of her bedroom, me awkwardly slumped over my too-big guitar and her leaning forward in eager attention.

Her green eyes shone in the dim yellow lamplight as I plucked out the first few chords.

I began to sing. My voice was shaky, but it didn't crack.

When you were here before,

Couldn't look you in the eye,

You're just like an angel,

Your skin makes me cry,

You float like a feather,

In a beautiful world,

You're so fucking special,

I wish I was special,

I raked my pick hard across the strings in the pre-chorus riff, and then Emily's voice, steady and clear as a bell, joined me.

But I'm a creep,

I'm a weirdo,

What the hell am I doing here?

I don't belong here

I set the guitar down, my hands shaking too violently too continue.

"Why'd you stop?" she asked.

"I just..." I didn't finish my sentence.

Emily looked at the floor, then back up at me through strands of hair that had fallen over her face.

"Do you ever feel like...." she trailed off.

"What?" I said.

"Nothing."

She bit her lip and seemed to decide something. She leaned in, and softly pressed her lips against mine.

Her hair brushed my face. It smelled like lavender shampoo. I closed my eyes, and there was nothing in the world but the softness of her lips and the smell of her hair as the strands gently swept my cheeks.

Our lips broke, and my world of bliss dissolved back into the patchy yellow light of Emily's desk-lamp.

"Did you hear that?" she whispered.

"Hear what?"

"Shhh, listen."

I could hear footsteps on the gravel outside.

"Is it your parents?" I asked.

"I don't have parents," she said. "Just my dad. You need to hide."

"Why? We weren't doing anything bad we just—" Emily kissed me on the lips again and shoved me into the open closet. I fell onto a pile of old coats. I scrambled to get back up, but Emily was already sliding the slotted wood doors closed behind me.

I could hear the front door open and close, and then Emily's door as it creaked open and Emily's father stood in the doorway. I couldn't see his face through the half-inch horizontal slits, but I could hear his voice perfectly.

It was the deep, rugged voice of a man who'd smoked for many years.

"What did you do?" the voice asked. The voice was flat and calm, although it might have held just the barest trace of anger.

"I didn't do anything," Emily said. Her voice had moments before been steady and clear, but now it was trembling.

"Don't lie to me, girl," her father replied. "The lies are written all over your face. You look just like your mother. Like a proud slut."

"I-I'm sorry dad, I didn't mean to—"

SMACK

The slap rang out loudly against the quiet night, and Emily tumbled to the floor.

I gripped the neck of my guitar tightly.

"Didn't mean to?" he asked. "Didn't I tell you not to lie to me?"

"Yes sir, I—oof"

Her father had sent his foot into her stomach, knocking the air out of her. He picked her up by the hair and threw her onto the bed, fumbling open the buckle on his belt and sliding it off.

He lashed it across her thighs, and she yelped in pain.

I could feel my face growing hot.

He lashed her again.

My hands poured sweat, slick against the neck of my guitar.

He lashed once more.

My ears rang. My heart jack-hammered in my chest.

"Take of your pants," he said, fumbling drunkenly with the buttons on his own.

"Daddy please I—" he swung the belt across her back, and this time she screamed.

I could take no more. I kicked the doors open and swung the

guitar as hard as I could at his head. It connected, and the wood splintered with the twang and vibration of broken strings. One of them lashed out and struck him in the cheek, and red blood began to blossom from the gash.

Mr. Ross stared dumbly at me for a moment before swinging the belt at my head. It caught me in the ear, and the side of my head exploded with pain and noise. I hugged the carpet and felt the belt whip down on my back. I rolled onto my back and swung the broken neck of the guitar wildly, slashing Mr. Ross across the belly with the jagged edge.

He roared with pain and dropped his knee into my stomach. The air disappeared from my lungs, and Mr. Ross knelt on me, lacing his fingers around my throat.

My face was hot. My eyes felt like they would pop from their sockets at any moment. A black haze drifted over the world, and I began to grow dizzy. Where had Emily gone?

I was faintly aware of a loud noise. Was it a train? An explosion? No, it was Mr. Ross, screaming in my face.

His hands weren't around my neck anymore, they were reaching, grasping for something unseen on his back. The cool night air rushed into my lungs.

It was a thin wooden rectangle. It looked like, no it was a knife handle. Emily was backing away from her father, shrinking into the corner of the room.

He had pulled the knife out of his back, and he held it in front of him as he walked towards her. Spit bubbled at corners of his mouth as he let out a tangled grunt of pain and rage. I felt something cold in my hand, and I realized I was still holding the broken guitar neck.

I staggered to my feet and planted the broken wood into the fat of his back. He grunted in surprise and dropped the knife, but he didn't turn around, instead leaping on Emily like a lion might leap on its prey.

His hands squeezed tight around her neck. Her face went red, then purple.

My heart sank as I looked at the bloody knife, gleaming in the yellow lamplight. I didn't want to do it, but I had no choice. I picked it up and plunged it into his back. His hands slackened a bit, but he didn't turn around. His eyes bulged out of his head, purple veins standing out against a red neck flushed with blood.

I stabbed him again, and his grip released. He grunted one final time and slumped over to the side. I fell on Emily, rubbing my hands on her face, but it was no use—she wasn't breathing. I ran to the landline, hands trembling as I punched the numbers in: nine-one-one.

I sat by Emily's bed in the sterile white quiet of the hospital room. The paramedics had been able to restart her heart, but she'd slipped into a coma, and when she'd woke up—if she woke up—was anyone's guess.

Her father was dead.

I had been coming every day for two weeks. It was winter break, and I had nowhere else to go, nothing else to do. I was alone. Friendless.

Today was a special day, though. I had read about something online that might help. The article said it was good to talk to comatose patients. It said that if they could hear you, it might help to keep them attached to the physical world.

So today was the day I would sing her Radiohead's Creep. If anything could reach her in there, that would be it.

I tried to work up the courage to do it, but every time I opened my mouth, my vocal cords twisted into a knot.

Trying is the scariest thing in the world, because once you've failed, you can't pretend that everything's going to be alright anymore.

I took a deep breath, closed my eyes, and laced my fingers through hers. They were warm.

My guitar was still shattered into pieces, and all I had was the sterile beeps of the heart monitor to keep time.

Slump-shouldered and shaky-voiced, I began to sing.

Whatever makes you happy,

Whatever you want,

I wish I was special,

You're so fucking special,

My hands raked imaginary strings as I strummed out the pre-chorus riff, and the heart monitor's beeps became a solid line of sound.

Emily was dead.

When I got home from the hospital that day, a shiny new guitar was waiting for me with a big red bow on it. The hospital had called my mother and told her.

I picked the guitar up and turned it over in my hands. It felt clunky, alien. It wasn't my guitar. An ugly rage began to bubble up inside me. My head was pounding. My ears were ringing. I saw red.

I screamed, and tears stung my eyes as I smashed the guitar on the floor, over and over and over again until I was winded, collapsing on the ground in a pile of tears and broken wood.

My mom swooped over me and we cried together for hours.

A few days later I came home to the same thing, except it was my old guitar that had been pieced back together. It was covered with splotches of blood and nicks in the wood. Pieces had been replaced, and yellow lines of wood glue seeped out from ugly scars in the wood, but it was my guitar.

I thanked my mom and she kissed me on the forehead. When she came away her eyes were wet. I picked up the guitar and took it to my room, sitting on the bed and cradling it in my lap.

And as I stared down at it, something amazing happened. The strings began to vibrate and indent in the unmistakable chords of Radiohead's Creep.

I closed my eyes, and my voice was steady as I sang with Emily for the last time.

She's running out the door
She's running out,
She runs, runs, runs, runs,
Runs

SEXUAL PREDATORS

David Maloney

"So uh... what do you do for a living?" I asked.

"What do I do?" the woman on the barstool replied as if I'd just asked her the square root of seven hundred and twenty-three. "You've been staring across the bar at me all night," she said. "You've bought me two drinks, you keep gawking at my tits when you think I'm not looking, and now you want to know what I do for a living?"

"Uhh..."

"You want to fuck me," she said.

I wasn't really sure what to say, but I wish I'd at least remembered to close my mouth.

"Does it really matter what I do?" she went on. "Would you not want to fuck me if I were an evolutionary biologist or something?"

"No, I—"

"Good, then let's get out of here."

"Wait, really?"

"Yes, really."

She grabbed my hand and practically yanked me off the bar stool, dragging me out the door to a black BMW sedan.

Once we were comfortably seated she turned and gave me an appraising stare. "You're not a murderer, right?" she asked.

"I—what? Why?" I said flabbergasted. "Do I look like a murderer?"

"No, but neither did Ted Bundy or Jeffrey Dahmer."

"Well—"

"Gacy and Manson did though, so I'd say the odds are about fifty-fifty."

"Okay..."

She didn't wait for my response. She just threw the car into gear and got us on the road.

When we reached her place the clothes flew off so fast I would've thought she had at least eight hands, and it wasn't two minutes before she was naked and lowering herself down onto my lap.

She gasped as she slipped me into her, rocking her hips gently back and forth. The way her body moved was unlike anything I'd ever seen before, the rhythmic, fluid contortions like a dance.

My face grew hot and my mind grew heavy, and soon I could not remember who this woman was, who I was, or even where we were. There was nothing but the sensual twisting of her body as we neared the climax in unison.

We reached the peak together, and the moans of pleasure turned into screams as the world dissolved into a haze of ecstasy. After it was over I couldn't move. The whole world was a mist of pleasure and warm comfort—soft and silent.

And then my lover's face began to twist, stretching and bulging out like a rubber mask about to burst at the seams. Just when I thought it couldn't stretch anymore, the skin split down the middle.

Out of the blood and torn shreds of face emerged a large insectoid head. I willed my muscles to move, but they would not cooperate; I realized that the insect must have done something to paralyze me.

The insect's jaw unhinged, stretching wide over my head, its hot breath invading my nostrils as a ragged black tongue slid down my cheek. It took my head into its gullet, and its throat squeezed me down like a fleshy vice grip. I held my breath and prepared to die.

But then something happened—my head was sliding back out of

the beast's maw, the putrid stink of its insides replaced by the cool, calm fragrance of fresh air.

"Huh," the insect said.

My heartbeat pounded in my ears.

"This is usually the part where I would eat you—but..."

My throat made an involuntary gurgling noise, and I realized I'd regained the use of my voice.

"I uh... I don't taste good?" I managed to squeak out.

What a stupid thing to say, I thought.

"No, it's not that," she said. "You just seem really sweet. I'm not sure that I want to eat you."

Her head morphed back into the beautiful woman I'd met at the bar, and my heart slowed down just a little.

"I don't think I will," she said, staring down at me from her mounted position on my lap with a slight smile.

"Oh, that's uhh... really great," I gasped out.

I wanted to shove her off my lap and run screaming in the opposite direction, but I feared that if I offended her she might decide to eat me after all.

I figured I'd better at least try to make conversation.

"So uh..." my voice sounded dusty and hoarse, "are you a m-monster?"

"What?" she seemed taken aback. "You think I'm a monster just because I eat people?"

"Uh..."

"Do you think cats are monsters because they eat mice, or people are monsters for eating chickens?"

"I'm really not—"

"Of course you don't," she said. "The chickens probably think of you as monsters. Then again, chickens are assholes. Who cares what they think?"

"Oh...okay?"

The room fell silent as we stared at each other for a moment.

"So—"

"You were about to ask me if I wanted to go again, right?" she cut me off.

"Um, yeah." She grinned, arching her back as she twisted her hips in circles. My last thought before consciousness gave way to pure pleasure was that I was lucky she'd interrupted me before I asked what she did for a living again.

END WITH A BANG

David Maloney

"I like to fuck."

Her dating profile was those four words under a picture of her that could have easily been a mugshot.

She was still beautiful. She couldn't hide that with the lack of makeup, the ratty clothes, or the unkempt hair.

Should I send the message? I thought.

On the one hand, all my life experience, my intellect, and my instincts told me to forget about it. There was no way a woman that beautiful had to resort to online dating to get laid. It had to be a trap. On the other hand, I was horny.

So I sent the message.

>Hey, it's John. Let's get naked and do the sweaty ugly dance.

No, I didn't actually send that. When I'm online dating, it's usually about the 47th draft that gets sent. But my cat chose that moment to sprint madly across my keyboard, and the message was sent like that. Actually, if I'm quoting the message exactly it was:

>Hey, it's John. Let's get naked and do the sweaty ugly dance aserkkjllll

I reminded myself to get Mr. Paws neutered before shutting my laptop in disgust. I promised myself I wouldn't check the site for at least an hour, and left my laptop behind as I strolled to the corner coffee joint. Five minutes later I had the dating site open on my phone. I figured just one quick look wouldn't hurt. I guess that explains why I can't quit smoking.

To my surprise, I had already received a response from the girl, Annie M.

> Hey John, I'm all for sweaty, but let's not shoot for ugly. Just in case we wanna film it.

I couldn't believe she'd messaged me back after what I'd sent her. Everyone knows the secret to online dating is pretending to be less desperate than you actually are.

I stared at my phone trying to think of a clever response when I saw the italics at the bottom of the chat window.

Annie M. is typing.

Her address popped up on the screen followed by a single word.

> Busy?

I thought for a moment before I typed my message.

> How do you know I'm not a serial killer haha

Annie M. is typing.

> How do you know I'm not?

It was a fair point. For all I knew it wasn't even a woman on the other end of my messages. She certainly didn't act like one. The smart thing to do would be to verify it somehow. Then again, I was still horny. I typed my response.

> On my way.

When I showed up to the house I knew there was no way I was at the right place. There were at least twenty cars parked in the yard. I triple checked the address. It was the one she'd sent me.

I sent a message to the dating profile.

We're sorry, but Annie M. is offline right now.

I sighed and got out of the car. If I was about to be murdered, then at least there would be plenty of witnesses. I strolled up and knocked on the door. An old woman in a black dress answered.

"Uh, hi," I said. "Is Annie here?"

"Of course she is," the old lady said, eyeing me suspiciously. "Are you a friend of the family?"

"Uh... family?"

"Henry's family."

"Who's Henry?"

The lady swelled up like a big indignant balloon, but before she could yell at me, a voice called out from inside.

"Is that John? Let him in."

The woman narrowed her eyes but nonetheless stepped out of my way. Everybody in the place was dressed in a suit or a dress, except for me. I was dressed in ripped jeans and a Metallica T-shirt.

There was a somber air in the place. Annie came walking up to me.

"Wow," I said. "You look a lot better in the flesh."

"Soon you'll be in the flesh," Annie breathed in my ear.

The balloon-shaped lady eyed me hatefully. "John, this is Henry's mom," Annie said. "Gertrude, this is my new lover, John."

"Uh, hi, I—"

The old lady turned around and stormed off in a huff.

"Don't mind her," Annie said. "She's been extra bitchy since Henry died."

"Ok, who is Henry?" I asked in exasperation.

"He's the stiff over there in the coffin. Used to be my husband before he got shot in the face."

My stomach dropped.

"Annie...is this a funeral?"

"It was," she said. "Now it's a party, lover."

Annie bit my earlobe.

"But, I don't... why would you invite a booty call to your husband's funeral?"

"One of Henry's favorite pastimes was beating the shit out of me," she said matter-of-factly.

"Oh... that's..."

"It's fine," Annie cut me off, leading me down the hall to a door at the end. "You know I asked everyone here for help. Not one of them raised a finger."

"Oh. Did you call the cops?"

"He was a cop," Annie said, pushing the door open. The room was lit by the flickering orange glow of candles, and a king-sized bed covered in rose petals sat in the middle.

"You can only push a woman so far, David," she said.

"My name's John actually aahhhh..."

Annie slid her hands down my pants.

I'll leave out what happened next. I'd like to think that my prowess in bed had suddenly and inexplicably gotten better, but I think it's more likely that Annie was playing up the noises for the crowd outside.

"You know what you look like?" Annie said when we'd finished. "A lost puppy."

I didn't know what that was supposed to mean, so I just said thanks and pulled my pants up.

"I need to check something," Annie said. "Then we can get out of here."

"Uh...okay?"

Annie left and shut the door, and the heavy lock clicked behind her. I suddenly became aware of the fact that the door was locked from the outside, and I was effectively trapped until she got back. I wasn't much for being trapped in a stranger's home, and quite frankly Annie seemed a bit unstable. But I was probably just overreacting.

BOOM

The door shook in the frame as the explosion rocked the house.

What the fuck was that?

But then I heard the gunshots and the screams, punctuated by Annie's laughter, and I knew.

I frantically tried the door, but it was a no go. I threw my shoulder against it, but my shoulder gave a lot more than the door did. I ran across the room to break the windows and saw that there were bars freshly installed on the outside.

BANG A gunshot sounded right behind me and I turned to see

Annie, shotgun in hand, standing in the doorway. The door swung pitifully on its hinges, a large hole where the lock had just been.

"Sorry about that," she said. "Lost the key. Ready to go, lover?" She flipped her hair.

"I uh..."

Annie was looking at me expectantly, her eyes so wide I thought they might pop out of her skull at any moment.

"Okay?" I said weakly, hoping she wouldn't shoot me.

The inside of the house was a carnage of shattered bones and blood, and I tried not to look at it as we made our way outside.

"Ohh nice car," Annie said. "Can I drive it?"

"S-sure?"

I tossed Annie the keys and we climbed in the car.

"That place really went up," Annie said. Her hands were shaking as she pulled out a pack of cigarettes. "Do you want one?" she asked, offering me one.

My mouth opened, but I couldn't form words. I silently shook my head no.

"It's just as well," Annie said. "It's terrible for you."

She stomped the gas, and the tires kicked up gravel as we spun out of the driveway.

"Uh... Annie?" I said.

"Yes John?"

"Where are we going?"

Annie took a drag of her cigarette.

"There's a few people who didn't come to the funeral."

FIGHT ME, FUCK ME, BURN ME

David Maloney

Some relationships are sustained by nothing more than the fact that at any given moment it's easier to make up, have sex, and go to sleep than to tear your life apart.

That's how it was with me and Marla. We met at a bar, fucked all night, and after-wards she forgot to leave. If only I had made her go, I wouldn't be about to die.

I was surprised when I woke up the morning after and she was still there. Usually they skip out on me during the night. I'm not really anyone's idea of "Mr. Right", more of a "Mr. Right Now". And that's only after a lot of drinks.

I wrote it off and figured I'd let her sleep late. She'd be gone when I got home from work that evening, right? Wrong. I got home and there she was, just staring at me like "Where have you been?"

That's when I realized that there was something seriously wrong with her.

I ate in silence, and she just stared at me, wide-eyed, unblinking. Her gaze made me feel like there were bugs under my skin.

I wanted her gone, but I was too weak. That night we wound up fucking again. When the sun came up and I was still inside her, reality set in and I was disgusted with myself. How could anyone be so weak?

I promised myself I'd make sure she was gone by the time I got back from work next day.

Of course when I got home that day, she was still there. She didn't even look away from the TV when I came in. I didn't bother asking her to leave; I knew she'd just ignore me. We had one of those relationships where your partner is just a better version of your right hand. We didn't talk, we had no connection, we just fucked.

We fucked on the counter, on the bathroom floor, on the dining room table, wherever there was space. Our sex started getting violent, and that's when I first noticed the puddles.

I came home from work one day and there it was: a puddle of unidentifiable fluid right in the middle of the living room floor. I couldn't figure out what it was, but it smelled like rotting fruit.

I was too tired to clean it up and told Marla she might as well do something to help out. We fought about it, fucked about it, and then we slept. Same as always.

The next day there was another puddle. Things went on like this for a while, every day a new fight, a new fuck, and a new puddle. I started pouring bleach on them and pushing them into the yard with a mop, but the house still reeked. I had nightmares about drowning in a giant puddle that smelled like rotting fruit.

It only got worse from there. One night while I was inside Marla I heard her whisper in my ear.

"Burn me."

"What?" I whispered back.

"Burn me."

I fumbled around in my pockets and pulled out my lighter, flicking it on an inch from her skin.

"Like this?" I asked.

I looked at her for approval, but she just stared, her wide black eyes unblinking.

"Don't just hurt me," she whispered, "burn me."

I moved the lighter closer and watched as her skin began to melt like wax.

"More," she whispered.

"M-more?"

"More."

She looked up at the bottle of Everclear on top of the fridge.

"M-Marla I don't think that—"

"MORE!" she screamed.

I tumbled off the bed and ran to the fridge to grab the bottle. My hands were shaking as I poured it on her arm. Had I poured too much? I held the lighter to her skin, flicked it on and—

"SHIT!"

I hit the ground as a column of flame shot up and licked the ceiling. Marla just lay there moaning like I'd never heard her moan before.

I ran to the cupboard and yanked out the miniature fire extinguisher, praying it still worked. I emptied out the whole thing before the fire was finally out. Marla's arm was a twisted mess of scorched bone and melted flesh.

"Good job," she whispered.

She seemed pretty pleased with me as I climbed weakly back into bed with her.

"Daniel?" she whispered.

"Yes Marla?"

"Burn me more."

"To...tomorrow I will. Just let me sleep."

"Do you promise?"

"Y-yes... I promise..."

But I broke my promise. When I got off work the next day I went to a hotel. I didn't even want to look at Marla, and I was sure she would be there waiting for me when I got back.

It took two bottles of whiskey from the mini-bar for me to start feeling drowsy that night. It wasn't until three in the morning that I finally started to drift off. Then I heard her voice.

"Burn me, Daniel."

I sat bolt upright. I knew I must have imagined it, but I couldn't shake the sudden feeling that I wasn't alone.

And then I smelled it. Rotting fruit.

"Wh-where are you?" I whispered into the darkness.

"You know where I am, Daniel."

"I-I just want to go home," I pleaded.

"So do I. But I need you to burn me first."

There was nothing for it. I knew what I had to do. I got up, got dressed, and drove home. I pulled into the driveway, popped open the trunk, and grabbed the can of spare gasoline I kept for emergencies.

I went inside the bedroom and emptied it all over Marla, along with the bottle of Ever clear. She didn't move. She just stared at me, looking pleased with herself. Then I went to the kitchen drawer for matches. No way was I getting close enough to use my lighter.

I dropped the match, and the bed burst into flames, turning the whole room into a glowing orange inferno.

"Thank you," Marla whispered as she burned.

"Marla," I said, "I'm sorry. I didn't mean to choke you so hard that first night. I didn't mean to kill you."

"I know," Marla whispered as her face melted. Maggots popped in the flames like overgrown, pus-filled pimples.

"I just need one more thing before I can leave you alone, Daniel," she said.

"Y-yes Marla?"

I thought I could see the barest trace of a smile steal over her face. "Burn with me."

SUNSET

Jake Healey

Harrison Samuel thought the barista was pretty cute. She walked away from him a bit flirtatiously, toward the counter, shaking her ass as she went.

That can't be an accident, Harrison thought.

He had just delivered what he judged to be a pretty smooth pick-up, and it had gone well enough, hadn't it? He supposed he would find out in a few minutes, when TAYLOR came back with the drinks—a black house coffee and a green chai.

TAYLOR. That was all Harrison knew of her, those six capital letters on her name tag, though he had visited the coffeehouse every day this week. Not quite a woman's name, Taylor. One of those androgynous names fit equally for both sexes to wear out. Harrison imagined breathing that name heavily, moaning it out in a darkened bedroom, and it felt...strange, like focusing too intently on the letters of your own name until they're not even recognizable as yours. That wasn't the kind of thing to stop him, though.

Harrison barely had time to form these thoughts before Taylor was back with the drinks. She smiled at him as she sat, briefly making eye contact, before turning her attention toward her tea. It had been less than five minutes since she first approached him, notepad in hand, asking what he'd have.

"You're on your break soon, right, Taylor?" he had said.

"Um, yeah," she responded. "Why?" There was hesitation, but not the bad kind. The intrigued kind. Almost playful. Harrison had never had any problems coming on to women, probably due to his strict adherence to the 'Two Rules for Successful Flirting':

1.Be attractive.

2.Don't be unattractive.

"Two coffees," he'd said. "Black for me, and for the second one… whatever you like." He gestured to the seat across from him.

Taylor blinked back surprise. "Oh, is that why you've been coming in here every day?"

"Yeah, it is," Harrison said. "I can get five better cups of coffee within a mile of here, no offense. But I'm picky about baristas."

"Huh. Well." Taylor gave a nervous laugh, but was clearly flattered. "I don't drink coffee. It makes me too jittery."

Oh. An awkward pause hung in the air. Now it was Harrison who had to regain his compos—

"I'll have the green chai, though, if that's alright. Costs a dollar more."

Thank you, God. "A whole dollar, huh? That should be fine."

Taylor smiled and turned to walk away.

"Oh, Taylor?"

She wheeled back around.

"My name's Harrison. In case you need to write it on the cup, or something."

That was the first conversation Harrison Samuel and Taylor Aubrey ever had. The second, over coffee and chai, went just as well.

Harrison walked out of his office building and into the cool air of the Rockies just as the last sliver of sun floated west beyond a mountain peak. The lake below the foothills shone like a mirage. It had rained not an hour before, and the dark gray clouds, no longer threatening, were still fresh in the sky to soak the entire landscape in a orange and purple glow.

Why don't I stop to appreciate these more? Harrison wondered as he strolled out to his car, eyes fixed on the remarkable view. Of course, since he'd met Taylor Aubrey, everything seemed a little more beautiful. He'd lived most of his twenties in a blur, building a life, working hard, yet rarely if ever pausing to find peace with the present moment. Now, at 29, he found himself feeling perpetually exhausted and a little cheated—if anyone had told him how quickly a person's twenties went, maybe he would've taken time to actually enjoy them.

But he was enjoying them now. He had seen Taylor every day for... was it three weeks now? Jesus. And it was going very well indeed. They hadn't slept together yet ("I want to take things slow," Taylor had said when Harrison's hand first slipped below her waist) but that would come in time. For now, Harrison was content to talk to his new companion every night until he literally couldn't keep his eyes open any longer. It seemed Taylor felt the same. They discussed philosophy, history, and art, but they also burned happy hours on Netflix, board games, and funny YouTube videos.

Find you a woman who can do both, Harrison thought as he drove, west, toward the sunset. Toward home.

Harrison lived on the other side of town from his job in a condo on the third-floor of a large building. Juice n' Java was a quick stop on the way.

When he arrived in the coffeeshop's parking lot, Taylor was already waiting for him. The dazzling display of colors had faded from the sky about five minutes before, but it was still fresh in her mind.

"Did you see that fucking sunset?" Taylor asked as she climbed in the car.

"I saw it," Harrison said. "Best one in a while. How was work?"

"It was work," she said dismissively before gesturing to a bag slung around her shoulder. "Toothbrush and my contact lens case, in case you're wondering."

"Why—" Harrison began, then stopped, suppressing a smile. He played it a lot cooler than he felt. "Sounds good."

∿

It wasn't the best sex he'd ever had, but it was the best first-time sex he'd ever had—which was much more important. One-night stands had lost their appeal years ago when Harrison realized that sex was a lot better with someone you were comfortable with. Someone who knew what made you go, and who wasn't afraid to tell you the same. It seemed Taylor was of a similar mind.

"We're gonna get good at that," she said breathlessly.

"Are we not already?"

"No, of course we are," Taylor soothed, but Harrison couldn't help wondering if she'd had better too. Of course she had, though. She'd graduated from State, hadn't she? Willing dicks were as commonplace as pennies on the sidewalk there. "I just meant, we're going to get even better."

Lying in post-orgasm fog, Harrison didn't have much trouble expelling the image of his new girlfriend (and she was his girlfriend now, she had to be) getting fucked by frat boys. He was in the moment, and it was a good one to be in.

"This is nice," he said after a long silence.

"Yeah," she said contentedly, head nestled in the crook of his arm, and a longer silence followed. Then: "So…Harrison. I want to ask you something. And I need you to promise you won't freak out."

"Ask away," he replied, a bit uneasy.

There was a heavy pause. "I have this friend. He's a, uh…drug dealer." A nervous laugh. "It's not hard stuff. It's like, psychedelics. LSD and mushrooms and that kind of thing. They're not bad for you in the same way other drugs are, and they're not addicting—they're just, like, consciousness-enhancing, right? Anyway, for a long time, this guy has been telling me about a drug called DMT. Have you heard of it?"

DMT. The Spirit Molecule. Yeah, Harrison had heard of it. Joe Rogan talked about it on his podcast all the time. The chemical was actually a natural product of the human brain, but when ingested or inhaled, it produced an astonishing display of hallucinatory pleasure. Perhaps the most attractive feature of the drug was its short duration, for unlike other psychedelics, a trip on DMT was over in ten minutes. Not exactly a big commitment.

"You want to use DMT?"

"Well, with you, yeah," Taylor said feebly. "I'm not into drugs, like, for recreation. I've smoked weed once and didn't even like it. But I think this could be a pretty life-altering experience, and I guess I'm excited that now I have someone to share it with."

Harrison was silent for a moment. He'd smoked weed far more than once, of course, but stopped when it had gotten him into some legal trouble back in his college days. He'd had to give back thousands in federal Pell grants. The penalties for illegal psychedelic use were likely to be similarly unforgiving—and ever since someone found a bong in his company's parking lot, there were rumblings about random drug tests. If it had been anyone else, he would've said no without a second thought. But Taylor…

"Fine. Only because I love you," he blurted out, then sat straight up, rolling Taylor off his chest and ungracefully onto her bare back. Holy shit. He did not just say that. He looked at Taylor in panic, but she didn't seem weirded out. Or angry. In fact, she didn't seem upset at all. She just looked at him with a light smirk on her lips, then responded, matter-of-factly.

"I love you too."

~

It took Taylor another month to get the drugs, but get them she did. By this point, Harrison's place may as well have been hers, so when Harrison heard the door open behind him as he perched on his couch, he didn't even turn around.

"Hey, babe," he called out to the mystery intruder.

"Hey yourself," Taylor replied, taking off her coat and boots. "You know, you should really think about locking your door. This isn't the best neighborhood."

"But then how would you get in?

"You could always…give me a key," she intoned, reaching around the back of the couch to embrace Harrison and kiss his cheek.

"Let's see if I still love you after my consciousness has been opened to the wonders of the universe," he said, but Taylor did not laugh.

"Shut up. I'm nervous about this," she said, waving an opaque bag which contained…well, Harrison could guess. "What if something goes wrong?"

"Then we can be buried next to each other, and we'll have "IT WAS HER IDEA" carved on the headsto—"

Taylor growled. "Fuck. You're not helping."

"It's just DMT. Joe Rogan uses it. And he's fine."

"Joe who?"

"Never mind." Harrison took a deep breath. "Let's do this."

She sat next to him on the couch. They kissed. She pulled a strange-looking pipe from her bag and placed it on the table. She told him that she would take the first hit, then him. Put the pipe back on the table right-side-up when you're done, she told him. Otherwise you'll lose motor control and drop it on the couch—maybe burn the house down. Okay, he said. She lit the pipe as a sunset battled the window shades, bathing the room in a faint orange glow. They drifted away, together, hand in hand.

After about a hundred thousand years, Harrison woke up.

His eyes were still closed, but he had a profound appreciation for all the curves and edges of his body. No…wait…not quite his body.

There were curves and edges, but they did not belong to him. There were no elbows, no hips, and no earlobes.

They were the curves of numerals. "8" and "3" The sharp edges of "4" and "7". Both edges and curves were present in "5". There was boundless knowledge here; power too, if only he could organize these numbers in the right way. And this was... him. In much the same way —no, in a far truer way than the earlobes had ever been. This was bliss. This was authenticity.

I'm code, Harrison thinks, and he is at an infinite peace. As he drifts away, a voice sounds from the distance.

"What the fuck is he doing there?"

Harrison was in a dark room, alone, his wrists and ankles strapped to a chair. It was cold. Metal. The shapes of the code—of him—were gone. He had earlobes again, and everything else too. His wrists were tied too tight. They stung with surprising clarity when he tried to wiggle free.

All at once, memories come flooding back to him, and he realizes what has happened. Illegal drugs. He's been caught. Stupid, he thinks. Any second now, a burly man is going to walk in, acting even tougher than he is. He's going to ask him: 'do you know why you're in here?' Jesus, it was just drugs...was it really necessary to tie him down?

But the time passed by slowly, or so it seemed to. Seconds became many minutes as Harrison sat in the immensely uncomfortable chair, unable to see much of anything in his nearly pitch-black surroundings. He wondered what had become of him and his lovely new girlfriend.

Finally a door at the far end of the room opened. Harrison blinked —a dim glow started to illuminate the room from nowhere in particular, growing brighter and brighter as his visitor walked toward him. Before long, he could see this was no tough guy. It wasn't even a guy at all. It was a woman, and an intensely beautiful one at that. The closer she got, the more powerless Harrison became to look away. She was short but strong, with very large eyes and silver-blonde hair. Harrison couldn't remember ever having seen a girl so lovely, but still, that wasn't enough to make him forget about...

"Where's Taylor?" he demanded as she grew nearer.

"Can you behave?"

Harrison blinked. "Sorry—what?"

"Can you behave?" The silver-blonde repeated herself patiently. "If I release you, do you promise to sit calmly? You won't attack anyone, break anything, do... anything stupid at all?"

"No. No, I won't."

"You promise?"

"I promise," Harrison affirmed.

"Cut him free," the silver-blonde said to nobody in particular. Harrison was very confused for about two seconds, then a massive, meaty hand grabbed his shoulder from behind with enough force to make his collarbone cringe.

"Hold still," came a deep voice from behind him.

"Who the fuck—" Harrison wriggled under the man's grasp, wheeled around the moment his ties were cut, and gasped. This man had Down Syndrome, or something like it, judging by his face, but he was enormous. Not the NFL lineman, 6'5", 315 pounds kind of enormous. The kind of enormous that made an NFL lineman look like a kid about to get his ass kicked if he didn't hand over his lunch money.

"Where did he come from?" Harrison asked the silver-blonde with more than a little panic. "Was he in here the whole time?"

"Yes," she replied simply.

"Why? Where am I?

"We didn't know if you'd be able to stay calm. We don't want an incident."

"You don't want—why—wait. Seriously, where am I?" Harrison repeated.

The silver-blonde sat in a chair across from him that had apparently materialized from nowhere. The room had become bright enough for Harrison to see his surroundings well. There was a window behind him with the shades drawn tight, and a few contraptions Harrison had never seen before hanging from the walls. The giant was still there, but he practically blended in. The silver-blonde was leaning forward in her chair, and her blouse fell open a bit to reveal the top of her breasts. He looked, and she looked at him looking, and her big, sharp eyes regarded him in a way that suggested... well, what, exactly?

That can't be an accident, Harrison found himself thinking again, as he struggled to wrench his eyes from her chest. But he couldn't. He physically could not.

This must be how perverts feel, Harrison thinks, shaking his head in an attempt to clear his thoughts.

"It's alright," the silver-blonde said, reaching forward to put a hand on his knee, exposing even more of her breasts. "You can look."

Harrison looked.

"You asked where you are. Do you still care to know?" Her voice was soft, yet somehow ethereal. Piercing. He'd never heard anything quite like it before.

Not particularly, Harrison thinks vaguely, but replies "yes" anyway.

"You're in the real world."

~

"I'm in the—the what?"

"The real world," the silver-blonde repeated. "With a real body. Your mind was unhinged from your artificial reality by the drug you ingested, so we had to help you out."

"You have to say that again. Slower."

The silver-blonde unbuttoned the top button of her blouse. She was practically bursting out of it. She laughed a bit at his reaction.

"I'll speak a language you understand. These," she said, cupping her breasts more than a little seductively with her hands, "are real. The first real breasts you've ever seen. That's why you can't look away."

This time, it was Harrison's turn to laugh. "Confident, are you?"

"Should I not be?"

Harrison had nothing to say.

"Your world is a simulation, Harrison. Nothing at all, really, except numbers and letters and code. That's what all your hopes and dreams are made out of. Your friends, your family... even your new girlfriend. You exist inside a computer."

Harrison cannot believe her, and yet, he must. Her presence, her voice, everything she's saying feels like the first unadulterated truth he's ever heard. And he remembers the code: the feeling of having no body, of being the numbers that made him up.

"Holy shit."

"You just... believe me? Like that?"

Harrison nodded.

"Huh. I must be prettier than I thought," she said flirtatiously. "Normally I have to prove it."

"Can you? Prove it, I mean?"

"Open the window," the silver-blonde directed the giant. He bumbled his way to the window and pulled the blinds up. Harrison gasped. The lights in the room dimmed as the light from the outside world poured out. The sunset was in its dying throes, washing the sky with colors more brilliant than any Harrison had ever imagined. He remembered the sunset from a few weeks earlier with disdain, however particularly stunning though it had been at the time. He remembered Taylor getting into his car, saying: "Did you see that fucking sunset?" That all paled in comparison to this, for as he sat, with this sunset and this girl, the clarity of his old world seemed to fade.

"Beautiful, isn't it?" the silver-blonde asked as the giant shut the blinds, dimming the room once more.

Harrison actually had to wipe tears from his eyes.

"That's a real sunset," the silver-blonde said.

"I never realized there was anything wrong with ours," Harrison replied feebly.

"Oh, yours are fine," she said. "All the beauty of our world is reflected in yours—we too have flowers, stars, cute baby animals—but not everything transfers into the computer. Your world just isn't quite as nice as ours."

Harrison wrenched his eyes away from her for just a moment. He looked at his hands. They looked a bit more real than his old hands. They felt a bit more sensation. It was as though his entire body, his surroundings, his senses, had all been upped from standard definition to HD. He asked the question that was growing in his mind.

"How am I here? How do I have a real body? If I'm just a simulated being, just code—"

The silver-blonde looked at the giant. "Leave us, please," she said. The giant lumbered out of the room, shutting the door behind him with surprising grace. The silver-blonde looked at Harrison as she stood up.

"You know, I don't exactly know how to answer that."

She slipped another button on her blouse, revealing the lacy edge of a sky-blue bra.

"We have experts, of course, who understand the science behind it all."

Another button.

"They're the ones who devised the whole experiment in the first place—and yes, your world is an experiment," she said, noticing the startled look on Harrison's face. "Nothing too cruel, mind you. Just an… observational study."

Another button.

"Nothing too cruel?" Harrison repeated, flabbergasted. He was trying to make sense of his surroundings, but even more baffling was this impossibly beautiful woman in front of him, her blouse now totally unbuttoned. Was this part of the experiment too?

"Children die of hunger in our world. Diseases. Bone cancer. Why not just… take those out of the simulation?"

With effortless elegance, the silver-blonde slipped out of her blouse entirely, looking at him with a mild but exasperated surprise. Maybe she couldn't believe he had bone cancer on the mind in the middle of her display.

"Your world was meant to reflect ours as closely as possible, Harrison. Still… we did take out a few things. Things we couldn't ethically include in the simulation. Things that are too horrible to subject another consciousness too, even if it is just code."

She flung her blouse at him playfully. It hit him in the face and slumped onto his shoulder. She tossed her hair back and adjusted her bra. And were the lights in the room dimming?

"Anyway," she continued, "your body. The best of my understanding is, it's part of the experiment. They want you to experience the best of what our world has to offer. See, every once in a great while, a consciousness becomes detached from its reality. It sees… the bigger picture. There was something slightly off, chemically speaking, with the particular batch of DMT you and your little lady friend ingested. That's how you lost your way."

Little lady friend. She'd said that with derision. As though Taylor were barely a grade above nothing. But then, in the face of this new knowledge, wasn't that exactly what she was? What everything was? Harrison was deeply disoriented. This high-definition woman was shattering his entire universe with a few short sentences, flipping everything he knew to be true on its head, while at the same time casually unclasping her bra to reveal a pair of breasts that rendered Harrison temporarily speechless. All he could do was puff out a huge breath of air.

She took the compliment.

"Thanks," she said with a light smirk before continuing. "So, Harrison, when a simulated consciousness like yours becomes detached, it takes a specialist to put you back in place. That usually happens without a hitch. But this time, our guys wanted to run a little test. They wanted to see if they could transfer your consciousness into our world, just for a short time, and then integrate you back into your own…"

She unzipped something in the back of her skirt, and let it fall over her legs onto the floor. She wore nothing underneath, now totally undressed save for a pair of crimson high heels. "I guess you're the lucky guinea pig," she said, in a voice barely above a whisper, walking toward him slowly, her high heels snapping on the floor.

"What… what are you doing?" Harrison stammered, his heart thrumming in his throat.

The silver-blonde (God, he didn't even know her name!) climbed on top of him, straddling him as he sat and caressing his hair with both hands.

"Just a little something to remember your trip by," she said.

Then she pressed her lips to Harrison's, and he was lost.

~

Harrison opened his eyes. He blinked a bit, rubbing his eyelids, trying to get his bearings.

"Hey, you," came a voice from his left. He turned.

"Taylor," he said, his brain emerging from the fog.

She smiled at him in relaxed ecstasy, practically slumped over the edge of the couch. "How was your trip?"

Harrison struggled to remember.

"Mine was incredible," Taylor said. "There were all these… numbers, and letters. It was like I was pure information, like computer code, you know? I felt—"

But Harrison held up a hand to silence her. With the other, he rubbed his head. It was all coming back to him. He had experienced the same trip Taylor had, yes… but there had been more, hadn't there? A room… a sunset… a giant. And a woman. Yes, a woman, with silver-blonde hair and a sky-blue bra and a skirt carelessly crumpled on the floor. That had happened too. It was only as he was in the stupor of an inconceivably real orgasm that he… that he what?

"I woke up," Harrison said, to himself.

He looked at his girlfriend. She did not seem beautiful to him anymore.

~

They tried to have sex a few more times, but Harrison couldn't get it up. These days, he couldn't do much of anything.

"What the fuck happened to you?" his girlfriend demanded, more than once, through tears.

"I woke up," was all he could say.

Taylor cried harder. Bitterly. "We never should have taken it, that stupid fucking drug…"

But they had taken it. And nothing could go back to the way it was. Nothing seemed real here. It was like looking at life through a window that hadn't been cleaned properly. It was infuriating.

The weeks passed, and they turned to months. Taylor had long ago left a post-it note on his bathroom mirror: "I'M GOING. GET SOME HELP". Harrison stopped showing up for work. The food in his fridge was all expired. Never mind. He only ate potato chips and cereal, dry from the box. He couldn't even boil water to make ramen.

Harrison wracked his brain constantly, searching for a logical way out of his existential purgatory. He once considered the possibility that maybe the silver-blonde's world was simulated too, but even if that were true, it didn't change his situation in the slightest. He was trapped in a fog of amotivation and apathy. It was maddening; he couldn't put his finger on why the fuck it even mattered that his world wasn't real; it seemed real to him, didn't it?

Well, it had. But not anymore. The other world had so much more to offer. Compared to the silver-blonde's naked breasts, Taylor's had been deflated and a bit blurry. Compared to the colorful rapture of the other sunset, this one—the one he found himself staring at now, from the 24th-floor observation deck of his corporate office building —seemed downright drab.

There had been one bright stretch when it seemed like maybe there was hope after all though. Harrison began to convince himself that he had imagined the real world and that it was no more real than anything people see on mushrooms or LSD. But deep down, he knew better. And when he finally extracted himself from his armchair to head down to Juice n' Java in search of his ex-girlfriend, he learned that she hadn't worked there in weeks. That she had moved out of state.

He got a hold of her dealer, though. He spent an absurd amount of money on DMT, demanding that his samples be selected from the same batch Taylor had bought. The dealer informed him that it was all mixed up, but that he'd do his best. And Harrison retreated back into his living room wilderness, drugs in hand.

His first trip was nice, but nothing to sell the farm over. Just lots of white and floating. If only that had happened with Taylor, Harrison thought. I could've woken up and gone on with my life. The second trip was a little less nice, and the third a little less than that. Even the most gratifying, sensual experiences this world had to offer were coming up short. Harrison was about to give up when a fourth and final trip catapulted him back into code.

If Harrison had tear ducts from which to weep, he would have wept. I'm back, screamed his consciousness through the thickness of the numbers. The words and numerals and commands drifted around him like pieces of garbage in the ocean. He was home. But his home became fuzzier, and fuzzier, and Harrison was losing his grip on it all. He was being sent back, being pushed, he could feel it—and before that world was closed to him entirely, he heard a woman's voice. He could practically see the silver-blonde tint to her hair as she said without sympathy: "I'm sorry, Harrison, but you can't come back."

That had been yesterday. But this was today, and the sun completing its final dive behind the Rocky Mountains to the west signaled that the day was nearly over. Just a few months ago, Harrison would have considered this sunset top-notch. Like the one he'd seen on that day he first made love with Taylor, it carried dark rain clouds through the colors in a breathtaking display of...of...of nothing. Harrison felt nothing. Not even fear.

His muscles had weakened from neglect, but he still managed to hoist himself up onto the high ledge of the observation deck. The wind rushed around him, raising little bumps on his flesh, and he let himself fall backward without a second thought. As his body tumbled through the air, he caught glimpses of a sunset so magnificent that people on the ground were actually getting out of their cars to admire it. He couldn't have cared less.

~

Somewhere both very close and very far away, a computer began to beep gently, then stopped. The code that had so carefully made up Harrison Samuel was obliterated into a meaningless jumble of symbols.

"Hm," said a man in a white coat, face expressionless, as he jotted a few notes onto his clipboard.

THE DEVIL'S WIFE

Tobias Wade

The Devil is known for his patience. He will see a ripening sin in our youth and wait all the long years of our life before the harvest. And why shouldn't he? What is one more soul to the untold billions in his dominion? What is one more year in the infinite span of his corrupted reign? Perhaps by waiting he is even giving us a chance to spend our lives repenting for what we've done, but I wouldn't know.

Sins such as mine are so terrible that no absolution is possible, so I suppose there was no reason for him to wait. He came for me in the woods while the mutilated woman I killed was still in my arms, warming my body with her blood. It's strange that I cannot remember why I killed her, or even who she is, but this feeling of guilt so permeates my being that I would have walked to Hell myself if I had but known the way.

I will not waste effort describing the Devil. The impoverished words at my disposal have only been designed for this material world. Even as he stood before me, he was more removed from my understanding than the glorious Sun was to a blind worm. It is suffice to say that he could not be perceived with any one sense, but the pressure of his presence so commanded my consciousness that I was aware of nothing else.

Escape was impossible. Words were meaningless. I let the woman slip from my arms and stood to face him with all the dignity remaining to a man so removed from God. When he turned from me and began to walk through the fading light of this dying world, I kept pace with him and did not turn to either side. Where we walked I do not know, but it seemed as though I could have relived my entire life in the time it took for him to stop.

As long as he was beside me, I could not make sense of what else might be. Even the thoughts in my head and the temperature on my skin were insignificant to his companionship. As terrifying as it was to know my fate, I had found certain tranquility in the mindless journey at his side. Now that I could feel him beginning to depart however, my mind revolted as though starting from a nightmare. I forced out the first thought I could muster to delay his departure.

"Who was she?"

"You will suffer more if you do not know."

And he was gone. And with him the curtain lifted within me to reveal the horror of his empire I now found myself mired within. Perhaps it would be more accurate to call Hell a person than a place however, considering the unceasing sentient screams which pummeled me from the land itself.

Writing shadows sensitive to the touch, grasping endlessly at me with hands that were not hands. Endless cities sprawled before me as open wounds upon the rotting corpse I stood upon. The sky was unobstructed by stars, instead vaulting endlessly into a timeless abyss, and looking at it I experienced the ghastly sensation of balancing on an eroding precipice which poised to tumble me endlessly into its yawning void. Charnel winds slithered their way into my nose and mouth with tangible substance, forcing me to let oiled coils like a writhing serpent penetrate my lungs with each breath.

Beyond the city in the distance rose the obscured ghosts of monstrous beings and Gods who roared in endless decay which fate had forgotten them to. Through this blasphemous temple to the end of the Universe I went, cowed constantly by half-conceived winged terrors which beat the air with a sound like the ceaseless wet bludgeoning of fists on flesh.

There are two kinds of pain which I had come to expect from the world of the living: the physical, and the emotional. Never had I experienced a physical pain so excruciating as the boils which began to swell across my body, nor a mental burden as debilitating as the taunting echoes which sneered at me from the living tissue beneath my feet. Every good memory of my life was poisoned against me, and each shame and guilt was magnified a thousand times over by the leering specters which narrated my ordeals with intimate knowledge and exaggerated effect.

Worse than either was the spiritual pain I endured however, the gnawing hopeless depression which robbed even my sense of self. I was not a person in Hell; I was Hell. I did not feel pain; I was pain—inseparable and indistinguishable. It was then, in the lowest reduction of my humanity as I crawled across the putrid ground in a trail of my own ruptured boils, that she took pity on me.

Gentle hands shed my skin from me; not as a torment, but a release. My disfigured limbs were cut away by her flashing knife, each slice bringing a pain so pure and clean that I welcomed it without question. Layer by layer she flayed me until at last there was nothing left to cut but my soul. Again it is difficult to describe her without the reliance of my mortal senses now stripped from me, but if you understood me when I told you that I was pain, you will understand again when I tell you she was beauty.

"My husband was wrong about you," she told me. "You didn't kill anyone, and you don't deserve to be here. I'm going to help you escape."

I couldn't comprehend how anything could exist outside of this. What universe would accept me, torn and broken as I was? What universe could I accept, knowing it had the capacity to so punish an innocent soul?

"I don't deserve it," what's left of me replied. "I know I killed her. It's something you can never cut from me."

"She killed herself by loving you, and for that you are not to blame. Do you see these hands?"

When she cupped my hands in her own, I knew that she was creating them as she spoke. Clean, strong hands, untouched by the blemishes of Hell.

"These hands could never be used for hurt. These eyes could never look upon such evil as its own creation."

I didn't even have a face before she spoke, but my entire body was growing with each word. It was as though the seed of my soul was sprouting new life; shards of bone lanced out and flourished with muscle like thickening bark, organs dropped and swelled like ripening fruit, and the network of veins and arteries blossomed toward her as though seeking nourishment from the sun.

Through the macabre landscape we sped, dancing across the festering world as softly as light through a drop of water. I could see her more clearly the further we traversed, although she never stayed still long enough for me to get a proper look. Bare feet skipped across the rotten land and twirled her through the looming specters which besought us on all sides. It is a wonder that the oppression of this unending night had failed to extinguish her spark, and invigorated by the purity of her wake, I was whole again.

"You are his wife then." It was difficult to speak to her as we raced, but I managed to slip in a few words every time I was able to draw near.

"We are bound to each other, yes," she replied, and then she was gone again; leaping fearlessly between fragile grips as she vaulted upward. I followed her up the tortuous, broken hand the size of a hillside which stretched vainly from the ground toward the vacuous sky.

"Of all the madness in this cursed place, that must king."

"My husband is not mad, and neither am I for being with him," she replied. She was pulling herself up through the fingers now, stopping to wait for me atop one of their monstrous joints.

"And if I were to love you instead," I asked. "Would that be mad as well?"

She smiled at me and stretched her slender hand to help me

clamber up beside her. We sat together staring upward from the bottom of an endless sky, the slightest brush of her leg against my own intoxicating me with rapture.

"All love is paradoxically mad," she replied. "It is an assault on reason, but in doing so it creates its own reason. But it won't do you any good, because this is where you have to leave."

"And you. Will you leave with me?"

She shook her head.

"You can't prefer to stay here!"

She nodded, saying: "But you are free now, and that is what matters. All you must do is jump from this point, and with the body I have given you, you will be able to fall all the way back up until you've left Hell altogether."

"I've already left Hell," I said, "since the moment you found me. And if I were to leave you here, then I know wherever I found myself would be Hell again without you there."

"You're being silly and wasting time. If my husband finds you with me—"

"He won't, because you're coming with me," I cut her off, preferring not to dwell on the thought of being found.

"I can't. I've made a promise—" she began.

"Then I can't either, and that's my promise to you." To prove my point, I even slipped down from the finger we sat upon and began crawling back toward the massive palm.

"Stop it! If he finds you he'll—"

"He'll what?" I shouted back. "What can he possibly do that he hasn't already?"

I saw in her something I could not live without, and she must have seen something in me which she could not let die. I hadn't even made it to the giant palm before her hands clasped me and heaved me back onto the twisted finger. We stood there for a long while together, hand in hand, staring up at the terrifying fall. Then the wet, bludgeoning drums of the winged creatures began, and I could feel the tension wash through her body. I watched her, although she could not meet my gaze, and just as the drumming began to close in around us, I felt her coil to leap.

We jumped together, flying and falling simultaneously in a dizzying tumble. The massive hand snatched at us as we began to depart, but it was too slow to prevent our liberation. The entire world screamed with more agony than could be contained, but though the land reverberated with its echoes, even this deafening cacophony was quickly falling behind.

The gut-clenching free fall distracted my attention, but I never let go of her hand as we whirled through the timeless void. It wasn't until the initial exhilaration began to fade when I could tell that something was wrong. I didn't have to look at her to feel her hand withering in my grasp. Her skin wrinkled and dried as though years of heat beat into it with every second we passed together. Soon she had begun to crack and bleed, washing me with her warm blood.

While I still felt healthy and strong, I was forced to watch with helpless terror as her body was devastated by the passage through the void. Her smooth hair began to mold and fall free in greasy clumps. Her face was torn as though blasted by relentless sand, and though her fingers clutched onto me ever more desperately, I could feel the strength fleeing from them.

No torment in Hell could match the guilt of knowing she was enduring this for me. As the spinning abyss began to slow, I was able to swim through the air and clutch her to me, cradling her in my arms as her body continued to deteriorate. Blood was now flowing freely from a thousand sourceless wounds. When finally the black sky relinquished us back into the woods where I began, I was soaked in her blood and my own freely falling tears.

Staring at her mutilated form, she was completely unrecognizable from before. My head was clouded as though freshly waking from a dream, and though I tried to hold onto the details, they were stolen from me with inexorable decay. Soon I could not even remember who I was holding, or how she had gotten there.

All I knew was that it was my fault, and the weight of the guilt which her death bade me carry. When the Devil came for me again, I knew I would follow him willingly. No matter what horror lay in store for me, I knew I deserved it for what I had done.

Letters from my
Dead Wife

The worst night of my life wasn't the night of my wife's death. The worst night was every night since.

I barely remember the actual accident. The phone call that sounded like a foreign language—swerving in and out of traffic on the way to the hospital—the surreal florescent lighting in that timeless waiting room: it's nothing but a blur. All I remember afterward was the surgeon who couldn't make eye contact with me, then sitting in my driveway for an hour and staring at the dark windows of my house.

It was a dream, almost like it was happening to someone else. Like it could only happen to someone else, because I couldn't understand how my life was supposed to keep going without her.

People keep telling me that things will get easier with time. The longer I wait, the more letters she writes though, and I don't know how much longer I can hold it together.

I recognized her handwriting immediately when the first one appeared. She'd written my name on the outside of a folded yellow paper which had been unceremoniously buried under a stack of junk mail. Inside, all it said was:

It's so quiet, but I can still hear you breathing. It's so dark, but nothing is hidden from me. Did we both die that night?

-Love M****

Cleanly printed in the same handwriting was "December 12th", the date of her accident.

It doesn't hurt, if that's what you're wondering, she wrote in a second letter which arrived a few days later. Not how things used to hurt anyway. Before when something hurts, you try to get away from it. Pull your hand away from the sharp stick, spit out the boiling tea.

Now pain feels more like being alive. When will you join me? I know you must be thinking about me because I can feel your thoughts race through my body like electricity in my veins. It gives me the strength to hold on, so I hope it never stops hurting. Is that how it feels for you too?

- Love M****

The written date was December 12th again, frozen in time. I stole from death each time I read and re-read those precious words. If pain was all she needed to feed, then she would never go hungry with me.

People have begun to disappear. Not all at once, but details and features keep slipping away until I can't even remember their names. Sometimes I'll call to the doctor and not notice until he turns around that he doesn't have a face. Conversations will sound normal in the background, but if I really focus I realize that the words are just random sounds that don't make any sense to me.

And the smell? Spoiled eggs. Festering meat. Rot and must so thick I can feel it trickling down my throat when I breath. It doesn't matter where I go, the smell is always the same. If you haven't smelled a flower today, do it now for both of us. What's it like? I can't seem to remember anymore.

- Love M****

You probably think I'm going crazy, don't you? I must be crazy for wanting to hold onto the comfort of this illusory connection. It wasn't the letters that were driving me crazy though. It was the smell which began to linger everywhere I went.

Spoiled eggs and festering meat were gentle words for the relentlessly condensing atmosphere. From the moment I woke up, air as thick as oil began slithering into my lungs. I'd wash myself with a rough sponge until my skin was bright and raw and burn incense night and day, but nothing ever cleared the vile intrusion of my senses.

Coats and hats are walking around without people in them. Whole neighborhoods are simply gone, replaced with a random clutter of empty buildings and blank earth. It's as though I've forgotten what goes there, but somehow my mind is desperately trying to cover up its own errors with a hodgepodge of things it steals from other memories. Every day the world becomes more "could be" and less "is".

I'll forget them if I have to. I'll forget where I was born and where I went to school. I'll forget all the places I've gone and the people I've known. I'll forget my own name, I don't care. As long as you keep reading these, then at least you'll remember. As long as I keep writing them...

Please don't let me forget you too.

- Love M****

The smell is getting worse. I didn't think it was possible, but I can't even breathe without gagging. I haven't left the house in three days, so I don't know if I'm the only one who notices. Everything I eat mushes into decay in my mouth and I can't sleep at night. I just lie awake thinking about what the next letter will say.

You did this to me. I don't know why, or how, but I'm trapped here because of you. The light that bleeds from your eyes is blinding me. Your thoughts are so loud that I can't hear myself think. Why does your house line every street of every block in the city? Why does your face peer from behind every door?

Why does it make me sad when you look through me and turn away?

- M****

The space between life and death had never been so thin. Tenebrous silhouettes are always squirming in my peripheral vision these days. Shadows behind furniture linger for a full second after the light has been turned on. I hear footsteps in empty rooms and I'm positive that I've closed more doors than I've opened. Then late at night when I'm lying awake in bed, I'll hear them open again.

And always always the pervading rot, so real and present that I need to constantly check myself to make sure I'm not the one who is decomposing. That's the only explanation that makes sense to me. Knowing that she's rotting while I must endure—it's killing me. I didn't think she understood that until the next letter.

When you're gone, there won't be anything left to keep me here.
 - M

If I thought putting a bullet in my brain would have helped her move on, then someone would have been scrubbing my brains off the walls by now. I just don't see how something as measly as a bullet is going to make me let her go. Or maybe I'm a coward and that's just an excuse. I couldn't go on living like this, but maybe there was something in me that wanted to keep living somehow.

I went for a walk that night, but I couldn't find cleaner air anywhere. Not even in the cemetery where she was buried. It's odd, because I distinctly remember thinking how pure it felt here during her funeral. The whole world is painted in shades of gray, but graveyards are only white and black.

The smell only grew stronger while I was digging. The laminated casket was harder to break than I expected, but I wasn't in a rush. The enduring rhythm of my shovel pummeling the lock was like the heartbeat of this place, and the pain which drove the blade was its blood.

Between my pain and the lock, the lock proved less enduring. There was a sheet of blue velvet covering her body, but I didn't need to see her as I poured the gasoline on top. The wretched odor will burn clean. Her rotting mind will burn clean. I will…

I emptied the whole gallon of gasoline and tossed the match. Not exactly how I imagined saying goodbye, but there was something cathartic about watching the flames rise from the gutted earth. As long as there was a body, I couldn't shake the feeling that she was that body. Now she was the smoke and the sky and all the vastness of space. Now she was free.

That's why I didn't expect a final letter waiting for me when I got home in the early hours of the morning.

Profane desecration. The defiler will burn. -M

The shadows don't have the decency to hide their intent anymore. The doors don't wait until I've left the room before they taunt me with their opening. More worrying still are the doors that won't open even when they're unlocked, and the sparks which have begun to breathe smokeless from the electrical sockets.

Whatever remains of my wife isn't my wife anymore. She doesn't even remember me, but I hope she recognizes me when we're together again soon.

Redefining Love

I didn't believe that stars were real when I was a little girl growing up in New York. My parents told me they were drowned out by the city lights, but that didn't seem possible. It just didn't make sense how something that big could be completely invisible. What was the big deal anyway, if they were duller than ordinary light-bulbs?

I was seven years old before I took a trip to the country and saw the endless heavens for the first time. One by one, little beads of light began sneaking through the dusk.

"Those are planes," I declared righteously. My parents only smiled. The stars kept coming—hundreds, thousands, webs and clusters, miraculously bursting out of nowhere as though they were being created just for me. I remember laughing out loud and flinging myself into the air, rushing to climb the tallest tree just to stretch a little bit closer.

It didn't matter if I couldn't reach them—it didn't even matter if I never saw them again. I knew they existed, now and forever, hiding there watching over me. And I swore with all the ferocity of a seven year-old's swelling heart that I'd never love anything less than this feeling for the rest of my life.

That's what first love is like. Feeling the world change overnight. Nothing into something, leaving you a helpless bystander while it rewrites everything about who you are and the reality you live in.

I was in sixth grade when I looked at a boy like that for the first time. We were hugging out of excitement for the last day before summer break when he snuck in a kiss, smiling sheepishly at me while the whole class cheered and laughed at the scandal.

I thought I suddenly understood what love meant. That was it for me, I decided. I knew how to love now, and I'd never need to learn again. How could I have known that "love" meant something new with every passing year? I didn't understand the anxiety, the jealousy, the doubt, or the soul-crushing rejection that would prove to be inseparable from such wonder.

After all the stars have gone, smothered beneath the fury of the inevitable sun, it's impossible to believe what fool could dream such a thing to be.

High-school, college, twenties and thirties. Excitement before disappointment. Hope before regret. They come and go, tugging and pulling at the heart, but not like they used to. They weren't the first, and they won't be the last. My forties passed, then my fifties, the frenzied march of years convincing me that I was too busy to waste time looking at an empty sky.

Then I met Jason and I knew what I had been missing all this time. I'd been wanted before, but I'd never been needed. Jason was already dying from cancer when we met. He'd given up, just like me. He thought he was going to die alone, just like me. I could feel the urgency of his hands like electricity on my skin. The desperation in his eyes when he confessed his feelings for me. It was intoxicating.

I cared for him through every laborious step of his treatment. I'd lay blankets down on the hard bathroom floor and setup his laptop on the toilet tank. We'd sit together watching his favorite musicals for hours until he'd vomited himself dry. Even when his face was plastered with sweat, his bloody gums would still flash a smile when I sang along.

Some days Jason would be strong enough to walk outside or play his guitar. He was a fantastic musician, and when he got going his husky dog would start wagging and howling along to the tune. I laughed so hard and loved so deep in those moments that they became frozen in time. Even his death couldn't steal this from me.

We cried together as he called his family and told them his time was running out. His pain was my pain, his love my love, and despite the ordeal, I can never remember being so happy. Then came the news: the chemo was successful. The cancer went into remission. We'd won.

Love means fighting for someone. I understand that now. Not letting go, not giving up, holding on like you'll drown without them. It wasn't easy, but what worth having is?

We didn't see each other as often now that he was able to return to work. We fought more, but we always made-up. He cheated, but I forgave him. Love survives, love endures. And the more I struggled to be happy with that man, the more I refused to accept how much of myself I'd have wasted if he were to leave.

Jason knew that his remission wouldn't last forever though. When he started getting sick again, he remembered how much he needed me. He was too tired to go back for another round of treatment and keep fighting, but it wouldn't have helped even if he had.

The arsenic in his food isn't going to kill him. Not at the levels I use. It's just enough to remind him that he needs me, and that I need him. That's what it means to love.

These were the blackest days of his despair, but at least he didn't have to suffer alone. Jason was shaking terribly all the time now, except when he lay so pale and still that I had to keep checking for breath. He was too weak to leave the house on his own, but he didn't put up much resistance when I decided to take him for a drive.

I brought him out to the country where my parents took me all those years ago and we lay side-by-side under the brilliance of an eternal sky. It's the same sky my seven year old heart went wild for, and after all this time, I finally realize that it's the same love I felt too. Love stayed the same while I changed around it, but I was finished now. Jason had made me into who I was meant to be.

I hadn't counted on that little expedition giving him so much hope. He started making a fuss about going back to the hospital to start his treatments again, but I knew that would only end in unhappiness for us both.

I kept making excuses why I couldn't take him. I thought he'd be too tired to keep pushing and give up sooner or later, but then I caught him trying to make an appointment behind my back. I had to increase the dose of his arsenic up to 75 mg a day, still half the lethal dose for someone his size. It was enough to make him too blind to drive, which at least bought me some more time to explain how he wasn't thinking straight.

I didn't expect Jason to take a taxi to his appointment. I thought he trusted me to know what was best for him. When I got home to the empty house I knew things were going to get rough from here.

As soon as the tests came back, a few days at the longest, they were going to tell him that his cancer was still in remission. He might even find out what I was doing. He wouldn't understand why I did it though, and he'd hate me forever.

I had no choice but to lock him in his room as soon as he got home. I took away all his phones and devices so he couldn't find out the truth. I'd sit with him and we'd watch his shows and I'd sing to him like we used to, but it wasn't the same anymore. He couldn't overpower me physically, but like the manipulative man he can be sometimes, Jason resorted to begging and pleading. I had to increase his dose again, just to get him to shut up.

Too much arsenic and I might as well be having a date with a body pillow. Too little and he'd start asking questions that I couldn't answer. I found the right dose eventually though, and it would have been almost perfect except that the dog was howling all the time now.

We were so happy until Jason caught me. It was that stupid dog's fault, barking and carrying on, making me chase it all over the house before I could get it to shut up. Jason wasn't in the room when I got back. He'd made it all the way to the kitchen, almost to the back door before—

"What's this?" he asked. The bottle that made our love possible in his trembling hands.

"Medicine. Go back to bed, you're not well enough to—"

But he wouldn't listen. I don't know if he could even read the label, but I think somewhere deep inside he already knew what was going on. Even if it was just unconsciously—he wanted to stay sick. He wanted to be taken care of. But he had a temper, and now that he knew for sure he was too stubborn to ever let it go.

"You're insane. You're absolutely insane," Jason shouted. He was running through the kitchen blind, smashing into cabinets and flailing through the hanging pots. He was acting so crazy that I think some of the arsenic must have gotten into his brain.

It was just too stressful. He was screaming. I was screaming. The dog was going wild again, barking and snarling and bristling up. Somehow Jason managed to get a knife into his hand, but he wasn't strong enough to hold onto it.

I was sobbing when I pinned him to the floor. I didn't know what to do. There aren't instructions to love. There isn't right or wrong. There's just happiness and unhappiness, and it broke my heart that he didn't want to be happy with me anymore. At this point it would be easier if he were dead and couldn't disturb the frozen memories where everything was still perfect. I didn't want to, but love sometimes means doing what is hard. I could feel that desperate energy radiating from his hands locked around my wrists again. Almost like when we first met...

But I was stronger. I forced the knife lower, inch by excruciating inch, until the blade was right up against his throat. I still don't know if I could have done it, but at least my intentions were good. The dog got me by the back of my neck first. I'd never seen him bite anyone before, but he had me good and dragged me all the way across the tile floor. I think I grazed it with the knife a few times, but the beast just clamped down harder and pinned me down until I heard the kitchen door slam.

The sky has never felt so empty. I let the dog follow its master without taking my revenge, and I'm completely alone now. I haven't seen either of them for over week, and I don't expect I will again. I'm not going to pretend that I didn't make mistakes. A lifetime of learning about love, but somehow I still know less than when I saw the stars for the first time all those years ago. That's what life is though. Making mistakes. Getting hurt. Learning and trying again. For me, that meant buying rope for next time.

FORKED TONGUE BEHIND A SMILE

Kyle Alexander

I live in a more rural area of Northern California. There's only one large shopping center within a 40 mile radius, so everyone tends to do their shopping there. Ever since I got out of prison on parole, I have switched to a plant-based diet in order to improve my health. I moved up north from Los Angeles in order to keep myself out of trouble and put the past behind me. I'm not a bad guy, just a man who grew up on the wrong side of the tracks and made a lot of poor life decisions.

There are a lot of freaks and weirdos in the city I came from. I thought that I'd find more of a normal demographic out here in the sticks, though I've recently come to terms with the fact that you can't hide from the crazies.

I'd regularly visit the grocery store in order to keep a nice stock of fresh produce. Most of the employees in the produce department are just young kids who are taking up a part-time job for pocket change while they work towards their high-school diploma. One man, Jeff, is the only adult who works in the produce department.

Jeff is tall, looks young for his age, but has to be at least mid 50s. He has thin brown hair with a bald spot on the top of his scalp, and he wears perfectly round glasses. Over the past years, Jeff and I became close acquaintances.

Jeff definitely was a strange one. He'd always get a little too close when we spoke. Other times he'd touch my shoulder or forearm during a conversation. I always brushed it off as Jeff just being a very eccentric dude. If only I knew it was just the tip of the iceberg.

Jeff held a package of strawberries in his hand. "Did you know strawberries aren't actually berries? Oddly enough, bananas are. The more you know!"

I'd always find something about his words to be enlightening. I felt that I'd learn something new from each conversation we'd have together. He was a very interesting guy.

"Bananas have a natural anti-acidic effect. If you ever suffer from heartburn, eat a banana and it will provide some relief." Jeff educated me as he stocked the stand full of fresh bananas. He was always so excited about his work: the way he spoke about food, his upbeat attitude, and the way he'd caress each item as if it were a newborn child.

The automated doors to the supermarket slid open, a relieving gust of air conditioning greeting me as I entered. I remember there was a popular song playing over the speakers throughout the store. I grabbed a basket and headed over towards the produce department where I was greeted by a familiar face. Jeff was there stocking red delicious apples—exactly what I came in for.

He turned his head towards me and smiled, revealing a set of perfectly white teeth. "Good morning, John. It's going to be another wonderful day isn't it?"

"Oh, absolutely. It seems like you knew I was coming since you're putting out some fresh apples. That's exactly what I came in for." I replied, turning a shiny red apple in my hand; examining it for blemishes.

Jeff chuckled as he put another handful of produce neatly on the stand.

"Interesting fruit they are. Apples are actually 25% air, did you know that? That's why they float if you drop them in water," Jeff announced, gracefully juggling 3 apples before setting them on the stack.

He broke down the cardboard on his little cart and took a glance at his wristwatch.

"Looks like it's about time for my break. You have a great day, John." He touched me on the shoulder and looked me right in the eyes. Normally I'd find it creepy as hell, but it was Jeff, and I was used to him by that point.

Jeff whistled 'I'm Walking On Sunshine' to himself as he wheeled the cart towards the stockroom doors. As he pushed through them, a slab of cardboard slipped off of his cart and fell to the floor. Jeff bent over to pick it up and his wallet fell out of his back pocket.

I jogged over to him, trying to get his attention, but Jeff already disappeared into the cold stockroom. I was left with his wallet. Fortunately for him, I have a bit of integrity and planned to wait around for him to return. Just because I have integrity doesn't mean that I don't get curious though. Jeff never showed me pictures of his family. He claimed that he didn't own a cellphone either. I went ahead and took the initiative to snoop through his wallet. There was $20 in cash, he had no credit cards, not even a store rewards card or ID. I found a discreet fold behind the empty slots for cards, and removed a few photos neatly folded into fourths.

Puzzled and a little disturbed, I couldn't believe what I was looking at. They were small copies of professionally taken photos of him standing in front of a scenic background in a studio. He had that same charismatic smile. In his arms were two petite potted plants. Alongside him stood a stool with a cantaloupe placed on top of it. He had his arm resting around the backside of the melon as if it were his best friend.

I didn't have much time to further examine the other photos as the stockroom doors swung open and a cart was being wheeled onto the sales floor. I quickly stuffed the pictures back into his wallet and slapped it shut. Behind the cart was same old Jeff, completely unaware of my intrusion.

He smiled at me, and I extended my arm to him with the wallet.

"Oh thank you! Wow, I would've been so upset if someone other than yourself picked that up. Some people really lack the honest quality of returning a man's personal possessions. You, my friend, are a saint." Jeff's eyes shifted back and forth between me and the wallet in my hand.

I shook my hand, gesturing for him to take his wallet back. Jeff slowly reached out and grabbed it, his fingers brushing against mine in an intimate way that not only lasted too long, but made me slightly uncomfortable.

"All in a day's work," I said as he tucked the wallet away into his back pocket. He smiled.

"Please, let me show you my gratitude. Join my family and I tonight for dinner. I'm doing the cooking, so you know it will be to die for!" Jeff pleaded. He didn't once break eye contact with me.

I started to conduct a reasonable excuse in my head. I didn't want to eat someone else's cooking as I had many dietary restrictions. I must've taken too long though, because he was speaking again.

"John, you must, I will not take no for an answer. Here's my address."

John pulled a small notepad and pen from his uniform pocket and scribbled on a piece of paper. He tore the page from the booklet and shoved it into my hand, winking at me.

"Dinner will be around 7. I suggest you show up early so we can have some fun beforehand." Jeff didn't wait for a reply. He pushed past me with his cart further into the sales floor, whistling the same tune as before.

I didn't really have any reason not to go. He and I had been acquaintances for quite some time, and it would be rude not to. On the other hand, I was terrified that he was a sick weirdo and would capture me and skin me alive. I convinced myself to go inside my own head. At the time, I should've trusted that feeling in the pit of my stomach. Something was trying to tell me otherwise.

I finished up with my shopping and headed home. For the remainder of the afternoon, I couldn't shake the sense of angst that I carried around with me. I should've listened.

I left my house around 6:30pm. It was transitioning into fall (although the temperature said otherwise), and the sun was beginning to set. The sky was painted a gradient mixture of purple, red, and orange that didn't seem to help with my anxiety. About 30 minutes later I was pulling down a long dirt road that was nearly hidden by trees. My GPS said my destination was just another half mile down the road. I must've had a bad signal because it felt like I drove at least 2 miles until I got to his driveway.

Jeff's house was a single-story rambler style home. It's paint was starting to fade, but you wouldn't notice due to the immaculate garden in his front yard. A brown wooden fence which stood about 4 feet high surround his yard, leading all the way to the back of the house. I pulled my car into the driveway and parked, leaving the door unlocked for reasons I couldn't recall. As I approached the front steps to his door I took a moment to appreciate the amount of effort he put into his garden. I passed by the line of shrubs that surrounded the edge of his lawn and kicked around an apple that had fallen from a tree in the center of his yard.

I climbed the couple of steps that led up to his front door. I pulled open the screen which was in front of it and knocked lightly. All of the shades were drawn, forbidding me from looking inside to see if anyone had noticed I arrived. A few minutes passed, and I knocked again, louder. No response. I wondered if I had misheard the invitation, but I was definite that he said to come over that evening.

I stepped down to the yard and followed a stone path which led around the side of the house into the back yard. It was almost full-on dusk by this point, and it was getting hard to navigate through the maze of foliage that cluttered his property. I managed to make my way around to the back porch when I heard that familiar tune. The back of his house was just as a giant fruit and vegetable garden. I could see the very top of a large greenhouse over the unusually tall artichoke plants and other assorted vegetable stalks.

I follow the whistling towards the green house that sat on the other side of the yard. When I got a few feet away from the door, the whistling stopped and Jeff's voice echoed from inside.

He was talking to someone. I crept up to the door which was slightly ajar and peered inside. There was no one around other than himself. I couldn't make out what he was saying, so I leaned closer to hear.

A branch snapped underneath my foot as I shifted my weight, and Jeff jumped in a startled jolt. He turned around and smiled.

"John! Oh I'm so sorry, I didn't even realize that it was time for you to arrive. Please excuse my messy self, I have been gardening since I got home." Jeff was covered in unidentifiable red liquid which had a odd resemblance to blood.

"Please, please come in. I want to show you something!" Jeff beckoned.

I was hesitant to come inside. Something about that greenhouse was just horribly unsettling. I should've left. I should've made an excuse to why I had to leave at that very moment. For reasons I still don't understand, I entered.

The greenhouse appeared even larger from the inside. Spider-like vines crawled up the interior walls and scattered across the ceiling in an sinister way. A partially transparent sliding glass door stood at the end of the room, leading to a smaller area where a strange green light glowed from behind the frosted glass. I could feel an ominous presence from within.

Outside of the door were two large barrels and an even larger ceramic pot. I couldn't even imagine how much it must've cost since it stood nearly five and a half feet from the ground. Did the produce business pay better than I thought?

Jeff gestured for me to come quicker; I didn't, taking my time to approach him. His expression was no different from the many encounters we had at the supermarket, so I couldn't trace the source of my discomfort.

"Take a look at this, John, isn't it magnificent!?" He stepped away from a large hole that had been concealed by his body.

The hole was about three feet wide and went down a lot deeper than it appeared from a distance. I took a step closer in order to see how far it went. Jeff hummed to himself in a very disturbing way. I was so distracted by inspecting the hole I hadn't noticed he sneak around my backside.

"What am I supposed to be looking at—"

I was interrupted by a loud shriek that pierced my eardrums like a sharp needle. Something pushed me forward with great force. I lost my footing and slipped into the hole feet first. I must've clipped my chin on the way down, because I felt a hard crack in my jaw and started to feel dizzy.

A splash of cold water to my face woke me. I tried my move, but I couldn't. I felt cold. When my vision cleared, I saw two perfectly manicured feet standing directly in front of me. This is when I realized that I was still in the hole, the empty space around me filled with soil. I was buried up to my neck.

"Wakey, wakey, John. It's time for your nutrients. If you're going to grow nice and strong, you have to be healthy. I can't have you dying on me."

I squirmed and wiggled, trying to loosen the dirt around me. The soil was too wet and heavy.

"Jeff, what the fuck are you doing to me? Let me go!" I cried. Jeff just kept whistling "I'm Walking On Sunshine" and squatted in front of me, holding a small brown bottle in hand.

"Open wide, John. You need your supplements." He held the bottle up to my mouth. I curled my lips tight, stopping him from feeding me the mystery drink.

Jeff pinched my nose and forced my head back. About 30 seconds went by until I was forced to suck in a large breath of air through my mouth. Jeff shoved the bottle down my throat and the foul-tasting liquid sailed down into my stomach. I coughed and wheezed, trying to reject whatever it was that he just fed me. Jeff only laughed.

"You know, John, I really liked you. But I love my family, and my family has to eat. Unlike us, they're carnivores and they have a very picky eating habit. I hope you can understand, even if you aren't a family man yourself."

Jeff walked towards the corner of the room, just outside of my limited vision. I heard some some rustling, and soon after Jeff came back into view. He was holding a melon, a silver dollar sized hole bored into the center of it. Jeff dropped his pants and underwear.

"My ex-wife left me because she felt I cared more about my garden than our family..." Jeff soon became erect and slid his penis inside the opening of the melon. I was in shock. I couldn't believe what was before my eyes. He slowly started to thrust his hips, sliding in and out of the melon.

"I came home from work to see she had packed her bags, as well as our two little girl's. She told me she was leaving. Just like that!" Jeff's thrusts became more rapid. He was groaning between sentences.

"John, what would you do if someone tried to snatch your life right out of your hands? Oh wait, you know exactly what I'm talking about. You were in prison, right? Armed robbery and assault with a deadly weapon, right? Four years in state? You're a burden on society, John. No one will miss you."

I screamed for help at the top of my lungs. My body thrashed beneath the soil. It was starting to loosen. I could feel my arms gaining a bit more mobility.

"I felt a rage inside me that I never felt before. It was overwhelming. I wasn't going to just let her take my family away from me. Not her, not anyone. So I did what I had to do to keep my family together... forever."

Jeff was thrusting even harder. He clenched the melon in both hands, holding it tightly against his pelvis.

"You are a sick fuck! You are a sick piece of shit! Fuck you! Fuck you!" I shouted. They were the only words I could muster. I was beyond angry. I was livid. I'd spent four years in anger management while incarcerated learning how to control my anger, but this time it was justified.

"John, I am not sick. I was a desperate man. I did no wrong, I only did what any man would do in that situation. Wouldn't you?" Jeff stopped thrusting for a moment and glanced over at the sliding glass door. Then he went back to fucking his melon.

"I tried to reason with her. I tried talking to my little girls. I wanted them to stay and we could be a happy family, but she wouldn't budge. So I did what I had to do. I can now take care of my wonderful garden and be attentive to my family at the same time. My wife loved cantaloupe, so I found it suitable that she be..." Jeff threw back his neck and arched his spine. He let out a long and satisfied moan. He finished. The swinging lightbulb over his head combining with the darkness of the greenhouse made him look even more menacing.

Now panting and covered in sweat, Jeff raised the cantaloupe up to his face. He whirled around in a circle, holding it above his head. He kissed the top of the melon and gently placed it on a mound of soil beside him. I couldn't hold it back any longer. My stomach churned and vomit sprayed out of my mouth with unrelenting force.

"John, maybe you don't understand. What do you find so revolting about a man making love to his wife? It's just natural." Jeff pulled up his trousers and squatted in front of me again.

"My children, my sweet little girls, they weren't fully grown. They were still young and innocent. I couldn't just bury them like their mother, they hadn't yet blossomed..." he stood up and walked over to the sliding glass door.

Jeff threw open the slider and two giant pots were sitting in the center of the small room. Inside were these horrifying Venus fly trap looking plants. The abominations were tall and flesh colored. Giant human-like teeth, only sharper, filled the insides of their mouths, stopping them from closing all the way. The rest of their faces were scaly but appeared to be soft like skin.

The ruckus Jeff caused must've startled the beasts; they snarled, large pointed tongues swirling around as a white foam oozed out their mouths and puddled onto the floor below. A high pitched "hiss" came from their throats as they swayed around aimlessly, biting at the air.

"Awwwe, they're awake. I'm sorry, girls, dinner isn't ready just yet. I know you're hungry." Jeff caressed the monsters and spoke to them in a baby-like tone.

During his distraction, I managed to loosen up the dirt to the point where I could freely move my arms underneath. I started to kick my legs around and wiggle my hips; the dirt loosened all around me. I pulled my arms up near the surface, just before the top of the dirt.

Jeff had stopped playing with his children and was heading in my direction. He was wielding something in his left hand: a syringe. I readied myself—I only had one chance to get it right. His smile had only grown wider and more sinister as he approached. He crouched down and got almost eye level with me.

"John, normally I let their dinner marinate for a bit, but this is an exception. You see, I got a little too excited and woke them from their nap. Now they're hungry and they won't stop crying until they're fed."

The hissing floated in the background of Jeff's voice.

"I need to prepare dinner."

Jeff turned and glanced at his disgusting creations. That was my opening. My hands shot out of the ground. With my left, I grabbed Jeff by his thinning hair and smashed his face into the dirt. He dropped the needle as I used my other hand to repeatedly punch him in the side of his face. He squirmed and thrashed in attempts to break free of my hold. I used all of my might to pull the upper half of my body out of the hole and reached for the syringe. With a stroke of luck, I managed to grab it. I jabbed the sharp steel into his neck and slammed the plunger down with my thumb. I then went back to wailing on his swollen face.

It didn't take long for the sedative to work. The creatures sneered and growled as I pulled the rest of my body from out of the dirt. After finishing off Jeff with the heel of my boot, I turned towards his children. I stepped into the room and one of those abominations snapped at me. I spit back at the beast, which growled at me like a rabid dog, it's long pointed tongue hanging out the side of its mouth. I've never seen something so disgusting.

Looking around for something to kill them with, I noticed a few gas containers. One of them had a small sticker with a picture of a little flame on it that read "flammable". Bingo. I turned the valve to release the contents of the tank and quickly exited the room, shutting the door behind me. With a tuft of dead shrubbery in one hand, my cigarette lighter in the other, I let out a light chuckle to myself and tossed the burning branches into the room.

I didn't even bother to look back as I exited the greenhouse into the warm night's air. The howling of Jeff's creations were assurance enough. I had an internal argument with myself as I walked back to my car. It was whether or not I should call the police. I chose not to. There was no explanation to why me, an ex-convict on parole, would soon be on dead man's property with possible charges of murder and arson. No fucking way I was going to take that risk.

A week later I read in the newspaper that the fire department had discovered the remnants of 75 bodies buried within his garden, three of which were his wife and 2 children. Apparently Jeff had been connected to a series of missing people that was going on for the better part of a year. They labeled him "The Green Thumbed Killer".

Jeff had been a busy man in his free time. He was one sadistic piece of shit. It's kind of funny when you think about it. Sometimes the happiest, most collected people are actually the ones you should be afraid of. They are the wolf in sheep's clothing. They are the ones who shake your hand and greet you with a wide smile, the smile hiding the forked tongue of a monster.

MIRROR WELL

.

Rona Mae

I grew up on a farm in the seventies in rural Minnesota.

I was an only child, but only by chance. Ma was a good, Catholic woman who wanted to have at least a dozen fat little babies, but after she had me the doctors told her that her body couldn't stand to bear another child. She was a sickly woman, small and much too thin, and carrying big ol' me was just too much for her. I was a whopping ten pounds twelve and a half ounces. She almost didn't make it through my delivery.

Ma settled for one healthy baby boy, and she devoted herself to me and my upbringing like nothing you've ever seen before. She was always the perfect mother, perfect housewife, perfect everything, and she liked it that way.

Pa was a good Christian man who went to church every Sunday morning. So, if he drank a little too much or was a little firm of hand with me, well, that can be overlooked. He was a good father, even on days when I wasn't a good son.

We raised hogs and grew beans and corn on our farm. We had a barn full of hay and another barn full of tractors, some nice John

Deeres that were my father's pride and joy. You'd never have seen him buying an International, that's for sure. Pa was the brains behind our operation, I did the chores, and Ma took care of the house. Though she did her fair share of chores, too, sometimes more.

Overall, I guess you could say that I led a pretty good life back in those days. Everything was good and wholesome and quiet.

Except for the well.

It sat on our yard, halfway between the side of the house and the tractor barn. It was always covered and, as far as I could tell, we didn't have much of a use for it. I asked Pa about it once when I was a kid, and he told me that it had dried up. I guess that answer was good enough for me because I don't recall ever asking him about it again, or showing much interest in it until the summer of '76.

By that time, I was fifteen, meaning I was young enough to take a lot of stupid risks, but old enough not to get caught most of the time. I had two good friends, Jacob and Augustine. Augustine's mother was an even more extreme Catholic than my mother, hence his name, but we called him Gus. Jacob's father was a drunk and his mother was dead, so he spent a lot of time at either Gus's or my house. My mother had a soft spot for unwanted children, and Jacob was definitely that, so she treated him with special care and tenderness. Even my father looked out for him.

So, it was Gus, Jacob, and I against the world. We spent almost all of our time together, and I wouldn't change those endless hours for anything. Even in light of what happened that summer.

It started in July. The day was hot and dry, like all the days before it. The corn was struggling out of the ground, combating the lack of moisture that could be my family's downfall. Pa wasn't in a good mood that day, probably because of the drought, so Ma told us boys to steer clear of him, which we did gladly.

Now, I'm not sure why it caught Jacob's attention. Even today I can't quite understand what was the catalyst for all of this. Did the blistering heat make Jacob think of water? Did he hear something echoing from the darkness that called to him? What is just pure chance?

I wish I knew.

Whatever the reason, Jacob walked away from us and whatever we were doing and started to head for the well.

"What are you doing, Jake?" I called to him. I don't remember what Gus and I were doing. Probably just screwing around like dumb kids.

"Why's this well all boarded up, Charlie?"

Gus and I made our way over to the well. Jacob had already climbed on top of the cement cover and was staring down at it.

"Pa said the well went dry. Probably covered it up so nobody would fall in. Why?"

"There's a hole," he said, kneeling down. And, of course, he was right—there was a little round hole that could give you a glimpse into the well if you had enough light. I'd never really thought to look down before. I just figured there wasn't anything to see.

"Fetch me a flashlight, won't you, Charlie?"

"Why do you want to look in there, anyway?" The heat made me feel sluggish, and I was far too lazy to make the short walk up to the house.

"Because I wanna see what's in it, that's all. Will you stop whining and just go get it?"

"I'll go," said Gus, walking towards the house. That suited Jacob and I just fine, so we sat down on the top of the well and waited for him to get back. A comfortable silence stretched out between us, filling the summer air until Gus got back.

He was munching on a chocolate chip cookie as he climbed up the well to us. "Your ma's makin' cookies, Charlie. She gave me the first one."

I rolled my eyes. "That's 'cause you're a suck-up."

"Gimme that," said Jacob, grabbing the flashlight from Gus. He struggled a little to avoid blocking the light with his face, but eventually he managed it, peering down into the darkness with one eye.

A few moments of silence passed before my curiosity got the best of me. "What do you see down there?"

"There's a... ladder. And something else... it looks like a magazine? Or a poster? I can't quite tell."

"A ladder?" I frowned. I didn't know much about how wells worked, but I didn't think the bottom of the well would be much bigger than the top. "Is the ladder standing up?"

"No… it's laying down. I can only see part of it. There must be some kind of a tunnel down here!"

"You're messing with us," said Gus, "That's not how wells work."

I didn't think so either, but Jacob pulled away and gestured to the hole. "If you don't believe me, look for yourselves."

So we did. And we discovered that he was right. There definitely appeared to be a tunnel on the left side of the well.

"Well, I'll be," muttered Gus. He was the last to look. As he pulled away from the hole, he glanced at us with obvious confusion. "What's the point of that, anyway?"

I shrugged. "I guess I could ask my dad…" Sometime in a few days when he's a little less irritable.

"Maybe that's how wells are supposed to work," said Jacob, although it was clear that he was doubtful.

"I don't think so," I said.

"But then why…" began Gus.

We were interrupted by the sound of Ma calling us from the house. "Boys! Dinner is ready!"

We each leapt down from the well and ran for the house, momentarily forgetting the most recent object of our curiosity.

Sometimes I wonder what would have happened if we'd just left it at that.

That night, Gus went back to his house, but Jacob stayed to lend Pa a helping hand as his father hadn't been home for a few nights and his house was running out of food.

We didn't think about the well for the rest of that day or night. We might have gone on forever not thinking about it, except that Pa woke us up roaring the next morning.

"Charlie! Jacob! What the hell do you two idiots think you're doing?!"

We, of course, thought we were sleeping. We were wise enough not to tell him that, though, and we just let him keep yelling at as, swearing a blue streak as his face got redder and redder.

"Did you think you were funny? Don't you have any idea how dangerous that is?"

We had no idea what he was talking about. When we told him as much, that made him even angrier. I'd never seen him so mad. I thought he might spit fire if this went on much longer.

We swore over and over again that, whatever had happened, we'd had no part in it. He didn't believe us for even a second. Eventually, he ordered us to our feet and marched us outside to where the old well sat.

The cover was missing.

That huge cement cover was just... gone. Like it had never been there in the first place. What's more, it was nowhere to be found.

"Where did you put that goddamn thing?!" shouted Pa, spittle flying from his lips.

Jacob and I were speechless. There was no way we could have moved the cover. It must have weighed a ton. Furthermore, even if we'd managed to push it off the top of the well, we couldn't have moved it any further than that.

"Pa, we didn't do it, I swear."

"It's true, Mr. Fisk, we didn't have anything to do with it. We wouldn't even be able to lift it ourselves!"

"Then who did? You're trying to tell me that some stranger came onto our farm in the middle of the night and took that well cover for no goddamn reason? I don't know how you little shits moved it, but you're damn well going to bring it back!"

We swore over and over again that we had nothing to do with it, but my father didn't want to believe us. He searched the entire farm for that well cover with us in tow, swearing up and down that we didn't know where it was. At first he was sure we were just pulling a stupid prank. After an hour of searching, he started to get quiet. After two hours, we had covered the entire farm and he was completely speechless, his face as white as a sheet.

Once he'd completed the most thorough search of anything I've ever seen, he walked back to the house. We followed him, terrified of what was going to happen to us. I'd never seen my father look like that: almost like he was going to be sick.

I was certain that he'd beat us black and blue for messing with the well, even though we really hadn't. Instead, he sat us down and said, "I don't want you boys going near that well. I don't even want you to get within ten feet of it. Until I figure out what happened, you just leave that damned thing alone. You understand?"

Jacob and I nodded, desperate to be out of the line of fire. Once my father was convinced that we were taking him seriously, he stood up and walked out of the house.

The next few days were tense in our house, to say the least. When Pa wasn't in the fields, he was searching for that well cover. And on the rare occasions he wasn't, he was trying to cover up the well with anything else—things like planks of wood held down by bags of feed, or sheets of metal…

But every morning when we woke up, Pa's impromptu cover was gone. And just like the cement well-cover, no amount of searching would bring it back.

For a while Jacob, Gus, and I were perturbed by what was going on. But we were young and adaptable. Eventually it simply became the new normal. The fear and aversion we first felt began to wear off and, as often happens with young boys, we got curious.

"What do you think is down there?" asked Gus one morning.

"Probably nothing," I said, although I didn't believe it. Gus and Jacob could tell.

"If there's nothing down there, why is your dad so upset about it?" asked Jacob.

"Probably because it's dangerous to have an uncovered well just sitting around. What if someone falls in?" I asked.

Neither of them looked convinced. Especially Jacob. I remember looking at his face that day and seeing a kind of determination in his eyes, one that meant he was going to figure out what was at the bottom of that well. It was only a matter of time… and opportunity.

∾

Well, the opportunity came just a day later. Pa and Ma had to go to the City. It had a real name, of course, but it was the biggest city for miles around so that's just what we called it—the City. There weren't any others to confuse it with—that's how rural our area was. It had about ten thousand people. That may not sound like a lot to you, wherever you are, but to us it might as well have been New York City.

A trip to the City took all day. Pa and Ma would leave in the morning before the sun had fully risen and would return long after it had set. They would do most of their yearly shopping then, stocking up on everything we couldn't get locally. Oftentimes they'd bring me with, but Pa was inclined to leave me home this time.

"Make sure nobody goes into that well. I mean it, Charlie. That well is bad news and I don't want to come home to find somebody dead from a broken neck, you hear?"

I assured him that I wouldn't let him down and waved as he and my mother headed out in his rusty pick-up truck. Gus had stayed the night with us, so he and Jacob were both next to me, watching our one and only obstacle leave.

The dust hadn't even settled back down onto the driveway before Jacob said: "Charlie, grab a flashlight. I'll go to your dad's shop and get some rope."

"You don't really want to go down there, do you?" I asked, but it was obviously a rhetorical question. In reality, I wanted to get down there just as much as he did.

"Forget the rope, we should just get a ladder. Easier that way," said Gus.

"If we get caught, Pa will have my hide," I said, even as I was heading to the house to get the flashlight.

"Don't be such a pansy! Nobody will catch us," said Gus, giving me a lopsided grin. Gus always looked a little funny when he smiled, on account of the fact that he was missing one of his front teeth. Got it knocked out in a schoolyard fight and never got a fake one. That was the last time I'd see that funny little gap, because he didn't smile much after what happened that day.

I'm getting ahead of myself. First, I went to the house to grab the heavy-duty flashlight that Pa kept around. By the time I got back outside, Gus and Jacob were standing there with a ladder and a length of rope.

"We're gonna tie the rope out here, too, in case something happens and we can't use the ladder to get back up," said Jacob.

"Why the hell would we need anything other than a ladder?" I asked.

Jacob shrugged. "Just a feeling."

In the grass a few feet away from the well was a loop of metal protruding from the ground somewhat like a croquet wicket. We pulled on it and it didn't budge, so that's where we decided to tie the rope. I wondered what it was for, but quickly dismissed it from my mind. They threw the rope down beside the ladder, which they'd already placed in the well. It wasn't very far to the bottom, so the ladder almost reached the very top of the well.

Our preparations complete, all of us just stared into the well, wondering what we might find down there. I wasn't sure why, but a shiver ran down my spine at the thought of going down the well. My instincts were telling me to abandon our stupid plan. Curiosity, unfortunately, got the better of me.

It got the better of all of us.

"Ladies first," said Gus, making a grand gesture over the well. Jacob socked him in the arm for good measure before crawling onto the well. I wasn't surprised that he was the first of us to make the descent.

I waited only until Jacob had made it halfway down the ladder before starting my own descent. It made me nervous to let him go down there by himself. I figured it would be best for us to stick together. Gus came down shortly after me, and soon enough we were all standing in the well, which was starting to feel just a little cramped.

I'd taken the flashlight down with me and turned it on as soon as I was on the ground. The darkness vanished and we were able to see exactly where the ladder on the well bottom led.

One side of the well opened into a tunnel. There was an archway leading into it, and the tunnel itself was much wider than the well. Before moving down the tunnel, Gus and I kicked at the archway—not the best idea we'd ever had, sure, but we wanted to be certain it was sturdy before going inside. It would have been better not to go inside at all, but by that point it wasn't an option anymore. We were firmly committed to our own stupidity.

"What do you think it down there?" asked Jacob.

"We might as well find out," answered Gus.

Without further ado, we set off down the tunnel. It seemed like we walked on forever, although in reality it couldn't have been very far—maybe twenty feet before we hit what we thought was a dead end.

Except it wasn't. The closer we got to the end of the tunnel, the brighter the light from my flashlight. Soon it was so blinding that I had to drop the beam towards the ground. Which is, of course, when we discovered what we were looking at.

"A mirror?" asked Gus, stepping forward to examine it more closely.

He was right. It was a mirror—covered in grime, but still beautiful. It was oval-shaped with an ornate gilt frame. Jacob yanked his shirt off and immediately began to clean the mirror off. I kept the light off the mirror but made sure it was still high enough that we could take a closer look at it. I saw our confused faces reflected back at us, but nothing more.

"Why would somebody put a mirror down here?" I wondered out loud.

Jacob was already feeling along the sides of the mirror. After a moment, he pulled it off the cement and stepped away, leaning it against the wall of the tunnel.

"There's a door here!" said Gus. I turned the light back to the end of the tunnel and discovered he was right. Beneath the mirror was a wooden door, fitted tightly against the cement. There were no hinges or handle.

"How do we open it?" asked Jacob.

"I'm not so sure we should," I said in response, a frown creasing my face. "What if something is behind there?"

"Like what?" asked Gus. "Don't wimp out on us now, man."

Jacob didn't even dignify my concerns with a response. He had already begun testing the door, trying to get it to budge with his shoulder. When it didn't, he pulled out his switchblade and shoved it between the door and the cement, using it like a crowbar. I kept hoping that the knife would break and we could leave. All of a sudden, I wasn't enjoying our adventure anymore.

Unfortunately for me, his idea worked, and the door came loose from its position. He grabbed it and pulled it out, placing it beside the mirror. The three of us walked through the doorway and into what lay beyond...

Which just so happened to be a room.

A large room, as big as my family's living room. I had to wonder how such a massive structure had managed to remain undetected for so long. In fact, how was it able to exist at all? It was the shape of a dome and made entirely of concrete. I couldn't imagine the kind of work it would take to build this underground.

While I was marveling at what, to me, was an architectural miracle, Jacob and Gus had moved towards something in the center of the room.

"What the fuck!" shouted Gus, stumbling backwards. Jacob didn't move a muscle.

"What? What is it?" I asked nervously. I took a tentative step forward, my heart pounding.

"It's a fucking corpse!" said Gus, his eyes wide. His hands were shaking slightly.

"It's not a corpse," said Jacob.

"You call that not a corpse?! Then what the fuck is it?!" said Gus. He sounded dangerously close to losing it.

"I don't know but, whatever it is, it's not dead," said Jacob. He turned around and looked at me, beckoning me closer even as I started to tremble. "C'mere, look at her."

Her? I stepped forward slowly until I was standing next to Jacob and was able to shine the light directly down on her.

She was laying on a raised cement platform, her arms crossed over her chest, her perfectly posed hands laying one on top of the other. I had to admit that she certainly didn't look like a corpse—or, if she was one, then she must have been a fresh one. She was wearing a long black dress with a high collar and long sleeves. I'd never seen a woman wear a dress like that, except maybe posing for pictures in the 1800s. The girl herself was beautiful: she had long, golden hair that fanned out under her body. It reached down to her waist and some of it spilled off the sides of the platform. Her skin was so white it practically gleamed in the light. She had long, sweeping eyelashes and rosy lips, parted ever-so-slightly as though she were about to take a breath.

She didn't, of course. She didn't breathe at all. I reached out to take her pulse. Jacob slapped my hand away.

"What the fuck are you doing? Don't touch her!" said Jacob. He'd never spoken to me like that. He sounded almost... territorial.

"I just wanted to take her pulse. To see if she's alive."

Jacob ignored me and did it himself, his fingers caressing the skin of her neck before pressing down to feel for her pulse.

"I don't feel anything... but she's warm."

"Maybe she's newly dead," said Gus, his voice no louder than a whisper. "She was murdered and the people who killed her and put her down here are the same ones who moved the well cover!"

"That doesn't make any sense," I said. "Why wouldn't they have put the cover back on if they were going to put a dead girl in here? And why would she be wearing such old clothes? It doesn't look like anyone's been down here in ages. Besides, look at her clothes... there's dust all over them."

I had noticed it after I'd started speaking. Her clothing was covered in a fine layer of dust, hard to see by the flashlight, but there nonetheless.

"She's been down here a long time," I said, my voice dropping to a whisper.

"That's not possible," said Gus in the same hushed tone.

"She looks like Sleeping Beauty," said Jacob. He was transfixed by her. His eyes were glued to her face. "She looks like she's just waiting for Prince Charming to give her a kiss."

As he said it, he began to lean over her, almost unconsciously. I grabbed him and pulled him back. "What are you doing?" I hissed.

"Dude, that's gross, what the fuck?" said Gus.

"We should get out of here," I said.

"What's the big deal?" asked Jacob, shaking me off. "It's just a joke." He forced a laugh and leaned back over her, brushing his fingers over her forehead. "She's so pretty. I'll just take one. That's not so bad, is it?"

"She's fucking dead, Jake, what the fuck, what the fuck!..."

"Shut up, Gus," Jacob said, pausing for a moment to glare at him. "She's not dead. She's just... sleeping, is all."

"She doesn't have a pulse!"

"I don't see why that should stop me," said Jacob, flashing a smile at us. I'd never seen him smile like that. It seemed cruel and was deeply unsettling. I found myself backing away towards Gus as Jacob finally finished his journey, his lips settling on the girl's in a long, drawn-out kiss.

"Oh fuck," whispered Gus. "We have to get out of here."

But he and I simply stood there, watching Jacob try to slip a dead girl some tongue. We could actually hear him licking at her lips. My stomach roiled and I was sure I was going to be sick. Eventually, the moment ended and he straightened his back, towering over her once again.

We all held our breaths and waited for something—anything—to happen.

But nothing did.

I was just opening my mouth to tell Jacob that Gus and I were leaving, whether he joined us or not, when she finally moved.

She stirred just a little, and then sighed, her voice lilting into the air like a song. She stretched her arms above her head and arched her back. Then, finally, she opened her eyes.

They were the deepest shade of red that I've ever seen in my life.

"Where am I?" she asked in a soft voice.

My head was spinning. Something about this was very, very wrong. Her every movement left me unsettled and disturbed. She moved like a marionette, a bit jerky and uncoordinated.

Gus didn't say anything. He just turned around and sprinted out of the room. I wanted desperately to follow him, but I felt rooted to the spot. Besides, Jacob was still in there, staring at the girl like she was some kind of fairytale come true.

"You're in a well," said Jacob, his voice soft and smooth. "What's your name?" He licked his lips.

The girl laughed—it sounded like the tinkling of bells. "In a well? How funny!" She giggled some more and then sighed again. "My name is Lily. Who are you?"

"M-my name is Jacob." I hadn't heard Jacob stutter since middle-school when he'd tried to ask Bethany Anne to go to the movies with him.

"What a wonderful name," said Lily. She moved to sit up, her legs falling over the side of the platform. "Have you come to wake me, then, Jacob?"

"Yes," he breathed, his hand reaching out to touch her cheek. She smiled at him and I swore her eyes flashed an even darker shade of red.

"Jacob, we need to leave. Now," I said. Every cell in my body was screaming at me to run. Soon I wouldn't be able to resist it. I had to try to get him to come with me. I couldn't leave him down here. Something was very, very wrong.

"Won't you come with us, Lily?" asked Jacob. "Won't you come with us out of the well?"

"I've been here such an awfully long time... I wish to see the sunlight again..." she said, closing her eyes for a moment.

And then, in a very small voice, so small I could barely hear it, she added, "But oh—first—I am so very hungry!"

Her words hung in the air and neither Jacob nor I moved. The silence was all-consuming, like the calm before the storm.

It was ripped asunder suddenly, just like her dress. The bodice of her gown tore open and four black tentacles burst forth, two of them wrapping around Jacob's arms, the other two coiling around his torso. Her eyes rolled into the back of her head and her jaw unhinged, stretching so far that her skin began to tear. Her gaping mouth revealed rows and rows of terribly sharp teeth and three black tongues that slithered out and began trailing over Jacob's face, leaving black slime in their wake.

But the worst part—the absolute worst part of all of this—is that Jacob didn't so much as blink. He simply stared into her maw with that same strange adoration that had seized him moments before. He stood there limply as she dragged him closer to her mouth, and I realized that she really and truly meant to devour him.

I screamed his name over and over, but it was like he couldn't hear me. I couldn't even go to him. To this day, I blame myself for what happened, but I was just a kid then. A terrified child who was seeing something impossible, a monster straight from my nightmares breathing the air of my own reality. I wish that I had reached out for him. I wish that I had fought whatever that creature was. I wished that I had done something.

I didn't.

Instead, I ran from the room, following in Gus's tracks, my ears filled with the sound of her feast.

Do you know what it sounds like when a human skull is crushed to pieces? I do. It's one of the few things that I will never be able to forget, even when I'm dead in the ground.

I did have the presence of mind to do one last thing before I left: one horrible thing that saved us all and doomed Jacob to an eternity trapped in that darkness. I grabbed the door and shoved it back into place in the cement. Then I hung the mirror back in its place. As soon as the mirror touched the wood, I heard a terrible roar from the room. Whatever that beast was began throwing itself against the wood and I was sure, so sure, that it wouldn't hold. I stumbled backwards and fell flat on my ass, watching in terror as the mirror shuddered on the door.

And then it just… stopped.

Everything stopped. The sounds, the shaking, time itself.
It stopped. And then my heart started. And I ran.

∾

When Ma and Pa came home from the City, there were a dozen cops on our farm looking for Jacob.

Gus and I had tried to tell them what happened, about the girl in the well that wasn't really a girl at all, but they didn't believe us. Why would they? When we led them to the well, the cement cover was firmly back in place. They couldn't budge it, not even with six men, so why would they believe that we could?

They searched for him for weeks, but all of us knew we wouldn't find him.

Gus knew. His parents sent him off to the hospital when he tried to tell them what happened. They had multiple therapists try to set him straight, but he stuck to his story. Eventually, they put him in an institution. They never spoke about him again.

My father knew. While the cops were searching the farm, he stood by the well, staring at it long and hard. Then he led me back into the house and hugged me with all his might, like he hadn't done since I was a child. He whispered to me that it wasn't my fault, that the well had made a calling, and when the well called, some poor son of a bitch always answered. And that's all he ever said about that.

I knew. I had nightmares every night for years about what was down in that well. I refused to take over the farm after my Pa died. I moved to the City and sold off the farm the first chance I could. Ma moved with me and lived in a nice townhouse until the day she died. I did right by her as best I could.

Since then, I haven't gone back. Never even thought about it. I know what's waiting there and I want no part in it. And even though I regret leaving Jacob behind all those years ago, there's no saving him now. I only hope that he's really and truly dead—that there's nothing left of him for that beast to torture down in her hell hole.

I've gone on with my life.

But then last week my life stopped again. See, I picked up the newspaper early in the morning—as I often do before work—and I saw a notice about a missing child. A young woman, only about fifteen years old. She is said to have disappeared from her family farm. Our farm.

The one that I sold to a young, unsuspecting couple. The same couple that was now searching frantically for their child, begging for her to come home. Offering hundreds of dollars in reward money for her safe return.

I've been thinking all week about what I should do. Because I know. I know where she went. I know what happened to her.

But worst of all... I know that she isn't coming back.

MY FIRST RELATIONSHIP WAS MY CRAZIEST

Hayong Bak

When I was 14 years old, my mother sat me down on the living room sofa and told me that she could not afford to send me to the private school I went to anymore. I tried to fake disappointment, but the excitement of going to a school with far less rules filled me with excitement. Don't get me wrong, I wasn't a bad kid, but at my old school we got detention for even saying the word "stupid".

I told her I was okay with that, and with relief on her face she gave me a hug and told me that she would try her best to make this as good of an experience as she possibly could.

Let me give you a little bit of background information about my earlier school days. From 1st-2nd grade I was the weirdo that walked around the playground and cried because no one wanted to play with him. 3rd to 7th grade I was the kid that kept speaking up at the wrong times and was the complete laughing stock of the whole school. 8th grade was the worst year for me. My only friend went to a different school, and I was stuck with kids that relentlessly teased me for being an outsider. While other kids started to date, I struggled to even get a "hi" from a person of the opposite gender.

The fact that I would be able to start again for high-school was an absolute relief for me. That plus the lack of rules made the deal pretty sweet for me.

The first week of my high-school life flew past I could even look back. I had already made fast friends with a couple of kids, and even managed to talk to a couple of girls. Basic high-school life for most kids, but for me this was heaven.

Around a month into my new school on the bus ride back, a girl walked up to me. She looked nervous, but still managed to mutter: "Wanna ride bikes with me later?" She was a very normal looking girl. She had brown hair, green eyes, and tight lips, but I had seen her around my neighborhood a couple of times and we got off on the same bus stop. When she saw me nod yes she smiled and walked back to her seat.

When we got off at our stop she walked right next to me the whole way back to my house. She didn't say a word, but I figured she was just shy. When I got to my house she told me that she would be over in an hour and continued walking to her house. I went inside and told my mom that I was going to go bike riding with a friend in an hour. She asked me who it was. I told her it was with the girl that lived in our neighborhood, and she started to gush about me finding a little girlfriend. I tried to act embarrassed, but I couldn't help but keep on smiling.

I ran to the kitchen and stuffed a couple of snacks in a plastic bag, waiting on the driveway until I saw her coming from a distance. I hopped on my bike and rode towards her. She gave me a little wave and we rode around the neighborhood a couple of times. After about an hour we stopped riding for a second to take a quick rest and snack break. I took out two granola bars and we munched in silence. After she finished her bar, she turned to me and stuck out a hand before saying: "Hey my name is June." I grabbed it and shook it while replying back with: "Hey my name is Jay." After the greeting, we hopped back on our bikes and rode around until it became dark. We parted ways with a quick hug, but I already knew I met someone special.

We spent hours together every day after the bike ride. Sometimes we'd go to the library, other times we would go to the Big Lots in the nearby strip mall, or hang out in her room watching a couple of her favorite movies. Three months into us hanging out, she brought up the idea for us to date. I gave her an excited "yes", but she told me that I had to ask her. I was still nervous. I knew she was going to say yes, but it was my first time and I didn't want to mess it up somehow. I tried asking a couple of times, but the words would not come out right. She kept laughing at my attempts, but I could tell she just wanted me to get it over with. Three minutes and over 20 attempts later, I managed to blurt out the question and she gave me a light peck on my lips.

The relationship lasted 5 months. 4 months of that relationship were amazing.

The last month of the relationship and the month following were the worst days of my life.

I could tell the relationship was going sour when June started to criticize every small thing I did wrong. If I went too fast on the bike, she would yell at me to slow down. If I talked too much, she would simply tell me to shut up. Every single day she would get more and more strict about how I acted, forcing me to act in a way that pleased her. After a couple of days, she lost patience with the yelling and proceeded to start hitting. It was never bad hits, but they were worse when we were alone.

I started to ignore her, but she still managed to catch up to me no matter how fast I walked after getting off the bus.

The day I told her I wanted to break up was the day that everything truly fell to shit for me. She started by knocking on our door at random times. At first she would only come on the afternoons to knock, but after a week she started to knock in the middle of the night. Several times my mother woke up to answer the door. I would hear June ask where I was. My mother was patient at first, but after the first couple of times she started to yell at her to leave us alone.

June still tried to talk to me on the bus on the way to school and back, but I remained silent.

7 months and 4 days later June was found dead in the entrance to the woods at our school. There were no witnesses or subjects. For the next two weeks they tried to find some type of evidence on June's body or through residential security cameras, but nothing was found. Her whole body was suspended in to the air hanging by a rope. Her midsection was sliced opened with some of her intestines touching the ground.

I am 21 now, and I'm working at the library that June and I used to visit. Today, for some odd reason, memories of June filled my thoughts. I decided to look through all of the books we claimed as our favorites. I got to the book that she insisted was her favorite book of all time.

"Of Mice and Men" by John Steinbeck. I rented it out and took it home with me when I got off of work.

When I got home, I sat on my couch and read the book. Near the end was a folded piece of paper which read:

"Jay, just know that I really do love you.

I know I yelled at you and hit you, but I was told to.

Don't roll your eyes. I know you are, but I'm not just passing off the blame.

On my way home your mother approached me. She told me that I needed to make you break up with me. She told me that you had a bunch of problems that made it important you were taken care of by your mother.

I tried to make you break up with me, but you just wouldn't. No matter how mean I acted towards you, you still kept trying to fix things. I know now that there is nothing wrong with you. There was never anything wrong with you.

I tried to talk to you, but you'd never answer me day or night, even though your mother made it very clear that I shouldn't talk to you anymore. That I should just leave you alone. I tried talking to you on the bus, but I know that I just ruined it all for us. I know everyone says young people like us don't know anything about love, but I did. I really did.

Tomorrow I'm meeting with a guy who your mom said is going to fix everything. She said she was sorry for everything and that she wanted us to be back together.

I hope I'm with you when you're reading this note, but if I'm not, just read the book one more time.

Sometimes we have no choice but to fuck up. It's how we are made.

Love,
June."

MY WIFE AND HER BABY DOLL

Hayong Bak

From the day my daughter was born I could tell that she was something special. We named her Zooey, and she was the smartest baby I have ever seen. Every single month I loved my special little girl more and more, but for some odd reason my wife distanced herself from Zooey. By the 6th month my wife barely even gave Zooey a glance. I could tell it made Zooey sad, but I didn't really want to bring it up. I just wanted my daughter to know that I loved her very much.

Zooey said her first word when she was 3 months old.

"Daddy."

She never really said "Mommy" or even "Mom", but my wife never seemed to mind. If anything, she finally looked to be in a much better mood.

At 6 months Zooey started to walk. She would still fall sometimes, but I was completely blown away by how strong willed her young mind was. Instead of crying whenever she fell, she would just pick herself back up and continue trying.

On Zooey's first birthday my wife was busy with work, so I shared a very special day with my daughter. I got a chocolate cake for her to smash and devour. She didn't touch it, but she looked perfectly happy with staring at the cake in wonder. We spent the rest of the day playing with her presents until it was her bedtime. My wife didn't come home until 10 pm. I asked her where she was, but she just put her hand up to my face and walked past me into our bedroom.

I sighed and watched TV until I fell asleep on the couch. I woke up to the sound of my wife and Zooey talking. My wife was trying to get her to say "Mommy", but Zooey kept clapping her hands while saying "Daddy!" with a wide smile on her face. That was the last time my wife tried talking to Zooey.

On the day of Zooey's 2nd birthday, my wife told me she was going to stay later at work. I tried begging and reasoning with her to stay, but she just told me it wasn't worth it. I heard sniffles from behind me when my wife left the house. I turned around to see a tear stricken Zooey staring out the door. She asked me if mommy didn't love her, but I just hugged her and told her that we both loved her very much. After I pulled away, Zooey asked me: "Why doesn't she talk to me?" I told her that mommy was just stressed, and to not let it bug her. I got her another cake, but she told me that she didn't like to eat cake. She thought it was too pretty to destroy.

I left the cake on the dining room table and took out three brightly colored bags instead. We have this tradition where I take out the presents for her and rip the paper as carefully as possible. She liked using the wrapping paper as decorations for her room. The first two presents were just little bow sets and a couple of new books. The third present was one of those baby dolls you can feed and change. She was really excited about the doll, and she played with it in the living room by herself until it was time for bed.

My wife came back home at 11pm completely drunk. She looked like she was crying, but I was far too tired to even acknowledge that she was there. This had become normal for her. Our marriage was falling apart, and I really didn't know how to fix it. I thought she was just going to go into the bedroom, but she walked into the middle of the living room and picked up Zooey's new doll. After a couple of seconds, she started to hug the doll and rock it back and forth. The bottle and the 3 toy diapers were lying next to it, and my wife picked those up as well. She put the bottle up to the baby and started whispering to the toy.

I was completely in awe at the sight of my wife showing the baby doll more attention than she ever gave Zooey. She sat down on the couch with the doll and took the bottle out of its mouth while continuing to whisper to it. The whispering overwhelmed me with curiosity, so I snuck up behind her and tried to listen to what she was saying. It was hard at first, but after a couple of seconds I noticed she was saying the same thing over and over again. "Please call me mommy."

After a couple of minutes, my wife fell asleep with the toy baby on top of her stomach. I walked into the bedroom and grabbed a blanket for her. After I got her settled in, I went back into the bedroom and fell asleep. The next morning I woke up to the sound of my wife laughing for the first time in several years. I rushed downstairs to see what the source of her laughter was. When I walked into the kitchen, I saw my wife twirling around in circles with the toy baby. Zooey was sitting down with tears falling down her cheeks. I picked up Zooey and asked my wife what she was doing. Each time she spun around, she said one word.

"Just"
"Playing"
"With"
"My"
"Daughter"

I told her that Zooey was crying, but my wife just shrugged and kept spinning around with the baby.

This annoyed me quite a bit, but I just took Zooey back into the living room and let her play with a couple of her older dolls. After about an hour, my sweating wife came out of the kitchen and said that she was going to the mall with her daughter. Zooey got up quickly and rushed into her room to change, but by the time Zooey came out, my wife and the doll were already gone.

Zooey's bed time rolled around and I tucked her in. While I put her covers over her, she asked me: "Does momma really love me?" I nodded and smiled. I just told her that momma wanted to surprise her with some new clothes. Zooey fell asleep a couple of minutes later with a tiny smile on her face.

Tonight my wife came home around 9 pm. I walked up to her and asked what was wrong with her. She tried to ignore me, but I kept blocking her way until she stopped and glared at me. She shoved the baby doll in my face and shouted: "She's at least fucking real! Do you know how hard it is to play fucking pretend with you? Zooey is dead. She's been dead. When are you going to stop playing this stupid game?"

I shouted back at her to stop lying, but my wife just fell into my arms and started sobbing. Zooey came downstairs and stared at us hugging. She gave me a smile and walked back upstairs. I started to sob with my wife as memories flooded back in. Our beautiful daughter died 10 days after we brought her home from the hospital. There was nothing wrong with her. She just fell into a deep sleep which she never woke up from. The doctors told us that it was SIDS, but I guess I never wanted to believe it.

After my wife finally settled down, I sat her on the couch and walked upstairs. I walked into Zooey's room and saw all of the little wrapping paper from her presents taped on the walls. The toys I got for her were there and the new bed I bought for her just 2 months ago was there, but Zooey was nowhere to be found.

With a heavy sigh I closed the door to her bedroom and walked inside. I looked through all of the photos on my laptop that I thought I took with Zooey, but it was just me taking photos of myself. I just wish I could experience one last day with her—what's so wrong with a happy lie?

A HOUSE OF ONLY MEMORIES

J.P. Carver

My house is a place of only memories, some that I want to share before I... move on.

Through the front door is a little table with a small flower plate. A lamp sits on the right side, its light filtered by a green shade. We found the items at a yard sale years ago in the heat of July. A memory now. A good one.

"I think I can make it work," she had said with a grin. Her hair was in a messy pony-tail, and she wore a white t-shirt with red sleeves. She knelt down beside the table and looked at the underside, then at me. "I can totally do something with this."

"And where are we putting it?" I asked.

She stood. "The place is already packed with your yard sale stuff."

"It'll fit beside the front door. It's so empty when you first walk in. A bit of paint and sanding, and it'll be perfect, don't you think?"

"I think there's no point in arguing."

"Oh, don't be like that. Do you hate it?"

I shrugged. "You like it, that's more than enough for me."

"Uh-huh, don't play the girl game, babe, you aren't good at it." I cocked an eyebrow at her, and she laughed. "You know what I mean. I'm the only one allowed to be passive aggressive."

"Ah, forgot that rule. Seriously though, we can get it, but you're helping me load it in the car."

"Aw, but that's what I married you for."

"Ha-ha."

My keys jingled when they landed on the little plate. I walked farther into our home and closed the door. There used to be the smell of food some days when I came home from work. She cooked better than even my mother. I went into the kitchen, my skin tingling and thoughts echoing out to different points of time. Every inch there was something to remember. I sat on the stool beside the kitchen island. I could see the cool, crisp fall day of a memory.

We worked hard to have a nice home, a home that I had dreamed of since I was young. She had come in from the backyard while I sat on the same stool, just staring out the screen door, watching leaves tumble while breathing in the smell of a far-off fire. A picturesque day made better by her being in it.

She canted her head as she came in, putting her purse down on the counter. "What are you doing and why are you smiling like that?"

"Just watching," I said flatly. She turned and looked back out the door, then to me.

"Okay, creepy dude. What, exactly, are you watching?"

"My old daydreams coming true." I finally looked up at her and saw her furrow her brow. "This was what kept me going when I was younger. I'm finally... what's that word? Content, yeah."

"Oh, content, are we?" She came over to me as she peeled off her purple jacket and dropped it to the floor. She sat on my lap and her arm went around my neck. Her perfume tickled my nose and I breathed in the scent of her. "Are you content with me?"

"There's nothing peaceful about being with you." She slapped my chest playfully. "But you were always part of my day dream. You make me a different kind of happy. An all-kinds of happy."

"Smooth talker, you just want to get into my pants." She started to pick at my shirt and rested her head against my shoulder. "I'm glad you're happy. For a while there I never thought…" She sighed and nuzzled my neck. "I never thought I'd get this."

"What? A handsome devil of a husband who is also a brilliant badass?"

"Yes, Mr. Badass, that's totally what I meant." She looked up at me, blue eyes hooded and seductive. "What else happened in those daydreams of yours?"

I grinned. "Want me to show you? We have to head to the bedroom though."

"Race you." She hopped off my lap and ran from the kitchen. I laughed and called her a cheater, chasing after her.

I stood from the stool, the memory tight around my heart, and looked through the cabinets. There came a sound from the basement, a muffled noise that I had been hearing all week. I stomped on the floor twice and the sound faded. Dinner was a can of raviolis. While they cooked I went upstairs. Each step felt like a mountain, my feet were lead. I was just tired, so tired of continuing to wake up.

At the landing I paused and looked at the pictures which hung there. We were two idiots, grinning and laughing at the stupidest things. I was a terrible photographer, though she always told me she loved my pictures. We'd tell little white lies to make sure our happiness stayed as long as it could. Simple, unimportant lies.

I entered the bedroom and removed my work clothes. The pants and shirt I'd been wearing all week lay on the floor. I pulled them on, then sat on the bed, staring out at the sun dappled wall. I dropped back onto the bed and watched the slowly spinning fan. I was engulfed by the comforter, one she had picked out and loved to just lay on. We laid in bed a lot of days, just talking; just creating memories.

"I've been thinking." She lay on her side next to me, half covered with the blanket, her hip and leg exposed to the air. We were in that bone-numbing, warm feeling that lays over you after good sex.

I looked over to her as she ran small circles over my chest with her nails. "Uh-oh, don't hurt yourself."

She squinted and crinkled her nose. "Oh, too late, ouch… Oh wait, that's just you giving me a headache." She stuck her tongue out at me then laid flat on her back.

"Remember what we talked about before we got married?"

"That I would never make fun of your mom's pot roast again? Look, I tried, but that roast was so bad last week that even the dog wouldn't take it as a chew toy."

"That's not what I meant—though it was terrible and so were your jokes—I'm talking about... our family."

"You're gonna have to spell it out, babe. Remember, you're talking to the densest guy this side of the Mississippi."

"Kids." Her gaze darted over to me, lips pursed.

"...Kids? Come on—"

She sat up. "Now before you start, remember that I'm the one putting up this awesome bod of mine and am willing to go through nine months of a tiny you or me kicking my bladder like it's a soccer ball."

I pouted. "It's not fair when you put it like that. Plus, it would only be like six months of your bladder being used for kicking practice. Maybe less."

"Yeah, that totally makes it better. Seriously, I'd like to try."

I sighed and closed my eyes. "If the baby becomes anything like me you may have to wear a diaper. I got some mad kicking skills that I'm sure will be passed down."

"I'm aware. Your mom told me when she was pregnant with you that you kicked so hard one time that she peed herself."

I shook my head. "Okay one: no more talking about my mom being pregnant with me. Two: are you really sure? We're doing pretty well with just the two of us. It'll... well, it'll change everything."

She shrugged. "It's just been us for years. We could do with a bit of a change. Add one more to our crazy lives."

When she had an idea in her head it was always hard to argue it away. I sat up and kissed her gently. "Fine, but you don't get to yell 'you did this to me!' in the delivery room. This was your idea."

She scoffed. "That's not fair. That's like the one thing women get, and besides, I'll be swearing like a sailor on shore leave who stubbed his toe. I gotta throw you into the mix too."

"Those poor nurses, you'll scar them all for life."

"If all the blood, grossness, and baby head coming out of my vagina doesn't bother them, I don't think me swearing will either."

"Okay, you shush now. No more words from you." I said, pulling her down to the bed in a tight hug, her face against my chest. She gave a muffled laugh and tickled me in retaliation.

The memories of us just talking, enjoying each other, are the most painful, the most suicide inducing. She would never forgive me if I did so, but it is sometimes a weight off my shoulders when I consider it.

The microwave beeped for what must've been the thirtieth time. I slowly got up from the bed and made my way down stairs. As I crossed into the living room a crashing sound came from the basement, like someone knocked over the shelf. I cursed and stalked over to the basement door. The small light bulb at the bottom of the steps flicked on with the switch and I went down. It was a mess.

The table had been knocked over, and what was on it now lay on the floor in a jumble. I kicked at the pile on the ground and sighed. Nothing can ever just stay the same. I painstakingly righted the table next to the other one. It was a struggle, but I was able to get everything back in place and secured again. Everything had to be perfect for later. Just one good thing to come out of all of this. That's all I wanted.

The raviolis were cold, but I couldn't be bothered to heat them again. I went and sat on the couch and stared at the blank TV, my reflection warped and distorted. We had a fight in front of the TV, one that I'll never be able to apologize for.

"Hey. What is this?" I was so angry when I came in from the outside. The trash bag had ripped open and in the mess of tissues and wrappers was an item I didn't expect to see. A used pregnancy test.

She looked up from the book she was reading, her eyes questioning until they landed on the little stick in my hand. She took a deep breath and closed her book. She removed her glasses, her lips a thin line.

"Where'd you find that?"

"In the bathroom trash. Bag ripped."

"You're mad."

"Always so damn perceptive. It's fucking positive."

"It did come back as that." Her calmness was aggravating.

"So what, you weren't going to tell me you're pregnant? Just one day start showing and be like 'oops, looks like I'm preggers.' Why the hell would you keep this from me? Or where you planning to—"

She closed her eyes slowly, as if she struggled to do so. "No, I didn't tell you because there was no reason to."

I stared at her, my brain trying to make sense of her reaction. It wasn't like her to keep things, especially good things, from me.

"No reason t—?"

"I lost the fucking child." The book that was on her lap hit the TV stand with such force that it buckled the little cabinet door. "All right? I lost the child and... and I didn't want you to have to go through that. I couldn't even—don't you fucking get it? I was protecting you."

"You lost it?"

Tears streamed down her cheeks, but her face was one of anger. "Do I have to repeat myself? I was feeling some pain and took the test. Pain got worse so I went to the doctor. She confirmed that I was pregnant and now I'm not."

I stood beside her, stunned, the pregnancy test falling from my hand. She didn't sob, but her shoulders shook and her lips were pressed so tightly together that they were white. All I could do was stand there feeling the emptiness left behind by my meaningless anger.

"We... but not now..."

"No, not now," she said. I wanted to comfort her, but my body wouldn't work. She stood and left the living room, her fingers tangled up in her hair as she stomped up the stairs.

We didn't talk for a few days, no more than murmurs of hello. I was still angry that she dealt with that pain by herself and didn't involve me... but I didn't know how to deal with my own pain, or how to come to terms with it. We were both hurting and for the first time we couldn't talk about it.

I finished my raviolis, but felt sick afterwards. The bowl clanged into the other dishes in the sink and I ran water over it before walking to the back door.

The window that I had been avoiding stood before me. Beyond was a scene framed for a painting. It was the middle of summer. The leaves were bright green on the trees in our yard and they shimmered in the sun.

It was the beginning of winter the last time I stood facing that window, another memory. The air chilled. The sky gray and purple, like a healing bruise. Everything heals in time except for maybe memories.

That night we were still not really talking, but I wanted to go for a walk. She did not, but went with me anyway for a few blocks. We ran into the neighbors and we chatted for a bit until my wife got cold and went home. I stayed a little longer as I was glad for the conversation, the worst mistake I had ever made.

I found broken glass on the tan throw rug when I came home. I can still hear the sound it made under my boots when I came through the door. The crackle and pop. I glanced outside wondering if some kids were out in the alley playing in the fading twilight. I saw no ball in the room.

Moments such as that night are slow: a sinking, twisting gut of a feeling that can't be placed or given a name. It's just wrong.

The lights were out in the living room, the fading light through the bay window the only thing to see by. I called out for her as I entered the room, but no one answered. The chill breeze from the broken window ran ice up my spine. My voice cracked when I called again, and I swallowed dryly when she still didn't answer.

The lamp was knocked over, right in front of the couch. I remember it clearly when I hit it with my boot and it made a hollow thump, the sound startling in the silence of the house.

A groan and then labored breathing came from just in front of me. The sound led me to the front door which was slightly ajar. There, in the thin line of twilight, I found her. A mess of a woman: a broken doll of limbs and fabric. I stumbled the last few feet, my voice caught in the depths of my chest and only a squeak of air escaped.

I smoothed her hair as I struggled for my phone. I murmured nothings to her as I dialed 911. I felt her hand grip mine as I said my address. I felt it drop to the floor as I hung up.

They arrived after what felt like hours in a show of sirens and lights. When they came into the room, I sat on my legs in a pool of her blood. Their flashlights shined across the room and showed its disarray. They shoved me aside. I barely felt it, only the motion of falling really registered. They went to work, but she had already said goodbye.

The police came. They spoke with me, asked me of my memories about the night. Asked me if I saw or heard anything strange. Asked me where I was when it happened.

I felt as if reality had torn itself apart and I was living a crude stitch job done by a kindergartner. They spoke in calm voices, as if I would snap at the first loud sound. They asked of our marriage, of our love, and I told them some of my memories. I told them that we loved each other.

Someone had broken in. The house was empty, but then my wife came home and they panicked. Two of them. They didn't stop, couldn't stop, until they were sure she wouldn't raise an alarm or call the police.

They got away with three hundred and twenty-five dollars' worth of items and petty cash. My wife's life was worth less than a thousand dollars. Less than five hundred. She died from her injuries.

The police had nothing. They tried, or said they tried, but there never was news no matter how often I spoke to the detectives. It was murder, but to them it was a tale to tell over jelly doughnuts between gibberings of gallows humor.

They never could find them, even when I brought them evidence that I had gathered on the killers, they still sat idly by. I was left alone, like a forgotten toy on a shelf who was missing half their body because a dog ripped it off.

This is my house of memories. Each scratch and nick, each scuff and smear, every item and smell, they all bring her back to me for a spring breeze of a moment: sweet and warm and soft, but fleeting. When it leaves I am left once more to pick up the pieces and to listen for the sound of her voice in the walls.

She's still here with me. I can feel her, the other half of my soul. She will enjoy the screams that I create for her from those tied in the basement. The work of the last few months I will finish tonight, and how they will suffer, even if it will always pale in the face of my own suffering. What happens after that... well, it'll just be another memory.

MILE HIGH CLUB

J.D. McGregor

It started as a dare.

By the time I strapped myself into seat 30A at the back of the plane, it had become more of a personal challenge.

The flight from Brisbane to Kuala Lumpur is a little under eight hours. More than ample time to finish the deed. It's just a question of whether or not you have enough backbone to pull it off.

Understand, my mates and I are some real hardcore types. A proper rowdy bunch. Sit down for a round of pints with us and you'll hear a few stories that'll make you rethink your place in the universe. On the most recent night out however, maybe a week before my vacation, we realized none of us was a member of the Mile High Club. Shocking!

But also an opportunity.

What could be more Alpha than being the first of your mates to join the club? Doing it on a whim with a complete stranger, no premeditated efforts, no giving myself the inside edge. Just straight up throwing myself out there.

The flight attendant was the first to catch my eye. She had this high-pitched, nasally voice. Sounded a bit like a wounded goat or something. Had to cover my ears as she raised the seatbelt above her head and showed us where the emergency exits were.

But, damn, was she cute. She was more than cute. She was hot. Couldn't ask for a better candidate.

All I needed was an In. And I found it in the breast pocket of my polo.

A Marlboro cigarette.

Smoking is strictly prohibited, the voice over the PA said. An alarm will sound if smoke is detected in the lavatory.

I wouldn't even need to light it. I just needed to bring it out at the correct moment. Right when she passed so she would have to start the dialog: Sir, please put that away. That's all I would need to see if she was game.

Right after the seatbelt sign switched off, I saw her point my direction down the hall. As casually as possible, I pulled out the cigarette and twirled it in my fingers.

It was in plain sight. There was no way she could have missed it. But she didn't say anything. She strode right on by and started arranging things on the food trolleys in the back.

Feeling a little disheartened, I put the dart away. I wasn't in the mood for hard to get.

A quick survey of the other passengers didn't do much to kindle my interest. I stood up and saw an empty row of seats smack in the middle of the plane. It was the perfect spot. There was bound to be a dance partner somewhere around there.

Sure enough, I was in luck. Right as I took my new seat, I found exactly what I was looking for, in the row right in front of me no less.

The girl was a platinum blonde stunner. 10/10, 1st overall in the draft type. She looked to be in her mid-twenties. To her left was a creepy-looking, middle-aged married man who obviously couldn't believe his fortune getting assigned the seat next to her.

The guy's head is permanently oriented to the side. He's babbling endlessly about God-knows-what. The girl must have a heart of gold or something to keep politely nodding her head the whole time.

I'm pretty sure I only heard her say four things. All part of a recycled response rotation.

"Yeah."

"Yep."

"Oh."

"Ha."

The guy doesn't take any hints though. He just keeps talking. Any moment of silence, he finds a way to fill it.

It was already starting to annoy me after five minutes of sitting there, and I wasn't even the target. I was still figuring out how I was going to break the ice. I was just a victim by proximity.

Finally, the dude's bowels grace us with a gift.

"Don't go anywhere", he said with a wink as he got up to go to the bathroom, close to where I was sitting originally.

The girl smiles. The moment the old creep is out of sight, it fades. Her shoulders relax and her head presses back into the seat. The poor girl was exhausted. I hoped she left something in the tank. She had no idea what kind of guy was sitting behind her, watching the entire thing.

I straightened my shirt as I stood up. My target still unaware of my presence.

I can't lie—I got a little nervous. I mean, wouldn't anyone? I'd never actually accomplished this badass feat before. I still wasn't sure exactly how I was going to pull it off.

This girl lets out a long, agitated sigh as my shadow casts over her. I could hear her hold it as I made my way to the back of the plane.

I slid my little shank through the crack in the door and slid the lock open. Piece-of-cake. Why would they serve food with metal cutlery after you get through airport security?

I looked both ways before entering the bathroom to make sure no one saw. Everyone was asleep or looking the other way. More good fortune!

I literally caught the guy with his pants down. The smallest squeak escaped his lips as I plunged my shank into his throat. Blood started pouring out.

Once he went limp, I turned him around and held his head over the toilet. I managed to get most of the blood into the bowl. Only needed a few sheets of paper towel to get the rest.

I was ecstatic. Couldn't wait to tell the boys. I wanted to scream to the heavens—I was so happy to be the first one in the Mile High Club.

After the cleanup, I poked my head out the bathroom. No one batted an eye. It was like no one even noticed I went in there in the first place.

The back area was empty as well. More good luck.

I hoisted the dude's body up. With one gentle motion, I brought him over my shoulder. I pushed the door open with my foot and stepped out. Quickly, I turned to the back and stuffed him behind the rows of dirty food tables.

I wondered how long it took after landing for the cleaning staff to find him.

So, here's my advice to you. Want to do something really Alpha? Join the Mile High Club. It's quite the rush.

Trust me!

VELA HAS A GIFT FOR THE WORLD

J.D. McGregor

I know what you think is cool. At least, I know what most people you know think is cool.

As you're reading this, there a couple dozen hipster bars downtown filled with every new age vegan, animal rights activist, and yoga teacher in town. Meditate. Don't work too much. Minimize your life as best you can. I bet even if you aren't vegetarian, you still felt a rush of guilt the last time you bit into a burger.

It's all about wellness these days, isn't it? Become the best version of yourself? Am I Right?

Of course I am.

But let me tell you something. This self-discovery, personal well-being craze is temporary. I know it doesn't feel like it, but I assure you, it's just like all the other fads that have come and gone. Like all things, it will end.

Trust me, we've already been through it here. I live somewhere so far ahead of the curve that it makes Silicon Valley look like its barely crawling out of the Stone Age.

So what comes next you ask? I bet you'd like to know.

Here's your answer. But understand, it may not be exactly what you want to hear.

The day will come where self-maintenance is nothing more than a memory of something people used to do. When that void gets filled, you'd be surprised just how different things become. A whole new world of worries comes in to take its place.

You think kids have it bad these days? Bullying follows them home over social media you say? Wait until they have to go through shit like I did. Wait until it's literally coming at them from inside their own heads.

The sky was black and the air brisk (exactly four degrees Celsius, to be precise). Few stars hung in the sky above scattered smoky clouds. I was the only one out in the streets that night. At least, that's what I thought at the time.

It was late November and the warm summer vibes had long faded away. Winter was coming and you could feel it in your bones.

I folded my arms through the front pocket of my sweater and pressed my chin into my collar. I kept my eyes on the ground, counting every block of the sidewalk as I passed.

I wasn't meant to be out so late. I was supposed to be tucked in bed and sleeping like the good boy my poor father thought I was.

Problem is, good boys seldom get late night invitations like the one I received. And it's hard to say no to such a rare prize.

Sneaking out through the little window of my bedroom basement proved both terrifying and exciting. A week before, I would have never imagined myself having a reason to move through the streets so late at night.

A notification came. I closed my eyes, ready to over-analyze every single word.

Sure enough, it was from my favorite sender.

You almost here?

I chose not to answer. Like I could possibly be the one playing hard to get.

She wouldn't hear from me again until I was right on her doorstep.

I was less than a block away, soon to be around the corner and over the hill and in sight of her house.

But what exactly was I going to say? I researched and turned a few topics over in my mind as I approached. Nothing stuck.

Her house came into view. It was massive by anyone's standards. The neighborhood was filled with custom houses, each tailor-made for the members of the 'Elite American Society' who resided, but her's stood out from all the rest. Her family is especially high up.

I had no business being there. My dad and I had no business even being in town. We were easily one of the poorest ones, living at the furthest edges of the outskirts.

But everywhere needed someone to do the dirty work. Dad said that if I didn't keep my head on straight and the transmissions coming through, I would end up as shit-poor as him.

Something rustled in the dark alley between her house and the one next to it.

The hairs on my arms stood up, but that was the only reaction I was willing to expend. I didn't have time to be startled by obscure noises. I was too focused on the task at hand.

I stopped at the edge of her driveway where the mansion loomed over me. There weren't any cars unless one was parked in the garage. Vela must have told me the truth. Her parents were really out of town for the night. Trusting her made me feel secure, and for a brief moment, I was calm.

Only two lights were on inside that I could see. The main foyer, behind the glass-trimming of the door, and one room on the second level.

I took a breath. I had come too far to let the opportunity slip. It was going to be a pivotal night, defining of my teenage years. Everything was in my hands. Was it going to be a night to remember? Or the grand low point of my loser high school career?

I scanned my vitals. There was a long delay. Something flickered inside my head as the results came through.

Accelerated heart rate, high blood pressure. Consider rest from high-level cardiovascular activity. That's the last thing it advised before it clicked off.

I started my walk towards the porch. Halfway there, the handle turned on its own and the door creaked open.

The most beautiful girl I knew poked her head out from behind it. The light reflected the golden color of her hair. I was just close enough to distinguish her features.

Vela smiled.

She sat on the bottom steps of the stairs opposite the main hall. She was dressed in a black t-shirt reading Need More Sleep. A tight pair of gray yoga pants constricted her lower half. Her bare feet rubbed against the tile floor.

I turned to close the door gently behind me. I pressed my hand, and then forehead flat against it. I tried to quickly check my vitals again, but the process failed.

It seemed my technology had failed me at the most critical time.

I left faint sweat marks on the door as I separated and turned to her. The house fell painfully silent. Like no one was even there.

I tried to remember the conversation topics I researched on the way over. I should have decided which one I was going to use before I even left my house. Panic set in as my mouth started to dry.

I was already blowing it.

"Thought you weren't going to show," she finally said. Her voice was so comforting, like she empathized with my struggling and wanted to save me.

I still didn't know what to say though. This was something I had never done before. I was unfamiliar with the etiquette. I wasn't capable broadcasting confidence or faking the impression that this was just a routine late-night visit to a hot girl's house.

"Isaac?"

"No. Just got out to a late start. Waited 'til I was sure my dad was asleep," I said, starting to untie my shoe.

"Well at least you made it one piece," she said, chuckling. "Can I get you something to drink?"

I shook my head no as I started to untie the other shoe. I used the wall for support as I did.

She shrugged her shoulders and stood up. Clearly, something about my presence in the house amused her.

"Alright then. Whenever you're done here in the hall, I'll be up in my room. Turn off the light down here before you head up, please."

The butterflies fluttered in my gut. I hadn't expected her to cut to the chase so quickly. The hours of thinking about all the small-talk I leading up the grand finale were out the window.

She accelerated us to the second stage already. I wasn't even ready for phase one.

Her hips swayed from side-to-side as the climbed the stairs. She ascended with steps that were calculated to be both elegant and efficient. The pants were tight against her, perfectly displaying her curves.

I held my breath, staring at her wide-eyed the whole time.

Unlike all the other girls, she looked lost in age somehow. She had some combination of youthful freshness and older maturity. Everything inside her was balanced and regulated to perfection. She stood out from all the other rich girls in town.

I tried to get an estimate on my chance of success, but was quickly reminded my Hivemind wasn't working. Not that the old piece-of-shit would produce an accurate prediction anyways.

She finished the last steps and disappeared down the hallway on top. The house fell quiet again, and only the smell of her perfume lingered in the foyer.

The light switch was just shy of the first step. I flipped it off and started to climb. I tried to keep my steps as steady as possible. I feared that if I went too quickly or slowly, she would detect them. Instantly she would run an analysis and determine that I was nervously out of control.

The shuffling from outside came again, but it seemed the exact spot had changed. Perhaps it came from the backyard. I stopped where I was and listened anxiously for it again.

In the dark emptiness, I realized just how big the space around me really was. There were seven different pitch-black rooms or hallways you could enter from the main landing. I gripped the railing and looked back down into the black. My eyes darted to every space around me, trying desperately to make something out.

Again, nothing.

It took every ounce of discipline to convince my body to climb the rest of the stairs at a normal pace. I don't think she picked anything up.

Only one of the doors on the second level was open. Faded Blue light from a computer screen shined from behind it.

My socks slid along the hardwood floor. My hands were out to my sides, fingers gliding along the walls, just below the rows of hanging family pictures.

I pushed the door open and stepped inside. The shag carpet was plush. The softness alone, that I could feel through the fabric of my cotton socks, was enough to tell me that it was purchased at some high-end specialty store. Probably like everything else in the giant house I still couldn't believe I was in.

Vela lay motionless in bed. The pressed white cover went all the way up to her neck. Her hair was neatly resting over her shoulders, disappearing under the blanket. Her head was tilted to the side, watching the giant screen projected on the opposite wall.

"How long are you going to stand there and stare for? I've been in bed alone for exactly three minutes and twenty-three seconds now," she said as she turned her head to me.

Her words took me out of the trance. I could have just stayed that way forever. Just watching her was enough.

"J-just a sec," I said.

It was the best I could think of off the top of my head. I wasn't used to having to think totally on my own.

She laughed. Again, it was the innocent laugh that said: I'm amused by you, not: I can't take you seriously.

"Do you need some motivation?" she asked as she brought her torso up, supported on her elbows.

The blankets started to slide down. She didn't look concerned over stopping it from happening.

I felt something move the moment I saw she wasn't wearing anything on her upper half. I was treated to a sight I had fantasized about in bed many times before. They were even better than I imagined.

My lower lip fell open. I rubbed a sweaty hand over my forehead and then back through my hair.

"Do you like them?" she asked.

"Yes," I answered as I loosened the buckle of my belt.

"Do you want to feel?"

Something moved again. I decided not to answer her. I'm not sure I could have found the words if I tried.

My jeans dropped around my ankles and my shirt flew to the corner of the room. I fell forward onto the bed. I brought my bony legs up and began to crawl towards her.

She held herself higher than she did before. Her back arched and her chest shot out closer towards me.

My shaking hand stilled as soon as it felt the flesh. At first, it was the smoothest, most pleasant thing I had ever touched. Then I felt the goosebumps start to form. Maybe she was cold. Or maybe she was just as nervous as I was.

One last time, something moved below my waist.

She grabbed me by the shirt and yanked me towards her. Her mouth was already open when our faces pressed against each other. It was violent. Like she was trying to suck my soul out through my mouth and into hers.

I just went for it. I pushed myself through all the nerves and hormones of my confused teen body that found itself in a dream situation. I was numb.

Suddenly, she pulled away and glared into my eyes.

"Have you done this before?" she whispered softly.

"No," I said. And perhaps that was the first truth I told all night.

She looked down and paused. She did something with her Hive-mind, but I wasn't sure exactly.

"Me neither."

She pulled the blanket up beside her and gestured for me to crawl under in the empty space.

I did as instructed. I wondered if I should slip my boxers off right away whether I should wait.

She made the choice for me. She pulled them all the way down and over my feet. She tossed them across the room, and they landed just next to my jeans on the floor.

I was trembling then. It was actually going to happen. I needed to be ready, but I didn't feel the movement below my waist any longer. Just more numbness.

My naked hip was against hers. She took hold of my shoulders and pulled me over her.

"Be gentle," she said as she pressed her lower half against mine.

But something was wrong. My body wasn't responding as it was meant to. I sent the command to my Hivemind over and over again. It just kept not responding. My body needed to regulate itself. I had never done that before.

Vela looked puzzled.

"What's wrong?" she asked.

"Just a second," I said, my hand working as hard as it possibly could.

"The Hivemind should regulate that for you. I had mine regulate before you even came upstairs. I've been ready for you the whole time."

"Just a second."

"Wait, you mean what everyone is saying at school is true? You don't even have a Havemind?"

"Yes, I do. I just don't like to use it."

"Thought this was your first time?"

"Err… Yes, it is."

"So have your Hivemind dictate the blood flow."

My hand moved violently below the covers. It was a feeble attempt at a manual function that I had only seen in textbooks or videos I wasn't supposed to be watching.

It was so painful. I couldn't understand how people did it on their own without their Hivemind just taking over the process.

Vela started to laugh.

"Do you even have anything in your head?"

"Yes."

"What is it, the first generation?" she asked mockingly. "The others weren't kidding, were they?"

"No it isn't. It's one of the new ones," I lied with desperation in my voice matching the desperation in my hand. What she said was exactly correct. My Hivemind was first generation. A hand-me-down as well.

But it was too late by then. She had already sprawled to the side, laughing uncontrollably.

"You're not going to tell anyone," I said desperately as I jumped out of the bed and over to where my boxers were on the floor.

"I won't need to," she answered. "Everyone at school was tuned in the entire time. It was all part of the dare. Why don't you say hi before you go?"

"The dare?"

"You seriously think I invited you over here just because? C'mon now Isaac, you're smarter than that."

By that time I was already sprinting down the hall, out of the house. As I ran across her front lawn and onto the street, I saw the source of the shuffling I had heard outside earlier. A group of Vela's friends were huddled outside the house, laughing just as hard as I imagine Vela still was in her bed.

We're coming for you pussy.

The message came through the moment I walked through the school doors. At least my Hivemind was working again.

I already knew it was set to be the worst day of my life, but it couldn't be anyone worse than who sent the message.

Greg Stanton.

That was Vela's EX. They had been broken up for over a month before she invited me over. At least that's what she told me.

I deleted the message and my Hivemind was blank again. I added him to my mental list of people to avoid all day. Exactly thirty-three people were on it in the morning. Probably the whole school would be on it by the end.

I showed up extra early for first-period calculus. I took an empty seat on the farthest part of the room. I locked my eyes forward on the plasma smart board.

I tried to check my Hivemind for notes from the previous class, anything to get my mind off what had happened the night before. The focus couldn't survive Vela's perfume which invaded my nostrils. I heard her and few others giggling as they came into the room.

Greg Stanton sent another message.

Shoulda made it count when you had the chance limp dick. Seriously think you're going to fuck my girl and get away with it?

I deleted the message immediately, turning back to the skimp math notes I had from the day before. I tried to avoid thinking about the seats filling up around me.

Greg sent another message. This one wasn't just to me. It was on the public server. Everyone could see it inside their heads. The laughter started to pop up over the room.

10 bucks for whoever brings Isaac to the cafeteria right now. Don't worry, his Hivemind is shit, he won't even know you're coming.

Mrs. Ryan noticed it and deleted it right away, but it was too late. Everyone in class and probably the whole school had seen it already.

I got up and ran out of the classroom. Most students still had their eyes half-open, indulging in Greg's message and anything else that was floating through the public server. They didn't even notice that I left.

I ran as hard as I could down the hall. My worthless Hivemind sent a signal saying that my heart rate was getting too high and that I should consider resting.

I took refuge inside the bathroom. I ran to the last stall and locked it behind me. I huddled there, wondering exactly what it was I was going to do. How foolish could I have been to think that Vela had actually wanted me to come over the night before?

Another message. I tried to delete it, but it stuck there. His Hivemind must have allowed him some kind of coding to lock it there and open itself.

He had literally gotten inside my head.

You think you could hide from us in the bathroom? C'mon now Isaac, we've been tracking you since last night. See ya real soon.

I heard sets of footsteps come into the bathroom. Shortly after, I heard the electronic lock of the door behind them.

I pressed my weight against the feeble stall door in front of me, like that was actually going to make a difference.

Hands bigger than my own reached over and rattled the door. Another message opened up inside my head as I braced myself against it.

Open up, Isaac.

A great force came against the door, knocking me back against the toilet. Pain splintered through my body as my spine smashed against it.

Another thump sounded, and the door flew off its hinges. Greg's outstretched leg was in the empty space. He had three of his buddies with him. The messages started to flood into my head. One stood out from all the rest. It was from Vela.

I'm sorry Isaac. I didn't mean for it to go this far.

Greg and his friends didn't say anything. They just stood there silently as I cowered before them. It was so much easier to send messages through the Hivemind than form the threats with their mouths.

"No, not that. Anything but that," I pleaded as I raised my arms in front of me.

They still didn't say anything. Greg stepped forward and grabbed me by the hair. With a simple twist of his arm, he was able to flip me over and press me against the toilet. I saw the glint of silver in his other hand as the blade came out of his pocket.

"Please, I begged him. Don't take it out."

But he had already started. He pressed the blade into the skin at the base of my skull. Then he started digging.

～

It's been a year since all of that happened.

Things have mostly blown over since the incident. Partly due to the passing of time, and partly due to the school flagging and suspending anyone messaging about it on the servers at school. I'm sure it's still messaged about in private from time to time though.

I wouldn't know. Pops doesn't have enough money to replace the old Hivemind Greg dug from out of my skin and flushed down the toilet. I only have a layered scar to enjoy back there now.

Poor rich-kid Greg had to withstand a little slap on the wrist for the whole incident.

I can't wait until I graduate. Think I'll move out and go somewhere where no-one knows my name. Where nobody even knows what a Hivemind is. I'll be the one ahead of the game when I move into your town.

Vela hadn't been to school for over a month. Before that, she was acting kind of strange as well, wearing different clothing and not talking much. I heard whispers that she gave up drinking and partying altogether.

Not that I really wanted to know too much about what she was doing anyways.

But she did finally come in today. Greg's arm was draped around her shoulder as she walked in with her little bundle of joy. Apparently, they had gotten back together a little while after out incident.

"Everyone," she announced to the class, the smile wide on her face. "Greg and I have some wonderful news for you. Last night we became loving parents of our newest family member, Ricardo."

She held the baby out in front of her.

Two demented, misshaped legs dangled in the open air. One arm looked smaller than the other and was pressed tightly against its bony frame. Its face was twisted. One eye shut, the other glaring wide with a dilated pupil to take in the new surroundings of the classroom.

"Doctor says he's the first baby to be born of two parents with Hiveminds implanted. He thinks the frequency coming from them affected him in the zygote. Isn't he beautiful?"

Mrs. Ryan held her arms out like a cradle and smiled.

"Thank you so much for bringing him in, Vela and Greg. He's adorable. I'm so happy for you two."

Vela took the hint. She set baby Ricardo down gently in our teacher's open arms. The baby reacted to the change. He started to squirm, calling out with the wet twisted squeal of a suffering animal.

Mrs. Ryan struggled to hang on to him. She brought him close her chest to try and hold him there. The baby reached up and pulled at her ears and hair. He was gunning for the back of her neck.

"Quite energetic," Mrs. Ryan said.

"It's the frequency," said Vela. "He can feel the waves from your Hivemind. He's already dependent, he craves to connect."

"Oh dear. And what do you intend to do?"

"Doctor said we only had one option. We have to get him his own. He will only suffer until it gets it in there. He will have a Hivemind nearly half the size of his own brain implanted next week. Brand new version too. He's going to be the youngest ever to get it."

Mrs. Ryan smiled as the baby kept trying to climb up over her shoulder. One demented arm clawing at the back of her neck.

Vela brought both hands to her mouth like she felt she had to reign her smile in.

"Can't wait for his first word. Hopefully, he'll send it to the server."

THE PROPOSITION

J.D. McGregor

My fate was sealed before the curtains drew. Sickness had already
set in.

Suspended lights turned and curled inwards. Center stage became
fully illuminated. There, standing in the middle of his fellow first
graders, was Jeffrey. My Jeffrey. The son who had made me so proud
when he first told me he landed the lead role in the school play.

No father was meant to feel ill at a time like this, yet sitting in the
rows of seats lined up on the gymnasium floor with the other parents,
it felt inevitable.

Jeffrey took a couple steps forward. He stood alone, ahead of the
other children. He began to recite the lines I had helped him rehearse
just a few hours earlier.

I heard his first words clearly.

"In the beginning," he said. "There were only a few of us."

I mouthed the words along with him silently. With deliberate
attention to detail, I tried to stay with every syllable. I tuned in. I
didn't want to leave the makeshift auditorium.

"But times changed, and now we are many."

His words sounded further away. The voice had gotten deeper. I started to slip.

"From this day forward, we will..."

The rehearsed words trailed off. The voice I then heard was no longer that of my son's. It was the voice of the daytime news anchor broadcasting a breaking report. He spoke with the casual professionalism of a man with no personal connection to the heartache his words would create. The buzzing static of an old TV was in the background.

It was a recording I could never forget. I had only played it over in my mind a thousand times before.

Tragedy strikes close to home today. The body of eighteen-year-old Westmount resident, Amy Bray, was found in a dumpster behind a bakery near the downtown core. The body shows signs of severe sexual assault and trauma around the neck. All evidence suggests she was strangled to death with a rope.

An anonymous tip was given to police this morning stating that screaming could be heard from the parking lot and a bald man was seen running from the area shortly after. Police were on the scene within minutes and have since taken homeless man, Troy McAllen, into custody. Authorities are urging whoever called to step forward and provide more information.

The mug shot of his wrinkled face came in into view. That bald headed mother-fucker left his DNA sprinkled all over the crime scene. His eyes glared back at me, just like they did from the TV screen for the first time nearly twelve years prior.

I was no longer in the school gym watching my son's play. I was somewhere else.

The routine of running through the same memory over and over against my will was not a new development. I had been trying to get over it with the support of family, friends and medical professionals for years.

But things weren't getting any better. They never got any better. Something needed to change. That much was obvious.

The bathroom floor was sticky. My dress pants clung to it as I tried to lift myself above the open toilet. As I knelt there dry-heaving, I dreaded two things.

First, the idea of having to wait alone in this school bathroom for the vomit (if there would be any) to come out.

Second, the fact that at some point in the evening, I would have to explain to my wife why I had gotten up from my seat. Why I embarrassed both of us as I ran out of the gymnasium with one hand on my mouth, the other on my stomach.

I gave up on the former after twenty-five uneventful minutes. There was no way I was going to try and squeeze my way back to the empty seat in the gym. Instead, I succumbed to the temptation. With shaking fingers, I dialed my brother's number.

"Hello," Noah answered. His voice sounded tired. He knew my reason for calling.

"Noah," I said. "It's happening again. I'm leaning over the toilet seat in Jeffrey's school bathroom right now. It's bad, it's real bad. Don't think I can get up."

The sigh was long on the other end of the line. I clenched my teeth and stretched across the closed toilet lid.

Perhaps even my brother, the one person I felt I could trust above anyone else, had grown weary of dealing with me.

I couldn't bring myself to blame him though. On our last phone call, I took the gamble and crossed the line. I mentioned the proposition. Surely, I sounded delusional. And perhaps, I was delusional.

After what I'm sure was much deliberation, Noah spoke again.

"Roger, remember what the doctor said. Relapses are part of the healing process. You need to keep the pills with you. Always need 'em on you."

"But I've been taking them, and all the other pills for almost ten years now, Noah. Doesn't help, it never fucking helped. I can't make it go away. I think I'm going to try to—"

"Stop it!" Noah interjected. "I don't want to hear that proposition shit again. It's nonsense, and you know it's nonsense."

I felt strong enough to lift myself off the bathroom floor. I stumbled out of the stall and used the nearest sink for support. I looked at myself in the mirror. The man who looked back didn't look crazy. At least, not to me.

"I'm not delusional," I said. "I was there. I was fully there both times. It was real. I remember what it said."

"Listen," Noah responded, his voice noticeably calmer. "There's no one I care about more than you, Roger. Fucking kills me getting these phone calls though. Amy died twelve years ago. It hurt everyone, not just you. Think about her parents. Think about her two brothers. Think about everyone who knew her at school and everyone else at the party who also could have done something. Hell, even I get nightmares about it."

I dug the phone into my ear. Guilt over the amount of stress I was likely putting on Noah ran through me. He never married, and I was the closest family that he had. And this is what I was doing to him.

"I know it's hard," he continued. "But this isn't just about you, don't forget that. You have a family now, and they need their father. You can't keep disappearing into some twisted fantasy world of self-despair. Amy is dead, and you need to move on. And you will move on. That much I promise you. Please don't go down this road. Amy wasn't for you. It's best you don't think about her. There is only pain for you there."

Click.

Noah's voice stopped coming through the phone.

Later that night, the bedroom was completely dark. I hadn't let my eyes close since going to bed, so they were well adjusted. I relaxed my neck and let my head roll to the side. The clock read 2:44 AM.

It was almost time.

Chelsea was asleep. Somehow I had managed to avoid explaining my absence during the play. We didn't speak a word about it, or anything else after leaving the school.

The truth is, she likely knew full well the reason. She was aware of the mental sickness that controlled my mind for all the years of our marriage.

It wasn't fair. All this time, she was stuck between being the supporting wife of a sick man and living with the hurt of knowing the source of his misery was longing for another woman. And it wasn't just any woman. She knew Amy well. They used to be best friends.

Chelsea had every right to be as upset as I was. More upset if anything. She was at the party that night as well. Her actions also indirectly led to the final outcome. That night was just like the morning after the party, the first time Chelsea and I shared a bed together. I had woken up and lay beside her for some time as she slept. I remember mixed feelings towards how things had played out the night prior. I was already fantasizing about sleeping with Amy instead.

I tried to take a mental photo of the scene. Separated by nearly twelve years, Chelsea and I lay together in bed before something terrible was about to happen. The first and last times were so similar in that way.

I rose and tiptoed towards the door.

Before I left the room, I momentarily considered looking back. I owed Chelsea that at least. Part of me genuinely loved her. She was the one who stayed up with me, running her hand through my hair on the countless, sleepless nights. She was the woman I made love to more than any other. She was the mother of my son.

But the burden was too heavy. I listened for the click as the door closed behind me.

I wish I could have been as decisive when I passed Jeffrey's room. His door was open a crack, just as it always was. It made a long, high pitched creak as I nudged it forward.

Jeffrey lay on his side, facing the wall on the far end of the room. His feet stretched outwards and rubbed together.

The sight of him made my knees buckle. I slid my hands up the door frame until they were straight above my shoulders.

For a long time, that room was where I would go to be alone. It was after Chelsea and I had bought the house, and before Jeffrey was born. I would often come to that room and stare out the window above his bed.

It was like a portal for me. When I looked outside I could go back to the night where it all went wrong. Where I had blundered and not acted as I should have. I was too cowardly to pick up on the cues. I didn't take the girl I longed for. That decision was what had ultimately led me to where I was then.

I resisted the urge to go up and rub his shoulder one last time. The view from where I stood would have to suffice. I wish I had the courage to say the three words I held in my heart.

For the rest of the journey through the house, my mind alternated between trying to keep quiet and considering the possibility of turning back. There was still time to turn around. I could easily return to the bed where my wife slept and simply pretend the whole thing never happened. And maybe, I could work it all out. I could live happily ever after with the family I built.

But if I really wanted to go back to bed, I would have.

Atop the flight of old wooden stairs leading to the basement, I paused. I looked down at the black pit below. No amount of adjusting to the darkness would allow my eyes to make out the shapes down there. I flicked the light switch. The single bulb hanging from the ceiling flickered before lighting the room up.

The gray concrete floor of the unfinished cellar was covered by a single yellow rug in the middle. Surrounding the rug was a collection of old furniture, sports equipment, partially opened boxes and of course - the mirror.

My breaths were short. Grinding my teeth, I took the first step down and nearly jumped when the old wooden board groaned. I had to force my legs to descend each of the next steps. With each one, the creak of the old staircase seemed to grow louder.

I reached the bottom and dead silence returned. I looked in every cranny, every shadow that was within my line of sight. There was nothing there.

My eyes told me that I was alone. And by all means, they should have been correct. However, it wasn't the truth. And I knew that before I had made the decision to go down there in the first place.

My phone read 2:58 AM. Only two minutes remained.

I allowed myself a few more moments of illuminated silence before I reached for the light switch. When the basement was dark again, I felt my way to the yellow carpet and positioned myself squarely in front of the mirror. My body trembled profusely.

I raced through the possibilities again, trying to reassure myself. As if through my endless hours of deliberation, I did understand everything. As if it were possible for a man to think through the infinite numbers of factors, responses, and outcomes and have some idea of how things were going to play out.

The arrival was imminent. Before it came, I remembered Noah's last words on the phone.

"There's only pain for you there."

The reflection in the mirror changed. Breaking through the darkness was one white spot just above my shoulder.

I turned to look at where it appeared to be in the reflection. But there was only blackness. This was no surprise, I had tested it before. But back in the mirror, it had developed.

There were now two spots and another line running below them. The face was there, clearly. It radiated a bright white that hurt the eyes if looked at directly for too long. The outlines of the facial features pulsed. Their exact shape was always changing. The corners of the mouth pulled upwards into a shape resembling a smile.

The breaths came. I could feel the moist air on the nape of my neck. And then, it spoke. Its deep voice seemed to come from every direction in the darkness around me.

"Back again I see? I take this means that you've been intrigued by my proposition?"

I didn't answer. I hated hearing the thing talk. It knew me too well. It spoke with complete understanding of my reason for being in the basement that night.

"Shall we get started then?" it asked. "You know this is the last time

I will come here. You must act tonight, or forever lose the opportunity."

"Lay the rules out for me one last time," I said.

I already knew the stipulations. But, I took comfort in hearing them again, as if I would have some brilliant flash of insight that would help me understand everything.

"One chance to go back. You cannot return here, and you cannot go backwards again. All outcomes are final."

"Tell me how it turned out for the others. What happened to the other people you've done this with?"

"You must decide now, Roger," it answered me abruptly. "I have no more patience for your concerns. I care only for your decision now."

My knuckles ached from gripping them so tightly. The eyes and mouth in the reflection slowly started to fade.

"Do it," I said. "Take me back."

The thing did as I commanded.

At first, it was all a blur. The darkness was gone, replaced by a range of opaque waves. They ran against each other, colours of all kinds shot out behind them. I heard the muffled sounds of conversation. My body felt lighter, newer.

One thing came through clearly. It was the audible voice of a young woman. I recognized it as Amy's immediately. My vision started to clear shortly after. She was right there in front of me. She was eighteen years old, she was alive. Her image matched the one I had kept in my mind for all the years.

"Roger," Amy said. "Still working on the first beer?"

All my surroundings became clear. The faint outlines of the shapes around me sharpened. I could see the familiar glass chandelier hanging from the ceiling. Recognizable, young faces were leaning on my parents grey, leather couch in the living room.

Condensation from the beer can dripped onto my fingers. I looked down at my hands and saw that they were young. A visual scan of my body revealed the same. I looked eighteen again. I was eighteen again.

Amy put her hand over mine. I felt the comforting softness I had fantasized about for what had felt like an eternity. She pulled the beer from my hands, bringing it to her lips.

Everything was in perfect order. I was back at the party. The thing had done exactly as it said it would.

Amy finished the beer and set it on the table. All the while, her eyes were firmly fixed on mine.

"Looks like you have some catching up do," she said.

As I anticipated, she took a step forward. She slid her hand in a straight vertical line from my chest to my stomach. As she let it rest there, I tested my recollection.

Next, she will grab me by the collar.

Sure enough, her hands slid upwards towards my neck and grabbed the shirt. I said her next words along with her inside my head.

"Why don't you grab us another?" she asked.

The first time through, I hesitated before speaking. That I remember clearly. My unconfident former-self would wait at least five seconds before spitting out the word "okay".

Not this time.

Blessed with the wisdom of seeing everything in hindsight, I spoke a new set of words. I said what I had been planning to say when all of this was a dream. A time when the situation I found myself in was nothing more than a distant fantasy, impossible to realize within the reality I thought I existed in.

"Maybe I'll do that," I said. "But I'll have to stop in my bedroom on the way back. Might be a little delay. Hope that's okay with you."

If they hadn't already, the two timelines officially diverged after that. I hoped that would make it easier to let go of the old life I had abandoned. Nobody would get hurt tonight. It was just a matter of execution.

I smiled and pulled Amy's hand from my collar onto hers. I released, looking at her one more time before leaving the room. I wished that moment could have lasted forever.

I stepped into the kitchen where Noah stood near the fridge, just as I remembered. He talked with some girls I hadn't cared to keep in my memory. I grabbed him by the shoulder and yanked him aside. My entrance caught him off guard.

"Can I help you?" he asked.

"Noah, I need your help," I said, reciting more lines from the mental-script in my head. "Remember how I told you about the Amy girl from my grade? I think I got her."

He bit his lower lip.

"I don't know little bro," he said. "I think you have the Chelsea girl all lined up. Don't try and bite off more than you can chew now."

"Yeah, but I've been secretly in love with Amy girl for like four years. You should see her, she's the hottest girl in my grade."

"I know," he said, much to my surprise.

"You know who she is?"

"Yeah, I think I've seen her a few times."

"Then why are you trying to talk me out of it?"

"I just think you're being over-confident," he said. "You've known for days that you have this Chelsea lined up. Take the sure thing, don't fuck it up."

The conversation was already taking too long. I saw both Amy and the younger version of my former wife, Chelsea come into the front hall. They stopped there and started talking privately. Amy's eyes cheated over in my direction. Chelsea was listening to her, nodding. She also peeked over. Her eyes were jealous. It was a look that I knew too well.

In approximately two minutes, Amy was going to head down the other hall toward the bathroom. Or, as I was almost positive now, my bedroom.

The first time through, I had been so unsure where exactly she had gone. Or perhaps more accurately, I was uncertain of myself. Instead of following her, I took the easy way out. I settled for the sure thing. I approached Chelsea instead. All because I didn't believe that what I wanted could possibly be attained.

That's how it happened. That's the way I fucked everything up.

Not this time.

I stared hard at Noah. His help was instrumental for this to work. My words were firmer than before.

"Listen, Noah. I'm going for this Amy girl. If it doesn't work, then fine, you can have her. I don't give a damn."

He shook his head.

"I need you to do one thing for me," I continued. "If you don't see me for a little while, trust that means things went well. But please, please just do me one favor. Walk Chelsea home if that happens. Bang her if you want, I don't care. I'm sure you could probably get her if you wanted."

"I'm not taking any girl to bed tonight."

"Fine, then just walk her home. I need you to do that for me."

Noah looked like he was searching for his rebuttal. I didn't stick around for any further deliberation. That part of the sequence was complete.

Right on cue, Amy had left Chelsea standing alone and disappeared down the hallway. I grabbed two beers from the fridge and started in her direction.

I always imagined that the walk past Chelsea would have been the hardest part. I tried to make it easier on myself. I kept my eyes on the ground, the door, the ceiling or anywhere that wasn't her.

Only from my peripheral vision could I see the look on her face. I recognized that expression as well. More so, I detested it. It was the insecure, desperate longing that I had seen so many times before in our life together that no longer existed.

A few feet away, I caught the scent of Chelsea's perfume. One more time, the thought of returning to my former life burrowed into my mind. I entertained the idea. Maybe I could still correct the sequence. Maybe I could somehow say and do the right things to converge the timelines. Perhaps I could recreate all the memories that we were supposed to make going forward.

I pushed the thought out of my head as quickly as I could. I passed Chelsea without giving her a glance. As I walked down the adjacent hallway, the burning sensation of her eyes into the back of my head eased with every step.

I didn't bother checking the bathroom on the way to my destination.

I pushed the bedroom door open. A slender female figure was sprawled across my bed. The light from the hallway provided just enough brightness for me to see that Amy was smiling. It felt like a dream. But it wasn't. It was real.

I didn't offer her a drink. I set the beers down on the night table and leaned over. She wrapped her hands around the back of my neck and pulled me down to her. Our lips met and I slipped away. I never thought that doing something that seemed so evil on the surface could have ever felt so right.

Hours passed. When the sex finally ended, Amy didn't take long to fall asleep. The adrenaline still coursing through my veins wouldn't allow me to do the same.

From outside the bedroom door, I could hear the party had grown quieter.

Much like the last time I was awake in bed while the woman beside me slept, I got out of bed as gently as possible. I tiptoed towards the door and pressed my ear against it. I tried to see if I could hear Chelsea's voice in the remaining bits of conversation. It wasn't there.

I went over to the window to see if anyone was hanging around in my front yard. I was relieved to see two people there. Chelsea stood at the end of the driveway, shivering in the cold autumn air. Noah was coming up the driveway with a sweater to put around her.

They exchanged a few words before heading down the street in the other direction. Her house was only a few blocks away. Nowhere near downtown and certainly not close to wherever that piece-of-shit, Troy McAllen camped out that night.

As they rounded the corner and went out of sight, a thought occurred to me for the first time. And it scared me.

I wondered what it would be like going forward. Would I have to live the rest of my life with all the vivid memories of a timeline that no longer existed? I could still remember my old life with complete clarity.

As I returned to lie beside the girl I loved, I prayed. I prayed that with time, the old memories would fade away. Hopefully, I could seamlessly adjust and settle into this new life as a young man once more. The thought lingered until I fell asleep.

A strange sound woke me the next morning. The sun was starting to rise and faint beams of light were coming in through the window. When I came to my senses, I realized that I was alone in bed. It was not how I was expecting to wake.

I heard the sound of the TV from the living room. Shortly after, I heard Amy whimper. I shot up and ran in there as quickly as my tired legs would take me.

Amy sat hunched over, curled into a ball on the couch. Her head was pressed into her palms, her cheeks red.

She had the TV on. It was set to our local news station. Before I had a chance to ask what had happened, I heard the familiar voice. With only slight variation from before, he delivered his report.

Tragedy strikes close to home today. The body of eighteen-year-old Westmount resident, Chelsea Arcobello, was found in a dumpster behind a bakery near the downtown core. The body shows signs of severe sexual assault and trauma around the neck. All evidence suggests she was strangled to death with a rope.

An anonymous tip was given to police this morning stating that screaming could be heard from the parking lot and a bald man could be seen running from the area shortly after. Police were on the scene within minutes and have since taken homeless man, Troy McAllen, into custody. Authorities are urging whoever called to step forward and provide more information.

The bald man's face came up onto the screen just as I heard the front door push open behind me.

Noah stepped in. His mouth was open wide as he took in long gasps of air. Clumps of hair stuck to his forehead where his sweat had dried. He looked up at us in horror. As if he thought it was impossible for us to be awake so early in the morning.

Blood dripped from the scratches on his face. From inside his half-unzipped jacket, I could see a piece of rope stained completely red.

"What's the matter, Roger?" he said.

"Where were you last night," I managed to spit out. "Didn't you walk Chelsea home and come back?"

"She's gone, Roger. Chelsea wasn't for you. It's best you don't think about her. There's only pain for you there."

THE DESERT STARS

Grant Hinton

oww.

I cracked an eye open, but all I saw was darkness like I was looking at the back of my eyelids.

What the hell..?

I couldn't tell if it was the low hum of a car's engine hurting my head, or if I had taken a blow. I tried to move and then realized my hands and legs were tied.

God, it hurts.

The darkness pulled at me, it promised sweet release from the pain, called at me with its warmth to just close my eyes and it would end all this, whatever this was. But something else kept me from its pull, I just had to remember what, It was on the edge of my mind but I just couldn't reach it.

The grogginess threatened to take me again, so I rolled over in the limited space, trying to lessen the discomfort, but the car hit a bump and my head bounced off the trunk. The last thing I felt before the darkness reached up to claim me was...

~

...The sting of my father's hand on my face. It hurt, but I didn't let it show. Pop's slammed the table hard enough for the salt shaker to roll off the side and smash on the floor to the disapproval of the other diners.

"Are you crazy? I worked my ass off, so you didn't have to go down that road."

I shrugged, and it made him angrier. I knew I wouldn't win the argument. Pop was old school Sicilian; I was better off trying to win a fight against Floyd Mayweather. A waitress in a ruby skirt ambled over with a dustpan. Pop's nose wrinkled as he smiled apologetically, then he turned back with a raised finger.

"I'm going to talk to Mr. Costello, tell him that you're a stupid boy trying to play a man's game, he will understand. He's got sons, right?" I blanched at being called a boy. I was 19 and although we sat in a diner behind the Las Vegas strip, where Pops was from you were already considered a man.

"Pop, you can't go and talk to these kinda people." He cut me off angrily as he repeated his question again only this time slower.

"Has..he..got..sons?" He didn't seem to care about the turned heads and muttered voices. I swept a strand of hair from my face and replied "Yeah, Frank junior and Fat Tony."

"Fat Tony? What sort of father calls his son fat Tony? Bah, I will go and talk to him, father to father."

I rolled my eyes and wiped my mouth with a napkin.

"Now who's being stupid."

I saw the hand come from a mile away and prepared for the impact...

* ...As the car crunched to a stop I smacked my face off a shovel. The car bounced as someone got out. I knew I was in trouble. The grogginess was still there, but I knew I had to stay awake. The indistinguishable murmur of voices penetrated the metallic sides of the trunk. The pounding in my head stirred again, as the voices became

clearer. A Moment later and the trunk opened, I squinted as torch-light blinded me.

"Get him outta there."

I couldn't help but groan as my body protested to being moved, the sharp pain in my head receded as the light moved off. The afterlife of the torchlight blinked before me in the night sky as a pair of big meaty hands pulled me over the edge of the trunk. I fell to the...

~

"...Floor, Yeah, that's her right there."

A young brown hair girl glanced up at me shyly as she danced in a crowd of sweaty bodies. Her yellow dress a stark contrast to the leather pants and dark tops of the other dancers. Fat Tony spoke in my ear; his spittle splashed the side of my face as the music pumped around us.

"Frankie likes her; he said that if anyone gets too close, you gotta deal with em." I frowned and wiped my cheek.

"What I'm Frankie's minder now, get outta here, If she's his girl, let him watch her."

The pretty little thing before me was suddenly swallowed by the sea of men trying to gain her affection. Tony laughed as a bottle blonde pulls at his arm wanting her share of his affection.

"It's your funeral, hey, see that Hispanic dude there?" He said pointing.

I followed his finger to a short Spanish guy decked out in the same fashion as half the club.

"What about him?"

"He's dealing on our turf."

I sighed as Tony disappeared into the gyrating bodies. The guy watched me approach and I likewise used the time to assess him as he sized me up as a potential customer or a threat.

"Hey, How you doing?" I said.

The man took in my expensive watch and Gucci suit.

"You looking for something my man?"

I grabbed the guy by the arm and showed him what laid in my waistband.

He didn't protest as I wheeled him to the back door.

I reckon he knew he fucked up.

Outside the crisp fresh air hit me like a truck as I tossed him into the trash bins, his silver top sparkled with the neon exit sign. I pulled the gun from my waistband and pointed it at him.

"What are you stupid or something? You do realize who's club this is?"

The guy went down on his knees and raised his hands in prayer.

"Please, I...I have kids to feed, I'm sorry, I fucked up, I didn't know. I...I won't do it again, I promise."

His pathetic plead annoyed me but the club didn't need a dead body in its alleyway so I put the gun away.

"Get the hell out of here and don't come back, You're lucky it was me you're dealing with and not Fat Tony."

The Hispanic guy couldn't stop thanking me as I turned back to the door. The sea of people still swayed to the music, and the girl was still there too. She smiled at me again, and I returned her infectious grin. A waiter walked past with a tray of drinks, so I snatched two and raised them to her. She parted the dance floor like Moses and took one of the drinks from me.

"Hey, I'm Michael." Her deep brown eyes swallowed me whole and I lost myself forever.

"Cassandra." She said as we clinked glasses and I winked...

...My eyes opened and the stars winked back.

Fat Tony pulled me across the desert floor with no regard for the sharp rocks. I wonder dreamily about the stars before being dumped unceremoniously in a shallow grave. The sound of a second person being dragged in a similar fashion aroused me enough against my plight, so I rolled over to better see just as a heavy boot came towards my...

"...Head? Did you hear me? Are you fucking crazy? Cassy is Frankie's girl! If he or Fat Tony finds out, you're a gonna."

Pop tried to sit up in the hospital bed, but I pressed a firm hand against his chest. The stroke had taken much of the man I love, but his firey Sicilian roots were still strong, He slapped his hands together, then pinched his thin chin. His eyes were sharp, and I could see his mind working fast.

"You have to run away; you can go to my cousin in Italy, leave the girl. It's the only way."

The machine at his bedside bleeped as his heart rate increased and a nurse in a speckle blue-white dress came over to check on it clucking like a hen. I glanced around as she inspected Pop, I thought again about bringing in a painting from home to cheer up the drab brown walls of his ward. The nurse tutted and told me not to excite my father as she left us to our talk. I reached over and cradled his cheek with one hand.

"Don't worry Pop. I'm ain't gonna do nuthin stupid. Shes Frankie's girl."

Cassie walked into the room with a cup of steaming coffee, and my father watched her like a doe seeing a wolf for the first time. She came and sat by his bedside and handed me a coffee with a smile that melted my heart. Pop saw it too but didn't say anything. She placed a hand on one of his and he smiled at her.

"So, Cassie, what do you do for a... "

"...Job? Father never told us to whack him. So why the hell are we out here?"

I could hear the two of them argue, I knew the voices, how couldn't I? I'd been working with them for the last few years. The Costello brothers. I tried to remember what had happened but my head just throbbed. When I brought my bound hands down from my head they were slick with blood. A new sound filled my ears, and I felt the vibrations of the shovel entering the dirt by my head.

"Don't worry about it; I'll take care of that. Just dig the fucking hole." He turned to me.

"You rat bastard, how dare you get with my girl." Frankie spat a glob of phlegm at me.

A faint whimper made my heart contract, I knew that voice even better than the two brothers. Maybe it was the blood loss or the beating, either way, the darkness started to collect at the corners of my eyes as the shovel sliced more dirt. I rolled again as my fading eyes saw Cassie tied...

∾

...up.

Frankie laughed and cheered his brother on as Tony panted and grinned. The girl's eyes were closed, but when they did open there were terrified. I looked away from the tears stream down her face to her husband's dead body two feet away with a clean bullet hole in his head. The smoking gun stills shook in my hand, he had been my first.

"Ah come on guys, The boss didn't say nuthin about this." I said to Frankie.

I look disgusted at Tony as he pumped the women over the table. His flabby belly rolled like waves and the girl looked at me pleadingly. Tony groaned and finally shuddered to a stop. I looked away again in disgust as the pervert pulled up his trousers and zipper. Frankie pointed the gun at my head.

"Well, I say this is what we're doing, so your next Micky boy."

The barrel of the gun pushed hard against my temple, and I closed my eyes for a brief second. My hand clenched into a fist as anger swelled in my chest. I heard Frankie taking the safety off. He looked at me and grinned.

"What you think about..."

∾

"...That?"

She pointed to a cluster of stars that shone like diamonds on a velvet sheet in the night sky before us. Her warmth next to me more than made up for the discomfort of the hard desert floor.

"That's the big dipper, and see those ones there?"

My finger painted a trail of stardust through the sky.

"The three stars in a row are called Orion's belt."

She snuggled next to me and placed her head on my chest. The night was clear in the middle of the Nevada desert, no man-made light reached out here. The multitude of stars made me feel insignificant and small but with Cassie at my side, somehow, the world felt right.

"So many stars." She said.

"Do you think that there are others like us."

The wind picked up, so I wrapped a thin blanket around her shoulders as we continued to watch the heavens. Falling stars blazed across our vision and Cassie gasped.

"We would be stupid to think that we were the only ones in the universe," I said as I pulled her closer.

"You know it's a huge place.

I think it would be rather lonely if there weren't others like us." Cassie reached up and pulled my chin toward hers.

Her lips were like honey and peaches; I could have kiss those lips forever, every time getting as lost in them as I could in the desert stars.

"As long as I'm with you." She said.

"I'll never be lonely, just me and... "

* "...You..sure..Frankie? She's a good looking girl. No? Last chance to keep her?"

Tony's voice seemed far off; I didn't know if it was the distance or the pain until Cassie screamed and I remembered with a jerk the situation we were in. Frankie stood over me as I tried to sit up.

"You mother fucker."

He hit me with the butt of the gun, and I slowly drifted again.

Then he spat and the last thing I saw was the blood roll past my eye and...

...Dropped from the cloud, soon fat heavy rain pelted the few black umbrellas that surrounded the grave. The priest was saying things I could barely hear over the canopy of raindrops. I was numb to all that was going on around me until a warm delicate hand clasped mine and squeezed. Cassie smiled at me, and I returned mine through the tears. Frankie, however, looked over the coffin at us. His face hidden in the shadows of his hat, but I saw the glance down at our hands. I met them on the way back up. Today was about my father's life and his deeds, not mine, and I didn't give a fuck about Frankie.

The priest held out a box full of dirt; I took a small handful. Cassie placed a white rose in my other, and I walked numbly to the front of the tiny congregation. The single rose smelt sweet, and the freshly turned dirt and rain added to the aroma. With nothing left of him to hold on to, I kissed the rose and tossed it down onto the ivory coffin lid. I hadn't been able to give my Pops a lot throughout his life as he didn't want to associate with bad money as he called it. But I was determined to provide him with the burial of a saint. I said a silent prayer as I threw the handful of dirt...

...Into the shallow grave dug by Tony. My side hurt from the kick and the short drop to the grave floor. I winced as new pain sprung up along my body. The few inches of dirt walls was a mountain to my tied hands as another volley of desert showered my face.

"Take that you fucking pig. Punch me in the face god damn you."

The wetness of the spit clung to my face and fat Tony laughed, I managed a tiny smirk. That punch taught Frankie not to put a gun to my head.

"Yeah you can laugh fat boy, at least he had the balls to punch me."

Tony's laugh was cut short, and his grunts coupled with a rhythmic slap filled the night air. We were in the desert that far I knew. I was in a grave, not great. I had dug a few graves and knew how this went so I worked on my bonds as the brothers conversed.

"You want a turn after?" Tony breathed heavily.

"You're sick; you know that? Sick. Ma must've dropped you on the head, you hear."

Tony chuckled and the air went silent except for his grunts and Cassie's whimpers. I managed to roll onto my back and looked up at Frankie surrounded by millions of stars. He looked majestically like the god of mob bosses as he pointed the gun at my face and sneered.

"Not gonna get out of this one, ahh Mickey. Not gonna punch me again Mother fucker." He stamped on my chest and I felt a rib snap. The blackness crept up and Frankie lunged into the grave.

"Oh no you..."

"...Don't. We have to leave if he finds out he will kill us." Cassie pulled the duffle bag from my unresisting hand and continued to pack it.

"And where would we go?" I flung my hands around the tiny room.

"He has connections in every city this side of the Pacific. Anywhere we go he will find us." The plasterboard wall folded around my fist. It had been the same argument for days.

"We can go to Europe or Australia or anywhere, just as long as it's you and me." Cassie begged, almost pleaded, and I sagged. I cradled her head in my hands and kissed her lips tenderly.

"As long as I'm with you, Just you and me. Remember?" She said and pulled me down onto the clothes. I struggled to speak from the side of my mouth as she kissed me again.

"What about packing?" I asked. "You gotta be ready for after the job tonight."

"I'll be ready." She said as I let her pull me down on her.

"Just make sure you come back..."

"...To me, that's it you rat bastard, you come back now you hear."

The burn on my arm brought me back with its pain alright. Frankie stood over me with a knife that glistened in the moonlight, the edge darken by my blood. I groaned and tried to sit up again.

Frankie aimed the gun back at my head.

"I want to look in your eyes when I kill you, fucker."

He bit the corner of his lip, I'd seen him do this before, right before he flipped out and somebody gets hurt. I closed my eyes knowing that my time had run out. I heard the muffled yell and a gunshot, then I blacked out, But...

..The light was so bright it blinded me so I threw up a hand to block out the source, but it didn't help. It came from everywhere.

Overwhelmed, I stumbled on.

The ground beneath me buckled and started to crack, soon they widened to reveal rivers of molten fire below. Beasts made from the bowels of Hell crawled from the inferno. The broken ground caused me to stagger as more climbed the scorched rim. They rose in horrid waves, some in the shape of men with horns and snake-like hands. Others resembled the beasts of the fields only twisted and grotesque.

Suddenly a pain tore through my leg. The creatures claw burnt through my pants and seared my skin. Its fiery arm extended from the broken earth and attached to a spider that glowed red with magma. The sickly smell of burnt flesh reached my nostrils. I screamed but no one was there to hear the desperate cry. The beasts of hell crawled closer, and the monster tightened its grip on my leg, the pain was unbearable, and my mind reeled with the agony. Suddenly, the grip loosened, and a wave of air refreshed the heat that racked my body. Through the tears of pain, I looked up and saw my savior.

We soared from the broken earth hand in hand, each beat of his enormous feathery wings concussed my ears as we gained altitude. As

I glanced at the ground, the hellish horde snarled back at me. As suddenly as we started we stopped in mid-air, and I saw my savior's face as he smiled at me. My father, as I saw him as a boy. Healthy and strong. His loving brown eyes filled me, encompassed me with all of his being and I allowed myself to be caught up in the moment.

Then he let me go.

My body convulsed, and I grabbed for his fingers as they slipped through my hands. I pleaded with my Pops as the monsters roared below, but the convulsion hit me again. He smiled as I scrambled to clutch his fingers tighter when another hit me, then I fell. My father's face smiled at me as I fell through the air, back to the ground when my body...

~

....Convulsed for the last time and my eyes fluttered open, a white light past overhead, then another and another. People talked rapidly around me, and someone held me down by the shoulder, the pressure too strong to fight, but I tried anyway.

"Don't move Michael, You're in good hands."

The voice was sweet, musical and soothing. I didn't have the strength to fight the hand and the voice. Plus, my body didn't respond as it should and soon the darkness came to claim me for the hundredth time, but I held on. The wheels of the bed clattered through the corridor. The lights changed and different voices assaulted my ears.

"Male, 22, Gunshot trauma to the right shoulder. Vitals are low but are holding."

A field of white and blue swum past my eyes and a doctor's face peered over me.

"Can you hear me Michael, Good, You hold on their buddy, we're gonna get you fixed right up."

A slab of hands shifted me to the operating table, and I noticed another body being wheeled out. The sheet closed forever over the face until a loved one came to identify them. The lifeless feet stuck out from underneath reminded me about Cassie and a sob escaped my lips. The darkness swum through my head like a shark searching for prey, defeated, I let it take me back into the abyss.

~

Time passed although I wasn't aware.

When I finally came to I dared not open my eyes. Instead, I laid still and listened to the sounds around me. The slow beep of the heart monitor and the steady breath of someone asleep. I tested my limbs with tiny movements to help determine if I was whole and not dead. My leg burnt and felt heavy. My left hand was free, and I caressed the smooth cotton sheet that covered me. My right one had pressure on it, a gentle but sweaty pressure, I flexed my fingers, and the hand responded. Cassie's slept with her head rested on the bed as I opened my eyes to see her. She must have felt me move as she too opened hers and they shone up at me. She moved to hug me and pain shot through my ribs and my shoulder ached in protest, but relief also washed me clean.

"Michael, are you alright?" I grinned, even though my mouth felt like sawdust.

"I feel like I've been dragged through hell, but, yeah I'm OK, what happened?" Cassie turned her face away, and I saw the dark blotches and bruises that cover the side of her neck and cheek. I moved to touch her and the pain flared again.

"Fat Tony collected me from my home, said that Frankie wanted to see me. I knew something was off, but before I could make a run for it, he grabbed me."

"That bastard." I spat. Cassie's tears shone like pearls, ready to fall.

"He said that you were dead. He said that Frankie had found out and he shot you after the bank job. I didn't believe him, but he just laughed and said I was next. That's when he tied me up, covered my face and threw me in the boot."

The tears trickled down her cheek, and she wiped them away furiously with the sleeve of her top. After a deep shuddering breath, she continued.

"When I heard the boot open and felt a body being put in with me, my heart sank. I tried to nudge you, but you didn't move. I thought Tony was telling the truth, that you were dead." I pulled Cassie into a half hug, and she sobbed against my chest.

"When we reached the desert, and I heard you moan, I knew I had to do something. That fat pig groped me, and I knew what Tony wanted. I saw his gun drop into the seat of his pants when he raped me and thought that if I could somehow reach it, I could save us."

She wiped away the last of her tears and sat up straight, I saw something in her then, determination, fortitude. Respect. She'd been raped, and there she was telling me the tale.

"It took me a long time to maneuver around, but I finally got hold of the gun. Tony went limp as I pointed it at his tiny dick. Fucking bastard," she spat on the floor. "I shot that mother fucker in the cock before I turned it on Frankie, but I was too late. Frankie had already shot you."

Her body racked with the shredded tears, and her mouth moved through her grief.

"I thought you were dead."

I pulled her closer and kissed the back of her head. I heard a small shuffle of bedding and looked about the room, A Hispanic guy with a body full of tattoos lay peacefully on a bed similar to mine. Although my wrists were free of handcuffs. The shackled man turned to me, and I recognized his face but couldn't place from where. I heard the door squeak open and a policeman looked through the small window.

My heart sank.

Did I just escape death to be put in a jail cell?

As the door crept open, I heard the slap of feet on lino. The police officer turned to the frantic nurse, and soon the door swung shut as the policeman ran up the corridor after her. Cassie looked at me urgently.

"Quick, I have clothes we need to get out of here."

Slowly I sat up, every fiber of me protested to the movement but soon I was stood limp on the lino floor. Cassie helped me into a pair of trouser and took the papery gown off my back. My body was covered in bruises, and the patch on my shoulder was sore, but not as painful as the burn on my leg that was in the shape of a handprint. I shuddered remembering. I reached for the heartbeat monitor on my finger, but the Hispanic guy stopped me.

"No, if you remove it the alarm will go off, they'll think you're dead." He showed his index finger attached to an identical monitor and offered his other one to me.

"Thanks." Quickly I attached it to his finger.

"No problem Esai." The guy rolled his head away from us and pretended to be asleep.

An intense five minutes later and we shuffled through the car park. Cassie helped me along as my leg burnt like hell, and I wondered again at the strength of this beautiful woman. My old black sedan waited for us in a dark corner of the lot. Thankfully this time I slid into the passenger seat and not the boot as Cassie jumped into the driver's seat and the engine came to life.

The head light shone on the tarmac road as Cassie slowed and turned off to a narrow dirt track.

She tried to take it slow, I knew that, but the off-roading had my shoulder in pieces, and my ribs flared up with fire.

"Sorry. Not much further, I promise."

I grinned at her, and I saw that smile again.

The one when a pretty girl smiled at me from the dance floor. It seemed like ages until eventually she stopped. I focused on anything but the pain. The orange dust flew skywards as the tires skidded on the loose ground. The headlight illuminated the cacti and a few frozen predators that have been lured to the scene by the scent of blood.

When I climbed out the car clutching my side tenderly I felt a warm sensation spill down my side. The bandage felt wet and sticky, and I knew the car journey had opened a stitch. I saw Fat Tony first.

He was dead; the animals had started to feed on him. He hadn't managed to pull up his trousers before Cassie had shot him, and his face was frozen in an eternal state of surprise. Cassie went to him, started to kick him repeatedly, I didn't stop her. She needed to release the anger inside. I turned, leaving her to deal with her oww.

I cracked an eye open, but all I saw was darkness like I was looking at the back of my eyelids.

What the hell..?

I couldn't tell if it was the low hum of a car's engine hurting my head, or if I had taken a blow. I tried to move and then realized my hands and legs were tied.

God, it hurts.

The darkness pulled at me, it promised sweet release from the pain, called at me with its warmth to just close my eyes and it would end all this, whatever this was. But something else kept me from its pull, I just had to remember what, It was on the edge of my mind but I just couldn't reach it.

The grogginess threatened to take me again, so I rolled over in the limited space, trying to lessen the discomfort, but the car hit a bump and my head bounced off the trunk. The last thing I felt before the darkness reached up to claim me was...

...The sting of my father's hand on my face. It hurt, but I didn't let it show. Pop's slammed the table hard enough for the salt shaker to roll off the side and smash on the floor to the disapproval of the other diners.

"Are you crazy? I worked my ass off, so you didn't have to go down that road."

I shrugged, and it made him angrier. I knew I wouldn't win the argument. Pop was old school Sicilian; I was better off trying to win a fight against Floyd Mayweather. A waitress in a ruby skirt ambled over with a dustpan. Pop's nose wrinkled as he smiled apologetically, then he turned back with a raised finger.

"I'm going to talk to Mr. Costello, tell him that you're a stupid boy trying to play a man's game, he will understand. He's got sons, right?"

I blanched at being called a boy. I was 19 and although we sat in a diner behind the Las Vegas strip, where Pops was from you were already considered a man.

"Pop, you can't go and talk to these kinda people." He cut me off angrily as he repeated his question again only this time slower.

"Has..he..got..sons?" He didn't seem to care about the turned heads and muttered voices. I swept a strand of hair from my face and replied

"Yeah, Frank junior and Fat Tony."

"Fat Tony? What sort of father calls his son fat Tony? Bah, I will go and talk to him, father to father."

I rolled my eyes and wiped my mouth with a napkin.

"Now who's being stupid."

I saw the hand come from a mile away and prepared for the impact...

~

...As the car crunched to a stop I smacked my face off a shovel. The car bounced as someone got out. I knew I was in trouble. The grogginess was still there, but I knew I had to stay awake. The indistinguishable murmur of voices penetrated the metallic sides of the trunk. The pounding in my head stirred again, as the voices became clearer. A Moment later and the trunk opened, I squinted as torchlight blinded me.

"Get him outta there."

I couldn't help but groan as my body protested to being moved, the sharp pain in my head receded as the light moved off. The afterlife of the torchlight blinked before me in the night sky as a pair of big meaty hands pulled me over the edge of the trunk. I fell to the...

~

"...Floor, Yeah, that's her right there."

A young brown hair girl glanced up at me shyly as she danced in a crowd of sweaty bodies. Her yellow dress a stark contrast to the leather pants and dark tops of the other dancers. Fat Tony spoke in my ear; his spittle splashed the side of my face as the music pumped around us.

"Frankie likes her; he said that if anyone gets too close, you gotta deal with em." I frowned and wiped my cheek.

"What I'm Frankie's minder now, get outta here, If she's his girl, let him watch her."

The pretty little thing before me was suddenly swallowed by the sea of men trying to gain her affection. Tony laughed as a bottle blonde pulls at his arm wanting her share of his affection.

"It's your funeral, hey, see that Hispanic dude there?" He said pointing.

I followed his finger to a short Spanish guy decked out in the same fashion as half the club.

"What about him?"

"He's dealing on our turf."

I sighed as Tony disappeared into the gyrating bodies. The guy watched me approach and I likewise used the time to assess him as he sized me up as a potential customer or a threat.

"Hey, How you doing?" I said.

The man took in my expensive watch and Gucci suit.

"You looking for something my man?"

I grabbed the guy by the arm and showed him what laid in my waistband.

He didn't protest as I wheeled him to the back door.

I reckon he knew he fucked up.

Outside the crisp fresh air hit me like a truck as I tossed him into the trash bins, his silver top sparkled with the neon exit sign. I pulled the gun from my waistband and pointed it at him.

"What are you stupid or something? You do realize who's club this is?"

The guy went down on his knees and raised his hands in prayer.

"Please, I...I have kids to feed, I'm sorry, I fucked up, I didn't know. I...I won't do it again, I promise."

His pathetic plead annoyed me but the club didn't need a dead body in its alleyway so I put the gun away.

"Get the hell out of here and don't come back, You're lucky it was me you're dealing with and not Fat Tony."

The Hispanic guy couldn't stop thanking me as I turned back to the door. The sea of people still swayed to the music, and the girl was still there too. She smiled at me again, and I returned her infectious grin. A waiter walked past with a tray of drinks, so I snatched two and raised them to her. She parted the dance floor like Moses and took one of the drinks from me.

"Hey, I'm Michael." Her deep brown eyes swallowed me whole and I lost myself forever.

"Cassandra." She said as we clinked glasses and I winked...

～

...My eyes opened and the stars winked back.

Fat Tony pulled me across the desert floor with no regard for the sharp rocks. I wonder dreamily about the stars before being dumped unceremoniously in a shallow grave. The sound of a second person being dragged in a similar fashion aroused me enough against my plight, so I rolled over to better see just as a heavy boot came towards my...

～

"...Head? Did you hear me? Are you fucking crazy? Cassy is Frankie's girl! If he or Fat Tony finds out, you're a gonna."

Pop tried to sit up in the hospital bed, but I pressed a firm hand against his chest. The stroke had taken much of the man I love, but his firey Sicilian roots were still strong, He slapped his hands together, then pinched his thin chin. His eyes were sharp, and I could see his mind working fast.

"You have to run away; you can go to my cousin in Italy, leave the girl. It's the only way."

The machine at his bedside bleeped as his heart rate increased and a nurse in a speckle blue-white dress came over to check on it clucking like a hen. I glanced around as she inspected Pop, I thought again about bringing in a painting from home to cheer up the drab brown walls of his ward. The nurse tutted and told me not to excite my father as she left us to our talk. I reached over and cradled his cheek with one hand.

"Don't worry Pop. I'm ain't gonna do nuthin stupid. Shes Frankie's girl."

Cassie walked into the room with a cup of steaming coffee, and my father watched her like a doe seeing a wolf for the first time. She came and sat by his bedside and handed me a coffee with a smile that melted my heart. Pop saw it too but didn't say anything. She placed a hand on one of his and he smiled at her.

"So, Cassie, what do you do for a... "

"...Job? Father never told us to whack him. So why the hell are we out here?"

I could hear the two of them argue, I knew the voices, how couldn't I? I'd been working with them for the last few years. The Costello brothers. I tried to remember what had happened but my head just throbbed. When I brought my bound hands down from my head they were slick with blood. A new sound filled my ears, and I felt the vibrations of the shovel entering the dirt by my head.

"Don't worry about it; I'll take care of that. Just dig the fucking hole." He turned to me.

"You rat bastard, how dare you get with my girl." Frankie spat a glob of phlegm at me.

A faint whimper made my heart contract, I knew that voice even better than the two brothers. Maybe it was the blood loss or the beating, either way, the darkness started to collect at the corners of my eyes as the shovel sliced more dirt. I rolled again as my fading eyes saw Cassie tied...

~

...up.

Frankie laughed and cheered his brother on as Tony panted and grinned. The girl's eyes were closed, but when they did open there were terrified. I looked away from the tears stream down her face to her husband's dead body two feet away with a clean bullet hole in his head. The smoking gun stills shook in my hand, he had been my first.

"Ah come on guys, The boss didn't say nuthin about this." I said to Frankie.

I look disgusted at Tony as he pumped the women over the table. His flabby belly rolled like waves and the girl looked at me pleadingly. Tony groaned and finally shuddered to a stop. I looked away again in disgust as the pervert pulled up his trousers and zipper. Frankie pointed the gun at my head.

"Well, I say this is what we're doing, so your next Micky boy."

The barrel of the gun pushed hard against my temple, and I closed my eyes for a brief second. My hand clenched into a fist as anger swelled in my chest. I heard Frankie taking the safety off. He looked at me and grinned.

"What you think about..."

~

"...That?"

She pointed to a cluster of stars that shone like diamonds on a velvet sheet in the night sky before us. Her warmth next to me more than made up for the discomfort of the hard desert floor.

"That's the big dipper, and see those ones there?"

My finger painted a trail of stardust through the sky.

"The three stars in a row are called Orion's belt."

She snuggled next to me and placed her head on my chest. The night was clear in the middle of the Nevada desert, no man-made light reached out here. The multitude of stars made me feel insignificant and small but with Cassie at my side, somehow, the world felt right.

"So many stars." She said.

"Do you think that there are others like us."

The wind picked up, so I wrapped a thin blanket around her shoulders as we continued to watch the heavens. Falling stars blazed across our vision and Cassie gasped.

"We would be stupid to think that we were the only ones in the universe," I said as I pulled her closer.

"You know it's a huge place.

I think it would be rather lonely if there weren't others like us." Cassie reached up and pulled my chin toward hers.

Her lips were like honey and peaches; I could have kiss those lips forever, every time getting as lost in them as I could in the desert stars.

"As long as I'm with you." She said.

"I'll never be lonely, just me and... "

∾

"...You..sure..Frankie? She's a good looking girl. No? Last chance to keep her?"

Tony's voice seemed far off; I didn't know if it was the distance or the pain until Cassie screamed and I remembered with a jerk the situation we were in. Frankie stood over me as I tried to sit up.

"You mother fucker."

He hit me with the butt of the gun, and I slowly drifted again. Then he spat and the last thing I saw was the blood roll past my eye and...

∾

...Dropped from the cloud, soon fat heavy rain pelted the few black umbrellas that surrounded the grave. The priest was saying things I could barely hear over the canopy of raindrops. I was numb to all that was going on around me until a warm delicate hand clasped mine and squeezed. Cassie smiled at me, and I returned mine through the tears. Frankie, however, looked over the coffin at us. His face hidden in the shadows of his hat, but I saw the glance down at our hands. I met them on the way back up. Today was about my father's life and his deeds, not mine, and I didn't give a fuck about Frankie.

The priest held out a box full of dirt; I took a small handful. Cassie placed a white rose in my other, and I walked numbly to the front of the tiny congregation. The single rose smelt sweet, and the freshly turned dirt and rain added to the aroma. With nothing left of him to hold on to, I kissed the rose and tossed it down onto the ivory coffin lid. I hadn't been able to give my Pops a lot throughout his life as he didn't want to associate with bad money as he called it. But I was determined to provide him with the burial of a saint. I said a silent prayer as I threw the handful of dirt...

...Into the shallow grave dug by Tony. My side hurt from the kick and the short drop to the grave floor. I winced as new pain sprung up along my body. The few inches of dirt walls was a mountain to my tied hands as another volley of desert showered my face.

"Take that you fucking pig. Punch me in the face god damn you."

The wetness of the spit clung to my face and fat Tony laughed, I managed a tiny smirk. That punch taught Frankie not to put a gun to my head.

"Yeah you can laugh fat boy, at least he had the balls to punch me."

Tony's laugh was cut short, and his grunts coupled with a rhythmic slap filled the night air. We were in the desert that far I knew. I was in a grave, not great. I had dug a few graves and knew how this went so I worked on my bonds as the brothers conversed.

"You want a turn after?" Tony breathed heavily.

"You're sick; you know that? Sick. Ma must've dropped you on the head, you hear."

Tony chuckled and the air went silent except for his grunts and Cassie's whimpers. I managed to roll onto my back and looked up at Frankie surrounded by millions of stars. He looked majestically like the god of mob bosses as he pointed the gun at my face and sneered.

"Not gonna get out of this one, ahh Mickey. Not gonna punch me again Mother fucker." He stamped on my chest and I felt a rib snap. The blackness crept up and Frankie lunged into the grave.

"Oh no you..."

~

"...Don't. We have to leave if he finds out he will kill us." Cassie pulled the duffle bag from my unresisting hand and continued to pack it.

"And where would we go?" I flung my hands around the tiny room.

"He has connections in every city this side of the Pacific. Anywhere we go he will find us." The plasterboard wall folded around my fist. It had been the same argument for days.

"We can go to Europe or Australia or anywhere, just as long as it's you and me." Cassie begged, almost pleaded, and I sagged. I cradled her head in my hands and kissed her lips tenderly.

"As long as I'm with you, Just you and me. Remember?" She said and pulled me down onto the clothes. I struggled to speak from the side of my mouth as she kissed me again.

"What about packing?" I asked. "You gotta be ready for after the job tonight."

"I'll be ready." She said as I let her pull me down on her.

"Just make sure you come back..."

~

"...To me, that's it you rat bastard, you come back now you hear."

The burn on my arm brought me back with its pain alright.

Frankie stood over me with a knife that glistened in the moonlight, the edge darken by my blood. I groaned and tried to sit up again.

Frankie aimed the gun back at my head.

"I want to look in your eyes when I kill you, fucker."

He bit the corner of his lip, I'd seen him do this before, right before he flipped out and somebody gets hurt. I closed my eyes knowing that my time had run out. I heard the muffled yell and a gunshot, then I blacked out, But...

~

..The light was so bright it blinded me so I threw up a hand to block out the source, but it didn't help. It came from everywhere.

Overwhelmed, I stumbled on.

The ground beneath me buckled and started to crack, soon they widened to reveal rivers of molten fire below. Beasts made from the bowels of Hell crawled from the inferno. The broken ground caused me to stagger as more climbed the scorched rim. They rose in horrid waves, some in the shape of men with horns and snake-like hands. Others resembled the beasts of the fields only twisted and grotesque.

Suddenly a pain tore through my leg. The creatures claw burnt through my pants and seared my skin. Its fiery arm extended from the broken earth and attached to a spider that glowed red with magma. The sickly smell of burnt flesh reached my nostrils. I screamed but no one was there to hear the desperate cry. The beasts of hell crawled closer, and the monster tightened its grip on my leg, the pain was unbearable, and my mind reeled with the agony. Suddenly, the grip loosened, and a wave of air refreshed the heat that racked my body. Through the tears of pain, I looked up and saw my savior.

We soared from the broken earth hand in hand, each beat of his enormous feathery wings concussed my ears as we gained altitude. As I glanced at the ground, the hellish horde snarled back at me. As suddenly as we started we stopped in mid-air, and I saw my savior's face as he smiled at me. My father, as I saw him as a boy. Healthy and strong. His loving brown eyes filled me, encompassed me with all of his being and I allowed myself to be caught up in the moment.

Then he let me go.

My body convulsed, and I grabbed for his fingers as they slipped through my hands. I pleaded with my Pops as the monsters roared below, but the convulsion hit me again. He smiled as I scrambled to clutch his fingers tighter when another hit me, then I fell. My father's face smiled at me as I fell through the air, back to the ground when my body...

∽

....Convulsed for the last time and my eyes fluttered open, a white light past overhead, then another and another. People talked rapidly around me, and someone held me down by the shoulder, the pressure too strong to fight, but I tried anyway.

"Don't move Michael, You're in good hands."

The voice was sweet, musical and soothing. I didn't have the strength to fight the hand and the voice. Plus, my body didn't respond as it should and soon the darkness came to claim me for the hundredth time, but I held on. The wheels of the bed clattered through the corridor. The lights changed and different voices assaulted my ears.

"Male, 22, Gunshot trauma to the right shoulder. Vitals are low but are holding."

A field of white and blue swum past my eyes and a doctor's face peered over me.

"Can you hear me Michael, Good, You hold on their buddy, we're gonna get you fixed right up."

A slab of hands shifted me to the operating table, and I noticed another body being wheeled out. The sheet closed forever over the face until a loved one came to identify them. The lifeless feet stuck out from underneath reminded me about Cassie and a sob escaped my lips. The darkness swum through my head like a shark searching for prey, defeated, I let it take me back into the abyss.

Time passed although I wasn't aware.

When I finally came to I dared not open my eyes. Instead, I laid still and listened to the sounds around me. The slow beep of the heart monitor and the steady breath of someone asleep. I tested my limbs with tiny movements to help determine if I was whole and not dead. My leg burnt and felt heavy. My left hand was free, and I caressed the smooth cotton sheet that covered me. My right one had pressure on it, a gentle but sweaty pressure, I flexed my fingers, and the hand responded. Cassie's slept with her head rested on the bed as I opened my eyes to see her. She must have felt me move as she too opened hers and they shone up at me. She moved to hug me and pain shot through my ribs and my shoulder ached in protest, but relief also washed me clean.

"Michael, are you alright?" I grinned, even though my mouth felt like sawdust.

"I feel like I've been dragged through hell, but, yeah I'm OK, what happened?" Cassie turned her face away, and I saw the dark blotches and bruises that cover the side of her neck and cheek. I moved to touch her and the pain flared again.

"Fat Tony collected me from my home, said that Frankie wanted to see me. I knew something was off, but before I could make a run for it, he grabbed me."

"That bastard." I spat. Cassie's tears shone like pearls, ready to fall.

"He said that you were dead. He said that Frankie had found out and he shot you after the bank job. I didn't believe him, but he just laughed and said I was next. That's when he tied me up, covered my face and threw me in the boot."

The tears trickled down her cheek, and she wiped them away furiously with the sleeve of her top. After a deep shuddering breath, she continued.

"When I heard the boot open and felt a body being put in with me, my heart sank. I tried to nudge you, but you didn't move. I thought

Tony was telling the truth, that you were dead." I pulled Cassie into a half hug, and she sobbed against my chest.

"When we reached the desert, and I heard you moan, I knew I had to do something. That fat pig groped me, and I knew what Tony wanted. I saw his gun drop into the seat of his pants when he raped me and thought that if I could somehow reach it, I could save us."

She wiped away the last of her tears and sat up straight, I saw something in her then, determination, fortitude. Respect. She'd been raped, and there she was telling me the tale.

"It took me a long time to maneuver around, but I finally got hold of the gun. Tony went limp as I pointed it at his tiny dick. Fucking bastard," she spat on the floor. "I shot that mother fucker in the cock before I turned it on Frankie, but I was too late. Frankie had already shot you."

Her body racked with the shredded tears, and her mouth moved through her grief.

"I thought you were dead."

I pulled her closer and kissed the back of her head. I heard a small shuffle of bedding and looked about the room, A Hispanic guy with a body full of tattoos lay peacefully on a bed similar to mine. Although my wrists were free of handcuffs. The shackled man turned to me, and I recognized his face but couldn't place from where. I heard the door squeak open and a policeman looked through the small window.

My heart sank.

Did I just escape death to be put in a jail cell?

As the door crept open, I heard the slap of feet on lino. The police officer turned to the frantic nurse, and soon the door swung shut as the policeman ran up the corridor after her. Cassie looked at me urgently.

"Quick, I have clothes we need to get out of here."

Slowly I sat up, every fiber of me protested to the movement but soon I was stood limp on the lino floor. Cassie helped me into a pair of trouser and took the papery gown off my back. My body was covered in bruises, and the patch on my shoulder was sore, but not as painful as the burn on my leg that was in the shape of a handprint. I shuddered remembering. I reached for the heartbeat monitor on my finger, but the Hispanic guy stopped me.

"No, if you remove it the alarm will go off, they'll think you're dead." He showed his index finger attached to an identical monitor and offered his other one to me.

"Thanks." Quickly I attached it to his finger.

"No problem Esai." The guy rolled his head away from us and pretended to be asleep.

An intense five minutes later and we shuffled through the car park. Cassie helped me along as my leg burnt like hell, and I wondered again at the strength of this beautiful woman. My old black sedan waited for us in a dark corner of the lot. Thankfully this time I slid into the passenger seat and not the boot as Cassie jumped into the driver's seat and the engine came to life.

The head light shone on the tarmac road as Cassie slowed and turned off to a narrow dirt track.

She tried to take it slow, I knew that, but the off-roading had my shoulder in pieces, and my ribs flared up with fire.

"Sorry. Not much further, I promise."

I grinned at her, and I saw that smile again.

The one when a pretty girl smiled at me from the dance floor. It seemed like ages until eventually she stopped. I focused on anything but the pain. The orange dust flew skywards as the tires skidded on the loose ground. The headlight illuminated the cacti and a few frozen predators that have been lured to the scene by the scent of blood.

When I climbed out the car clutching my side tenderly I felt a warm sensation spill down my side. The bandage felt wet and sticky, and I knew the car journey had opened a stitch. I saw Fat Tony first. He was dead; the animals had started to feed on him. He hadn't managed to pull up his trousers before Cassie had shot him, and his face was frozen in an eternal state of surprise. Cassie went to him, started to kick him repeatedly, I didn't stop her. She needed to release the anger inside. I turned, leaving her to deal with her grief and found Frankie sprayed out on his back looking at me. His hand clamped over a wound in his stomach. Blood stained his white shirt, and a torrent of blood had soaked through his trouser into the orange desert dust. His face white from blood loss sneered up at me.

"What you looking at you cock sucker."

I stumbled over to him and with my good foot, rolled him into the shallow grave that he had dug for me. I spat on him this time and bent to pick up the shovel. The pain seared my side, but with every shovel full of dirt, I felt a bit better. Soon Cassie helped me, and she continued while I rested.

The sunrise crested the horizon when we finished with Fat Tony, all evidence of the struggle had been erased. I hugged Cassie and together we made our way to the car. In the pain of the gunshot and the haze of finishing off the Castello brothers, I never thought to look in the back seats. My memory jolted as I did. It came back in waves, the prep for the bank job; entering the bank, the jobs smoothness, and the loading of the car. Frankie had crept up on me while I piled the bags in the back seat and hit me over the head with his gun. The rest, as they say, is history.

The sunshine glistened off the scratched glass of the passenger's door window, and two large black bags bulged on the back seat. I opened the door and unzipped one, Green smiles glared at me, and I couldn't help but smile back. Cassie jumped into the driver seat, as she looked over her shoulder pushing her dust-covered hair out of eyes she asked.

"What you got there?" I couldn't help but grin, wouldn't you?

"Our future baby, our future."

LOOKING FOR LOVE

Grant Hinton

Have you ever had an experience that you didn't know was real or not?

The blood on my hands suggests it's real, but I'm in too much shock to think straight.

I have this friend Tracey who has always made me jealous. She's drop dead gorgeous: tall, slim toned body, a great backside, blonde hair the color of wave foam, and deep set blue eyes that looks as if a storm is brewing within.

She's the only one out of my girlfriends that haven't settled down, and I often wonder why.

Having two kids and a husband of 10 years, with not enough time to get down the gym or even wipe my ass has warped my body to a lumpy mess. I loath my wide child bearing hips, big booty, dirt colored hair, and tired baggy eyes. I can't stand to even look at Tracey when we meet up. =

She invited me out for a coffee two weeks ago, and before I went I decide to go to the nail salon for a manicure and pedicure. Afterward

I had my hair cut and went in search of an outfit to wear, determined to look my best.

The next day I put on my nice new clothes and my makeup, gave a quick kiss to my husband Tom and our kids, then headed out of the house. The moment I stepped into the coffee shop I knew she had out done me without trying. A random guy had just sat down at her table to engage her in conversation when I walked over, clearing my throat. Tracey bounced out of her seat and hugged me with a squeal of delight.

I looked to the young man for an introduction, but she just smiled and leaned over him and his stupid grin.

"My friend is here now so, if you'll excuse us?"

The guy's smile faded. I realized that he was trying to pick her up. I laughed a little at his discomfort, but Tracey picked up on it and burst out laughing. The guy slumped off to his table, defeated.

It felt really good to see Tracey. The jealousy fell away as we continued to laugh and catch up on everything that happened since we last saw each other. Tracey told me she had just broken up with her banker boyfriend over some petty argument. I really couldn't keep up with her romances though; she seemed to be on a new one every few weeks. I think her longest relationship only lasted about two months, although I might be wrong.

She starting telling me about this dating app that appears to be all the rage with the youngsters though. She called it Tinder.

Apparently you put up a profile and do something with swipes that I didn't really understand. The app matches you up with potential partners, and away you go. It all sounded a little dangerous to me, and I expressed my opinion to Tracey. She agreed, but she had really wanted to try it. She told me that she already set up her profile and got her first match.

She showed me a picture of her prospected date, Jake, and I was surprised to see a well groomed man staring back at me. To say he was handsome would have been a understatement. Dark smoldering eyes captured my attention, and even when I glanced to his chiseled chin with a small thin smile, I found myself springing back to the eyes. I passed the phone back to her and blew out my cheeks.

After discussing what the night might be like, we settled on pre-writing different texts. Each one for a different outcome.

One to let me know that everything was going well and not to worry. Another for me to call her so she could make her excuses and leave, and the final for me to call the police and get to her as quick as possible. We laughed a little at the last one, and I teased that it would probably be the one she would use.

I had just finished cooking dinner when I got the text from Tracey. To my surprise and relief, it was the first message: she was having good time. After I cleaned up the family mess, I poured myself a glass of wine to relax on the sofa. Tom was snoring slightly, and I marveled at how lucky I was to have found my man early. No more worrying for me, and definitely no dating game.

The next day I called Tracey to hear all about the date, and not to my surprise, the activities that followed. I found myself blushing when she told me all about how he was a gentlemen throughout dinner, and how wild he was in the bedroom. We agreed to meet the next day for coffee and a potential shopping trip as my kids needed new clothes.

Problem was, Tracey never showed. I tried calling, but she didn't answer, so as a last resort I dropped the kids with Tom and went to her house. She lives in a small complex of six apartments. Tracey lived on the second floor, apartment two. As I approached the door, the smell of pizza hung heavy in the air. I knocked, and Tracey's voice sounded from behind.

"It's me," I called.

I heard her shuffle to the door and pull at the latch. When the door swung open I grabbed at the side to steady my legs. Tracey looked horrible. Her hair was lank and greasy, her face white and clammy, as if she'd been sick for days. But what really shocked me was the small pot belly poking out from her tight care-bear pajama top.

I couldn't believe what I was seeing as Tracey crammed pizza into her mouth. I voiced my concern, but she just shook it off saying that she must have the flu or something. She was always hungry and felt drained all the time.

She didn't let me in her apartment because it was a mess, but she reassured me that she would be all right in a few days and that all she needed was rest. I told her to call me if she needed anything and left.

That was two days ago. This afternoon she called me in a panic. The fear in her voice made me drop the vase I was carrying and it shattered around my feet. Tom was at work and the kids were at school, so I grabbed my bag and ran to the car. Ten minutes later I was banging on her door.

She wasn't answering so I tried the handle, expecting it to be locked. It opened. I took a deep breath before pushing at the door. The heat, and the smell hit me as if Mayweather had just stepped up and punched me square in the face.

The pungent decay of rotting food and something else made me cover my nose. As I walked through the apartment I could hear Tracey's labored breathing. I first thought that maybe she was doing some exercise to shift the belly she'd gotten from the illness, but as I crunched yet another fast food container underfoot, I knew that something was amiss.

Tracey had always taken great care of her appearance and was incredibly proud of her house too. I was shocked to see that the apartment looked in such an abysmal state. All the curtains had been closed and the heat was starting to get unbearable, and rounding the corridor to the living room, I saw Tracey squatting by the couch.

I initially thought that someone else had taken over Tracey's home until my friend looked up at me with tearful eyes. Her stomach had swollen so much that she looked like she was in the later stages of pregnancy.

I've had friends carrying twins that looked small compared to her now. I couldn't wrap my head around the size of her belly—it seemed truly bizarre. I rushed to her side and she held out a hand toward me for a moment before snapping it back to her swollen stomach, groaning in pain.

The skin around her bugle was stretched so tight that it appeared dry and flakey like when you pull pastries just before they tear. I didn't know what to say or do, and just stood like a zombie until she grabbed at my sleeve pleading for help. I couldn't think, could breath, as I watched her stomach move like something was within. Tracey screamed and I stumbled back, falling hard on my ass. My friend's stomach rolls and moves, an outline of a face pressed against her tight skin. I could clearly see the chin and eye socket underneath.

Tracey panted heavily, screwing up her face in pain. She let out a shrill scream and my blood froze. Her eyes rolled back to whites and her head tilted backward to the ceiling. She clawed at her clothes and tore off her pajama top. Her breasts were huge, her stomach grotesque, and she screamed again as a small tear appeared at her chest.

I watched in horror as the skin tore apart and two bloody hands pushed through, the tear stretching down to her pubic hair. The blood covered hands stretched out, and a slimy hairless head followed.

I kicked back into the TV cabinet as Tracey groaned and slumped to the side. The child thing fell from the rip and landed on the floor in a pool of blood and amniotic fluid. My eldest child is seven years old, and I swear this thing was bigger than her. I didn't think my blood could run any colder until the child-thing moved sat up.

As it smeared the blood away from its face and eyes, a noise behind me startled me into turning around.

Jake, her tinder date, stood smiling in the doorway. He extended a hand forwards me and I scurried back. I started to cry as a wet slap made me turn again to the child-thing. It had gotten to its feet, wobbling unsteadily as it made its way over the messy wooden floor toward Jake.

The creature took Tracey's date by the hand and its legs grew steadier. Jake looked up from his child to smile at me, the same thin smile that Tracey had shown me 4 days ago. Jake winked and turned around. They slowly walked down the hall, leaving a smear of blood on the wooden floor as they left the building.

I sat there for what seemed like years trying to comprehend what had just happened, until a small gasp sounded in the hall. I instantly shrank back in fear that Jake had come back, but it was only the lady who lived below Tracey. She had called the police. When they came, I had to relive the whole traumatic event again.

The police said that they are looking into the case and with Tracey's phone and the CCTV at the restaurant, they may have enough to find this Jake. I'm not sure if the police will ever find him, or exactly what they will charge him with if they do. Somehow I don't think their jurisdiction reaches to whatever world he's is from.

SOME SMELLS SHOULDN'T BE IGNORED

P. Oxford

You know when people say "if something seems too good to be true, it usually is"? Turns out they're right.

I recently moved in with my boyfriend. He has a beautiful flat in an old building. It's a penthouse and everything. We hadn't been together that long, but I knew from the first time I met him that he was the one. We'd be together 'til death do us part', if it was up to me at least.

At the beginning of the relationship, I wasn't sure if he felt the same way. He was always a bit distant, always referring to me as babe, honey, or some other nickname, but never calling me by name. According to "John Tucker must die", a movie filled to the brim with advice for life, this is a clear way of knowing that a guy is two timing you. I'm sure he was seeing multiple girls at the beginning, but that was okay. It's the 21st century after all. But that's not what this story is about.

When he asked me to move in with him, I was thrilled. I had been living in a crappy flat share with 6 other people and owned no furniture. Packing up my stuff was easy, and his apartment was a dream. I had only been there two or three times before I moved in—for some reason he always seemed to prefer staying at my place. Maybe it made him feel young, who knows.

Cal worked a lot, so I would spend the days alone in the flat. I'm a painter and Cal was very supportive of my art. He told me I could use the spare bedroom as an atelier, and he even convinced me to quit my waitressing job so I could dedicate all my time to my art. I loved him so much.

The first days in the flat, as I was setting up the atelier, I heard sounds coming from the wall. "Rats. Damn." I've lived in my fair share of crappy flats, so I'm not unfamiliar with the sounds of critters in the walls.

Then the flies appeared. I was taking a break from painting, sitting on the floor of the atelier, eating a slice of pizza, trying to figure out what my latest art piece was missing. A fat fly landed on my pizza. I shook it angrily. Another fat fly was buzzing right next to it.

I looked around the room. There were at least 5 flies there.

When I told Cal about it later, he got really annoyed.

"What the hell have you been doing in there?"

I shrugged, frowning. His anger surprised me, made me uncomfortable.

"You don't eat in there, do you?" he asked, disgusted.

"I... Sometimes?"

"Well, maybe if you weren't such a pig this wouldn't happen! God, if you're gonna make a mess, at least don't complain to me about it!"

"I—I'm sorry!" I exclaimed, distressed. His whole demeanor changed so fast. "It didn't occur to me that it was my fault!"

"Aw, babe, no. I'm sorry. It's just—I've been under a lot of pressure lately. I didn't mean to take it out on you. Just ignore the flies, I'm sure they'll go away eventually."

The next day there were even more flies. I didn't say anything to Cal—I was too worried about his reaction. There was also a strange smell in the room though. I was sincerely worried that I had accidentally dropped food somewhere, so I cleaned the whole room. Didn't make a difference. I had left the window wide open since I moved in

—I like to paint in the cold—so I decided the smell and the flies must be coming from somewhere outside. I closed the window.

I when I returned to the room after getting lunch, the smell had gotten much worse. I hadn't really noticed it as I painted, but after the fresh air from the outside, the stench was impossible to ignore. A rank stench of decay. I closed the door and opened the window. I decided I had to talk to Cal about it later. I guessed one of the rats had died in the walls or something.

"Yeah, it does smell a little funky in here. Rats? No, we don't have rats here. No, I'm pretty sure we don't. I don't know why you would think that. Too much paint fumes in that little room?" His eyes went dark with anger before he managed to pull himself together. I hadn't realized how temperamental he was before I moved in with him.

"You know what, I bet it's from that downstairs neighbor." Cal relaxed as he spoke. "You remember the weird guy we saw in the lift that first day?" I shuddered. I remembered. "I bet it's him. His flat would be right under this room. I don't wanna know what he's doing down there... You just spray some febreeze, and I'm sure it'll go away eventually."

How could I forget the downstairs neighbor? I had only seen him once, the day I moved in, but it had made an impression.

We had been taking the elevator down to get the last of my stuff, and it stopped on the floor below the flat. I noticed Cal looking uncomfortable, probably anticipating the neighbor. The doors opened, and I felt my nostrils flare in objection. The man waiting outside was tall, skinny, dressed all in black, and smelt worse than anyone I have ever encountered. He locked eyes with me, then let his gaze slide over to Cal, then back to me. I shuddered involuntarily. He frowned, staring at me for several seconds. Then he entered the lift without a word. We rode down in silence.

Every time I took that elevator, I worried that I'd run into him. I tried not to think about what he could be doing in that flat to cause a smell like this one floor up.

The next day there were more flies, and the smell was even stronger. I called Cal at work.

"You're exaggerating, it can't be that bad. Just get some febreeze, and get over it. And don't disturb me at work unless it's actually important. If there is a rat there, the smell will go away eventually. Don't be such a damn princess."

I didn't really want to press the issue; he seemed to be really stressed. I just kept the door closed and the window open, spraying the whole room with febreeze like he told me to. I spent the day sketching outside instead, not able to take the smell.

The smell only got worse. I wanted to paint, but I couldn't stand being in that room. I was probably being a bit of a princess, but Cal didn't have to work in that smell. I thought about the sounds I'd heard the first days. To me, that had sounded like some damn big rats. One of those dying in my wall could definitely stink up a room. But maybe Cal was right after all, maybe it was the downstairs neighbor. I figured I had to talk to that weird guy. At least I'd give it a shot.

After talking myself up, I went to ring his doorbell. As the door cracked open, the smell of stale sweat and cat-piss rolled over me. I almost staggered backwards.

He opened the door just as much as the security chain would allow.

"Um, excuse me sir, I live right upstairs, I just moved in with—" I cut myself off as I saw him start to slowly close the door. "Sorry, I'll be fast! It's just a bit awkward, but there's kind of a smell in our flat?"

His eyes went wide, but he didn't say anything. He just stood there, staring at me. The door stopped moving.

"I—uh—my boyfriend suggested that maybe you..." I faltered. His gaze didn't waver for a moment.

I stood there for ten seconds, considering whether I should run. In the end, my social conditioning not to be rude took over. I tried again.

"There's a bit of a weird smell in our apartment, and my boyfriend suggested that you might know something about it."

His face contorted into a frown. He still didn't say anything.

"I mean, I don't know. I—you—" I was flailing. "Uh, do you know if there are rats in the building?" I finished, defeated.

He smiled. "No-oo. No rats." Then he laughed. "Cats!"

"Um, OK, well bye then!" I turned, walking quickly down the hall. The door slammed shut behind me.

I heard it open again.

"Lady! Maybe you shouldn't be here, lady!" he called after me. I turned, only to see his door slam shut for the second time. I continued walking, thoroughly unsettled. The door opened again. I didn't turn around, just started walking faster. "Maybe not so safe, lady! With rats!"

I shuddered, frantically pressing the elevator button over and over. I heard the door click shut behind me. I sighed in relief. I swore to not ever talk to that guy again. Whatever the hell he was doing to make our beautiful flat smell like death, I didn't want to know.

Back in the apartment, the stench had started to spread into the living room. I realized I was scared that Cal would get mad. I knew he thought I had messed something up in the atelier. The idea that I was scared of his reaction unsettled me. He was the love of my life, after all. I decided I was nervous because I wanted him to be happy, that I didn't want him to be stressed about anything else. I decided I wasn't scared of him. I loved him, after all.

As I went over our relationship in my head, it hit me that the smell here was completely different from the downstairs apartment. There, it smelled like stale sweat and old cat piss. Here, it smelled like death. "No rats my ass", I mumbled. I knew a fat rat in the wall was the only explanation.

I figured it was time to call an exterminator. I briefly considered calling Cal to see if he minded, but he had been so mad the last time I called him at work. He thought I was being a princess. I decided I'd just do this on my own, dipping into the little money I had left. I couldn't paint in a room like that. I was a grown woman who could handle her own problems.

I called an exterminator. He referred me to a guy that specializes in getting dead rats out of walls. Apparently, that's a thing.

Lucky for me had a cancellation, so he could come right over. So damn lucky for me...

"Oh yes, you have a dead rat. Probably several. You know this happens sometimes when people put out rat poison. Their nest is probably in your wall, and they crawled back there to die. Don't worry, I'll take care of it. I have to cut a hole in the wall though, is that OK?"

I frowned, thinking Cal would get mad. But he never goes into the atelier. I figured I could just put a canvas in front of the hole and get it fixed.

"But don't worry, hun, with these exposed bricks it's really easy to patch it back up. Just slap on some mortar and chuck the bricks back in place. Anyone could do it—you wouldn't be able to tell at all!"

I told him to go ahead.

I was sitting in the kitchen when the police showed up.

I was sitting in the interrogation room when they told me about the dead body they found behind the wall.

I was sitting in the lawyer's office when they told me it was the remains of Cal's previous girlfriend.

I was sitting in the witness box in the courtroom when they told me he had left her there to die a slow, horrifying death.

I was sitting in the stands when they gave him life without parole for premeditated murder. But I was sitting all alone in a cheap motel when I realized that she had still been alive when I moved in.

The building really didn't have rats.

MY BOYFRIEND AND I WERE TAKEN

P. Oxford

In the interest of full disclosure, I should probably tell you that I was recently released from the loony bin. When you read my story, you'll probably understand why they put me there. Frankly, I understand why they put me there. Saying I'm crazy is a lot easier than believing my story. But I'm not crazy. There's something out there. Something evil.

You don't need to know about the first awkward date I had with Sean after chatting on Tinder. I'm skipping the glorious first few weeks with my wonderful new boyfriend, even though they were some of the best weeks of my life. It's not just because it would bore you—somehow that part is even harder to think about than what came after.

I never knew much about Sean. He recently moved to town. He grew up all over. He didn't speak to his parents. No siblings. Worked as a bartender. Thought I was the most amazing thing to ever walk the earth. And that last part was all that mattered to me.

I had heard the term whirlwind romance before, but I had never experienced it in all it's glory. We were in love, and we loved it. We decided to go away together. He had a cabin in the woods somewhere, and we wanted to get away from everyone and everything and just be together.

We started the drive after I finished work. After about an hour on the road, the sun had started setting. Sean was behind the wheel, and I was enjoying the sunset and the music and his presence next to me. I had the window down, my feet on the dash, and my hand out to float in the wind. I was completely at peace.

The glorious red and pink turned into purple and then black, and we were still driving. By then we were deep in the forest. Tall pine trees lined the narrow road. I could only see a few meters into the dark on each side. I remember that it occurred to me how easily this could be the opening scene of a horror movie. The happy couple on their way to their little vacation, going through the dark, scary forest, falling into the web of the evil killer. I told Sean. He had laughed and told me I was crazy.

"More like the final scene of a romantic comedy, babe," he said, flashing me the smile that still made me weak at the knees every time.

Sean had brought hot tea in a thermos which I drank it happily. The warm liquid and the steady movement of the car made my head groggy like always. Nothing puts me to sleep faster than being in a car in the dark. I nodded off, waking disoriented and tired to find us on an old logging road.

"Mmmm, where are we?" I yawned, stretching.

"Oh, you're awake." He almost sounded disappointed. "Do you want some more tea, maybe?"

"Mmm, I kinda have to pee. No thanks. Are we far from the cabin?"

"Nah, we should be there in like half an hour. I can stop if you want, though."

"Noo, it's fine, I'd rather not have to nature squat if I can avoid it."

"Oh." He frowned. "Ok."

I put my head against the window and stared into the darkness between the trees. Huge firs towered like giants over us. I felt uneasy. I didn't like the fact that I couldn't see into the woods. It was so dark, and our lights were so bright. I felt too visible.

Then I saw something. It was gone before I fully realized what I had seen.

I let out a little yelp. A man had been standing at the side of the road. Someone was out there, in the dark. He had his back turned, but when the lights hit him he'd turned his head towards us. I swear I felt him look right into my soul.

Sean asked me what was wrong.

"You didn't see that guy there?" I asked surprised.

"What guy?"

"The guy at the side of the road?"

"What? No! Are you sure that's what you saw?"

"Yeah, it was a man! He was wearing a red hat!"

"That's just really weird, that's all," Sean said, frowning. "There aren't a lot of houses around here. As far as I know."

I shuddered.

"God, I hope he doesn't follow us to the cabin."

"He'd have to run pretty fast to keep up with the car, so I wouldn't worry about that. And that's only if he wasn't just a human shaped tree..."

"I guess." I shrugged. My heart was still racing. This did not seem like the closing scene in a romantic comedy. "Where are we?"

"In the woods. We should be getting close. Don't worry, just go back to sleep."

I did as he said, letting my eyelids droop as my mind slid into the warm comfort of sleep and safety.

Suddenly, I was jolted out of my sleep and out of the seat.

Panicked, I turned to Sean. He was slumped over the wheel, blood seeping from a cut on his forehead.

I looked outside. The car was in the ditch.

I could feel my heart pounding in my chest. I could feel the panic threatening to take over. What do you do in a car accident? What are you supposed to do?

Stay calm. I took a deep breath. Check for injuries. I looked over at

Sean. He was injured alright, that was clear. Was he alive? I gingerly stretched my hand towards his neck, afraid of what I might learn. I took another deep breath, letting my fingers press against the spot I hoped was his jugular vein. A pulse. I sighed with relief. Sean was alive.

I got my phone out of the glove compartment. My fingers shook so much it took me three tries to get the pattern right. I fiddled until I got the phone screen up. Everything was taking way too long. I pushed 9-1-1 into the phone, pressed call, and waited. Nothing. I looked at the phone. No service. Of course, no service. We were out in some backwoods, God knows where, we had been in a car accident, of course my phone had no service.

Now what?

I looked around desperately. I was in the middle of the woods. I had no idea where we were. I had no helpful skills. I felt the panic building. What the hell could I do? Sean wasn't moving. The car wasn't driving anywhere anytime soon, and I didn't have reception on my phone.

I'd have to go see if I could get reception. That was the only solution. If I got to higher ground, I might be able to get a call out.

I looked at Sean one last time, opened the door, and started walking back along the road. Not thirty meters from the car my foot hit a rock and I tumbled to the ground. I got up, dusted myself off, and turned on the flashlight on the phone. I kept checking it every minute or so to see if I was getting any bars. I was walking uphill, so I kept telling myself I'd eventually find the elusive reception.

I angrily clicked away the low battery warning.

After about five minutes, my panic subsided to a dull, throbbing fear. I had a task. Reception. I would get that 911 call through. I would fix it. I would save Sean.

I made it five minutes into the darkness, surrounded by the tiny bubble of light my phone allowed me before I remembered seeing that man. When had that been? Not five minutes before the crash! He had to be close. A small rational part of my brain tried to reason that he could help. He could get an ambulance for Sean. A much larger part of my brain was convinced that there was something wrong, that I should be scared of him. I still don't know what made me so sure that man was malicious. I just knew it in my bones. In the end, I decided to ignore my bones. I needed help.

"Hee-eelp!" I yelled into the darkness. "Help us please!!"

Nothing. Maybe he had been a figment of my imagination after all.

"Please? Help!" I tried again. Shrugging, I kept walking.

I felt so small and so alone walking through the dark woods in my tiny little circle of light. The dull fear turned to pure terror as I let my mind wander. All the horrible things that could happen to us out there.

What if I got back to the car and Sean was dead? No. What if I couldn't make the 911 call. No. What if that man came out of the woods. No, don't think about it. What if Sean died. What if Sean died? No, don't think about it.

My mind spiraled slowly into what I can only describe as a slow, controlled panic. I kept it in check because I had a goal. I was making that 911 call.

Then my phone died.

My insides fell. It was like a punch to the gut. Why the hell had I used the phone flashlight? There was a damn flashlight in the car! I cursed myself and my stupidity. The anger was short lived. It turned to fear. I started crying. I had never felt so useless.

Sean's phone. I could go back and get it. I'd go back and get it, and try again.

Maybe Sean was awake.

Maybe Sean was dead. No.

I kept walking. I started running. I tripped, skinned my knees. I got up, forced myself to walk slowly, carefully.

After an eternity I spotted the car. I was so afraid of what I'd see there. I had to force myself to walk up to it. I took a deep breath and opened the driver side door.

The car was empty.

I just stood there, frozen. Millions of thoughts fought each other in my mind. I blinked several times.

He's fine. He left to get help. That was the thought that won. I started breathing again.

He had left to get help. I had no phone, and no idea where we were. My best option was to stay in the car. I sat down in the passenger seat, leaning the seat back to get comfortable. I closed my eyes, hoping I'd drift off to sleep and wake up in a different reality.

I don't know what possessed me to check for his phone. I knew he would have taken it. He was a smart man, not taking it would be silly. Sean was not silly.

But I did check. And it was right there. In the glove box. What the hell?

The relief that I had felt was immediately replaced by chilling fear. I was frozen in indecision, staring at the phone. I should go after him. I had no idea what direction he had gone. Wait, no, I would've ran into him if he had walked back. He must have walked forward. So I'd go after him. I'd take the phone.

I was about to get out of the car when I thought I saw something move. I strained my eyes against the darkness. Nothing. I looked all around the car. Then I looked back to the right. I screamed. A masked man, not ten centimeters from the window. I scrambled to lock the door. I fumbled with the button. The door was torn open. I tried to grab it, to pull it close again. He was stronger. The force of the pull unseated me. I spilled out of the car. I felt a hand grab my arm, pulling me to my feet.

I panicked, tried to squirm free.

"Let go!" I screamed. "Let go of me!"

I managed to wiggle out of his grip. I turned and ran.

I heard steps behind me. He was following. I knew he was getting closer. I heard it. I ran for my life. I felt his hand brush against my arm. A hand covered my mouth. A hand twisted my arm behind my back. A strange smell. I struggled, fighting for my life. I lost.

Then blackness.

The first thing I noticed was the pounding headache. I tried opening my eyes, and for a moment I thought I couldn't. Then I realized my eyes were open, but wherever I was, it was so dark that it made almost no difference.

The second thing I noticed was that I was contorted in a very uncomfortable position. My whole body ached. I was sitting on a floor, leaning against a soft wall, hands behind me.

The third thing I noticed was the ropes. My hands were tied tightly behind my back, my legs tied tightly together in front of me. There was something around my neck. Cold fear spread through my veins like wildfire. I panicked.

I pulled and pulled on the ropes to no effect. Probably just tightened the knots. If I thought I had been scared before, it was nothing compared to the pure dread that filled my whole body when I realized I was not getting loose. I tried to move, but immediately realized that whatever was around my neck didn't allow much movement.

My heart pounded a crazy tattoo in my chest. My blood rushed in my ears. I stifled the scream rising in my throat with my last sliver of sanity. The one clear thought in my mind told me to not alert anyone that I was awake.

The sliver of sanity grew. A voice in my mind told me that I had to get out of here and save Sean. I had to save myself. I had to stay calm.

I tried to make an inventory of my options.

I needed to find some sort of weapon. I was tied up on the floor of a dark room. Impossible.

I needed a way out. Also impossible.

I needed to loosen the ropes. It was the only thing I could possibly have a shot at. I knew it was a long shot, but I had to try. For my own sanity, I knew I had to fight.

I tentatively moved my wrists. The rope was tight. I twisted my hands painfully, trying to reach the rope. I let my fingertips glide over the coarse material, desperately feeling for a knot. There it was! I couldn't believe my luck. It occurred to me that whoever tied me up wasn't very good at it.

I tried wiggling my finger between the rope in the knot. It didn't budge at all. Maybe whoever tied me up wasn't that stupid after all.

The rope was not moving one bit, but I kept going. It was all I had, my one and only hope.

I'm not sure how long I worked on that knot. Maybe an hour, maybe three.

A door was slammed open. Blindingly bright light filled the room. I closed my eyes and tried to look away. Someone entered.

"Drink this," the man said brusquely, shoving a glass to my lips, tilting it.

I choked on what I can only describe as the most disgusting smoothie I have ever encountered. It tasted like meat, milk, and fruit mixed into one. I turned my head away, trying to spit it out. He slapped me, hard.

"Drink," he repeated in a calm voice.

I drank. I choked. I retched. But I got it down.

"Good girl!" the voice said, patting my head.

Soon after, I felt my mind slide into unconsciousness.

I have no idea how long I was out for. When I came back, I was still in the dark room, still tied up on the floor. I felt around until I found the knot again. I kept on the slow, painstaking work to undo it. It made no difference, but then I didn't have a whole lot else to do. Working on the knot was the one thing I could hold on to. My only hope.

And then again, the door. The blinding light. The dark outline of a man feeding me that disgusting slop. The intermittent bucket for bodily functions. The loss of consciousness. Waking up, still in that dark hell. Over and over. Sometimes he slapped or punched me if I didn't drink fast enough. Once I threw up, and that was the time he broke my nose. But that was only once. The ritual? Eat, shit, pass out. Eternal.

I don't know how many times that door opened. I tried to keep count, but the last number I remember clearly is seven. But there were more. Many more. Twenty? A hundred? A million? I couldn't say. All I knew was sleep, drink, knot, repeat. I lost all sense of time. I didn't know if I was unconscious for hours, days, or mere seconds. I started losing grip on reality. I didn't know if I was awake when I was awake.

Sometimes I had dreams of being outside. Sometimes I had dreams about being buried alive. I'd wake up, sweating, only to find that it was true. I really was buried alive. The room became a universe that I floated through, a submarine at the bottom of the deepest ocean, a hole in the ground, the center of the earth. It became my own personal hell.

I only have flashes of memories from the time I spent in that hell hole. Disjointed, distorted, terrible flashes. When I try to think of it now, it's like a black hole of fear in my mind.

Most of the time the room was dead quiet. Sometimes I would wake up and hear ragged breathing somewhere in the room. I thought it must be Sean. I remember trying to talk, to yell for him. I remember screaming until my throat hurt and my eyes watered. But never a response. Never any response. The frustration, the powerlessness, the intense loneliness, the horror all faded into one single feeling. I thought I was dead. I knew I was in hell.

Then suddenly, something was different. The clearest single memory I have from that time. I don't know what happened, whether the man made some mistake, or if he did it on purpose to screw with my mind and torture me further. Whatever the reason, he was slower. He stayed in the room longer. My eyes could adjust to the light. I saw him, for the first time.

I don't remember what I thought when I saw that face. I don't remember if I screamed. I just remember the feeling of my mind in a frenzy, trying to understand.

It was Sean. The man was Sean.

I couldn't react. I could only stare. For what felt like an eternity I stared at the face that I loved with so much passion.

Then I saw it. There was something off about his face. It was Sean, but it… wasn't Sean. His smile curved differently, and his eyes didn't have that warm twinkle I fell in love with. It was like someone had seen photo of Sean and tried to sculpt his face from it. It was like the angles were wrong, the muscles not moving like his muscles moved.

"Who are you?" I think I asked. "What are you?"

He looked at me like I was something disgusting.

"I'm Sean. I'm your boyfriend. You know that, right?" His voice was so full of hate, so unlike Sean's warm, loving voice.

"No, no, you're not Sean. Sean loves me, Sean would never hurt me."

"I'm Sean. I'm really Sean." He laughed before putting the glass to my lips. "I'm really Sean, baby." He whispered as I gulped down the horrible concoction.

"Why?" I yelled when he was done. "Why are you doing this to us?"

"Because I can." He laughed. "And because I want to. And because you look like such a delicious little lady, I just had to have you."

And then he was gone.

When I woke up the next time, I was in the dark as always. I heard the breathing again. The ragged breathing.

"Sean?" I whispered tentatively, not able to give up hope that I'd get a response. That man—that thing—it hadn't been Sean. He was keeping Sean too, keeping him drugged into unconsciousness. I knew it. I know it. "Sean?"

"Wh-what?" A weak whisper. I can't begin to describe the joy I felt at that moment. I wasn't alone in that darkness.

"Sean, baby, I'm here, I'll get us out!"

"Sean? Out? No." He sounded defeated.

"Yes! We're getting out of here! Don't worry!"

"I—no…"

And then nothing. I kept trying to talk, but there was no response.

I attacked the rope with new vigor. I had to save us both now. Something evil was holding us. What was that thing? Why was it wearing Sean's face? It had to be some sort of shape-shifter. A demon. He was wearing Sean's face to torment me. To break my spirit. I didn't know what kind of nefarious plan it had, but I wasn't hanging around to find out.

Finally, my sore fingertips managed to shift something in the knot. I can't describe how wonderful that felt. It might have been the best feeling of my whole life. That first sliver of hope after days, weeks, years, centuries in that hole. I was free. I would be free. Another painstaking infinity, and the knot was loose. My hands were free.

I was getting out of there.

I felt the thing around my neck. It was a simple dog collar which opened like a belt. Easy.

I fumbled in the dark for the knot that tied my legs together. I worked on the knot in a quiet panic, the dull dread that the man would come back before I got loose looming over me. But then, suddenly, the knot gave, and I was free.

I carefully got up. It had been days since I could last feel my legs. The pins and needles I felt when putting weight on them were like a whole new form of torture. I steadied myself with my hand against the wall. Oh, I was getting out of there all right.

I needed to find the door. I let my hand trail the wall. It was covered in foam. Soundproof, like a recording studio. I passed a corner. I knew the door was on this wall. My fingers detected a small gap in the foam. I stopped, letting my hands glide more slowly up and down. My left hand touched the door knob. I gripped it and paused. I had no plan if the door was locked. My only chance, my only hope, was that whoever was keeping me captive trusted in the rope. I turned the knob slowly. It moved. The door was unlocked. The door was unlocked! I slid it open, carefully, slowly. The light was blinding as always. I turned to look back into the room, blinking.

And that's when I saw Sean. Well, what was left of him, anyway.

I almost screamed.

I almost fainted.

I almost threw up.

That image still haunts my dreams.

Both his legs were amputated. The right below the knee, the left somewhere higher up. His left arm was gone from the shoulder, and his right hand was missing. A part of his cheek was gone, the hole large enough that I could see the teeth beneath it. His face was swollen, almost unrecognizable. His beautiful hair was shaved.

I ran over to him, shaking him, caressing his mangled face.

His eyes blinked, then focused.

"Get out of here!" he whispered accusingly through cracked lips. "Get help!"

"I'm not leaving you here!"

"You have to," he said weakly. "I can't run."

He was right. How would I carry him? I started desperately at the stumps where his legs used to be, where his arms used to be.

Then he uttered the single most chilling sentence I have ever heard in my life.

"He's eating me. He'll start with you once he's done with me." His tone was calm, stern. "Get help!"

I remember freezing, blinking, swaying on the spot. Staring at the horror that remained of the love of my life. Trying to comprehend what he had just said.

In a horrible moment, I realized he was right.

"Go…" he whispered, using the last of his strength. Then he slumped over, passed out again.

"I love you!" I said, leaning over to kiss him. "I love you so much!"

I turned, tears forming in my eyes. I was determined. I was getting him out. As long as I didn't get caught. I remember the chilling fear that I felt when I realized I had to get out of there too. I had been so focused on the rope, so relieved at the door, so shocked at the sight of Sean that I had completely forgotten our captor.

I snuck up to the door and peeked out. I don't know what I expected to see there, but it sure wasn't the interior of a cozy log-cabin with a fireplace and deep, comfy looking chairs. The room was empty. I tiptoed over to the next door. Heart beating, I reached out a hand and tenderly pressed the door handle down. Also unlocked. Why were the doors unlocked? I didn't give the question much thought. I was in fight or flight mode, and the flight path was wide open.

So I ran. Without any goal, without any idea, I just ran. The cabin was surrounded by dark woods. I dodged between trees, jumped over roots, ducked under branches. My breath grew short and ragged, my heart pounding loudly in my ears, I could taste blood and bile in my mouth. Still I ran. When I couldn't run anymore, I walked. When I couldn't walk anymore, I crawled. The sun set, and darkness fell. I needed to keep going, I needed to find help, I needed to get Sean out of that hell. But I couldn't. My body wasn't going any further. I rolled under a bush, immediately passing out.

Escaping the room didn't mean the nightmare was over. I ended up wandering that fucking forest for days. It became my new hell. I was hungry, tired, in pain. My bare feet were swollen, covered in cuts. If it hadn't been for Sean, I would have laid down to die. I cursed myself for leaving him. I should have stayed. I should have fought. I could have found a weapon and hid, waiting for the shape-shifter to return. I could have saved Sean. Why didn't I ever think? Why hadn't I gotten him out of the room at least? I could have hidden him in the woods. I could have done something. I decided to turn back, but I had no idea where I was anymore. At that point I was just wandering aimlessly, but I kept going. For Sean.

Finally, after another eternity, I stumbled over a path. I tried to keep going. I really did. But my body just gave out. The last thing I remember is falling.

~

I woke up in a bright, white room that smelled clean. A hospital. I remember screaming for Sean. Then nurses came running, drugs were administered, and I slid out of consciousness.

I woke up again. I think.

The FBI showed up. I tried telling them about the shape-shifter. They asked me questions about Sean. I told them they had to help him. They told me they'd get him, not to worry. More drugs. More questions. My mother crying. Telling me everything would be okay. Telling me they'd get Sean.

That was such a confusing time. Reality and nightmare faded together. I didn't know what was going on.

Now I know more.

I was found two weeks after Sean and I left for the trip. We had set out for the cabin in Washington, and I was found on a hiking path in Southern California. Our car was never found. Sean was never found.

I do remember the moment I realized that the FBI didn't believe my flesh eating shape-shifter story. I think that might have been the worst moment of the whole ordeal. In hindsight, I'm not surprised that they didn't believe me. I know I must have sounded crazy.

In their version of events, it was Sean all along. He had been spotted at a gas station after I had been missing for a week. They showed me the tape. I told them it was the shape-shifter. They had exchanged worried glances, but I pretended not to notice. They told me that his name was fake, that there were no records of him anywhere. They couldn't find any family, and he didn't have any friends at the bar, or anywhere else as far as they knew. He had set up a whole fake life so that he could take me to the woods and disappear. They said it sounded like he was grooming me, or something.

Well, I knew better. Sean loved me. He had always been a lone wolf, he told me that. He had some friends from his childhood he was still in touch with, but I didn't know who. I had never met any of them, but to be fair he had never met any of my friends either. I didn't think it was strange at all since we spent all our time together anyway. And we didn't talk about the past, we talked about our future.

They seemed to think that my Sean was some sort of psychotic serial killer. That was the most ridiculous thing I'd ever heard. Sean was the best thing that ever happened to me.

At first, I didn't really care if they believed me. They were searching for Sean, that was all that mattered. When they found him, it'd be pretty clear that he hadn't amputated his own body parts. But then I learned that they weren't searching for the cabin. They told me he wouldn't be there anymore. He would be on the run.

On the run? He didn't have legs anymore!

I remember screaming at them. Screaming for them to save Sean.

When I tried to sneak out of the hospital to save him on my own, I got moved to the psych ward. The closed psych ward.

Another hell hole. Another prison where days turned to weeks which turned to centuries. Doctors trying to convince me that I was crazy, that I had invented the shape-shifter story because I couldn't handle the truth. The truth that Sean had kidnapped me, tortured me.

They told me that my mind had broken when I saw that it was Sean holding me. They told me shape-shifters don't exist.

When I got better at lying, they let me out. It had been months. I didn't bother searching for Sean. I know he was dead because right after I was found, there was a massive forest fire in the very same area of the forest. I knew in my heart it was the shape-shifter covering it's tracks and destroying the evidence. Burning the remains of Sean to a crisp so that he'd never be exonerated.

That thing is still out there, and that terrifies me. I think about how many people he has eaten. How many times he set up an innocent man to look like a serial killer. Like Sean.

Sean was a good guy.

I know this. I knew this. I think.

But sometimes I wonder. Maybe I did go crazy.

And then I drink. It's easier that way.

LAST ROOM OF THE CAVE

Tara. A Devlin

A few days ago I heard about this place called Sorrow's Cave. I've never been there, but supposedly deep within the cave there's a room. If you find this room, you'll be granted five minutes with a recently departed loved one. No more, no less.

Three months ago the love of my life passed away after a long battle with breast cancer. She passed before I could reveal to her the secret I was keeping the whole time we were together. If there was even half a chance it could be true, I wanted—no, needed—to try it out.

There's a certain feeling that comes over you when you no longer have anything left to lose. When Shelley passed away, it was like the last light in the house had turned off. I was surrounded by darkness. Shelley was the reason I was still alive. During my darkest moments, she found me and she saved me, asking for nothing in return. Even so, I had betrayed her. I kept a secret from her, and with each passing day, it was eating away at me. The guilt was so violent that some days it was a struggle to wake up, let alone get out of bed. But the more I slept, the more nightmares I had. They were consuming me. I needed to let Shelley know, but she was gone. This was my only chance. I needed to find it, and I needed it to be real.

Bushes rustled in the wind. Clumps of dirt and rock blew by. A branch even hit me in the face as I pressed through the mounting storm, but the pain didn't register. There it was, just ahead of me. A tiny entrance, barely large enough for a full grown man to crawl through. Good thing I wasn't claustrophobic.

I got down and squeezed into the hole. My shoulders got stuck halfway, but after a little wiggling I made it through. The cave was pitch black. I fumbled around in my pocket and pulled out my lighter. It cast just enough light to see the area before me. There was a torch on the wall beside me. I smiled; without a doubt, this was the place.

I took the torch and made my way down the tunnel. The last room of the cave was where I could find Shelley. It got colder the farther I went, but I was too excited to care. There was a single door at the end of the tunnel. I grabbed the handle, but my heart was pounding in my throat. I'd been rehearsing what I wanted to say for weeks, but it always sounded too impersonal forced. In the end, I decided to just see where the moment took me. I braced myself for what I might see inside and opened the door.

The room was large, hollow, and empty. Looking closer, it wasn't even a room. This was the cave proper. Several tunnels snaked off in different directions, each blacker than the last. Something like a dog's growl rumbled down the middle tunnel. I jumped. Whatever that was, I didn't want to be around for it. I took the tunnel on the left, picking up the pace just in case. I walked for about five minutes before I was faced with three doors; one in front of me, one to either side. They were nondescript, exact replicas of the one I used to enter. I went through the middle door.

"So, you're back to ruin even more lives, huh?"

It was the voice of my mother. But that was impossible, because my mother died five years ago.

"H-hello?" I stammered, my voice betraying my attempt at confidence.

"You always were good for nothing. Knew it from the moment you were born." It was the tone she took with me ever since I was a child. I was nothing but a hassle. A time hog. A money drain. A nuisance. I held her back. Kept her from achieving her dreams. For the longest time, I even believed it.

"M-mother, is that you?"

"Well, I certainly ain't Santa! Not that he ever came to visit a naughty boy like you." My brother Kyle always received presents. Me? I got the joy of watching him receive them. But where was the voice coming from? How was she here?

"I don't understand—"

"Of course you don't. Moron."

The words stung. I didn't think my mother could hurt me anymore. It had been five long years now. I'd grown up and moved on, but not so far as to be safe from her.

"How are you here? Why are you here? Where are you?" Aside from my torch, the room was pitch black. What little I could see from the flickering light only showed a large, empty space before me.

"You didn't think this would be easy, did you? That you wouldn't be tested? You don't deserve to be free of your guilt."

My heart pounded and my chest seized.

"Oh yes, don't think I don't know your dirty little secrets. I know them all. Every. Single. One." The voice enunciated slowly and pointedly, but the final words weren't the voice of my mother. It was something else entirely.

"Who are you?" I screamed. Shadows danced in the corners of the room. It was empty, but I wasn't alone.

"I know why you're here." The voice was deep now. It was no longer pretending to be my dead mother. "You long for release from your guilt. Well, I'm here to give it to you."

"I-I'm just here to see Shelley." I didn't know why I was trying to reason with a disembodied voice, but in my confusion, it was all I could think of.

"You don't deserve to see Shelley. The only thing you deserve is death."

I heard the growl again. It was coming from the other side of the door. I took off running, finding myself down yet another winding tunnel. I heard the click of the door opening as my feet pounded on the rock below. 'Keep moving,' I told myself. 'You just need to keep moving.'

I reached a dead end. There were two doors, once again exact replicas of the ones before. I took the one to my right.

"It's not gonna be that easy, you know." It was the voice of my best friend, Terry. Well, former best friend. "All you do is leave a trail of death in your wake."

"Shut up. Shut up!"

"If it wasn't for you, my daughter would still have a father. My mother would still have a son."

"It wasn't my fault!"

There was nothing to distinguish this room from the one I was just in. For all I knew, it was the exact same one.

"No, it's never your fault, is it? It's always everyone else's but yours. Isn't that how it goes? Ol' Johnny boy gets off scot-free while everyone else takes the fall."

"I always knew he was trouble. From the moment he was born." It was my mother's voice. Now they were talking to each other.

"What do you want from me?!"

"To face the truth," they said in unison.

"You never did tell your mother about what really happened the day I died, did you?"

"Terry, please…"

"Go on, tell her."

"Yes, go on. Tell me."

"You're not even rea—"

"Tell her!" The voice boomed. I covered my ears, but the sound echoed throughout the empty room.

I'd done my best to forget about that day. We were only 19 and looking for a cheap hit. Terry had first introduced me to marijuana six years earlier, 'to take the edge off,' and by the time I was 19 we were both full-blown addicts. I spent a long time rehabilitating myself, and it was not a period of my life I liked to remember.

"W-we went to the park downtown," I began, feeling like a child before my mother's disapproving glare again. "Terry said he knew a guy. We could get some good cheap bud."

As much as I tried to erase them, the images were forever burned into my mind. We arrived and the first thing I saw was Shelley sitting on a bench. The light hit her hair just right and it was like looking at an angel. My heart actually fluttered. Then I saw who she was with: my brother, Kyle. He took a bite out of her ice cream cone. They were on a date. In a single instant my hopes and dreams were crushed. I wasn't even surprised, not really. Kyle was always the favorite. Kyle did well in school, was popular with both students and teachers, had a solid job and even more solid plans for the future. Me? I was a high school dropout living on my best friend's couch getting high every day.

"Let's get out of here," I said, putting a hand on his shoulder.

"What? We just got here!"

"I don't feel well. We can come back tomorrow."

"You can come back tomorrow. I'm gonna get this shit now."

I shrugged. "Whatever, I'm outta here. Do what you want."

"Hey, isn't that your brother? Who's the chick he's with? She's hot. I'd hit that with the fist of an angry God, if you know what I'm saying. You should ask him for her number, we can invite her over sometime and—"

"I said I'm outta here."

I swallowed.

"I was around the corner when I heard the gunshots," I said to the thing using my mother's voice. Maybe it really was her. I wouldn't have put it past her to come back to torture me some more. "I went back and saw Terry running towards me. Turned out his guy was actually an undercover cop, and Terry had his gun. I freaked out. I mean, who wouldn't? He started running across the road, calling out my name."

I closed my eyes. No matter how hard I tried, I couldn't erase the sounds.

"He called out to me again. He was standing in the middle of the road, calling my name with a gun in his hand. I saw the car coming towards him, but I—"

"But you let me die." It was Terry's voice.

"I-I was in shock. I didn't know what was going on."

"You knew exactly what was going on. You didn't just let me die. Go on. Tell your mother what type of son she brought into the world."

"Yes, boy. Tell me."

"Tell you what? There's nothing to tell." That was a lie. I knew it was a lie and they knew it was a lie. I didn't just see the car coming for him.

"I... I wanted it to hit him," I admitted. "He made a comment about Shelley and seeing my brother there with her like that just made me angry. I wanted to take it out on someone. Anyone. It was just for a moment, but it was long enough. The car hit him and he died before he reached the hospital."

I'd never vocalized my feelings out loud before. I actually felt a little better.

"I should have aborted you when I had the chance. If it wasn't for your brother—"

She was speaking, but her voice wasn't the only sound in the room. Something was scratching at the other side of the door.

I took off.

"Running like usual," my mother called after me, but I didn't care. I didn't want to be around for whatever that thing was. I couldn't let it stop me from finding Shelley. The sound of my feet pounding on the ground below echoed off the cave walls around me. Through endless tunnels and open spaces, I kept moving forward until I was sure I could no longer hear the thing behind me. Before I knew it, I was lost.

"Alright. It's okay. You can do this." I leaned hard on the wall, waiting for my breathing to return to normal before I could walk on. The farther I went into the cave, the more doors appeared. They were all exactly the same. I was starting to suspect it didn't matter which door I took if they all went to the same place. The longer I traveled without entering a door, the more doors appeared. The cave wanted me to go inside. There was a growl. It echoed down the tunnel. I grabbed the nearest handle and turned.

"John."

No. It was the one voice I didn't want to hear right now.

"Cat got your tongue?"

I couldn't respond. My body refused.

"Probably weren't expecting to hear from me today, were you?"

It was my brother, Kyle.

"I have someone with me."

No. Anything but that. Anyone but her. I dropped to my knees and covered my ears, but it was futile.

"Hi, Uncle Johnny."

"S-sarah? Is that you, sweetie?"

"Daddy says to say hi. We miss you."

"I miss you too, sweetie. H-how are you?" It was a strange question to ask a dead child, but the entire situation was strange.

"I'm okay, but it's dark here. Are you going to come visit soon? I asked daddy if we could go and see you, but he said no. I wanna play with Rollo again."

Rollo was my dog. He died a few months before Sarah did.

"M-maybe next time."

"Don't lie to my daughter. You've lied to everyone else your entire life. Don't lie to her."

It was like I was eight years old again, standing in front of mother and being told off for yet another thing I'd managed to screw up. Of course my brother would be off playing with his friends: his reward for being such a 'good boy.' Other than my mother, Kyle was the one person who could always make me feel small, no matter what. He was the perfect son, and I was the failure.

"I'm not—"

"Do you really think you can lie to me, John? Me, of all people? Your one and only big brother? I was the only person who ever believed in you, Johnny. Look where that got me."

I continued staring at the floor. Old habit. If I raised my head when I was being told off it was an instant beating.

"I hear you finally told mum what really happened with Terry that day."

"I—"

"I saw you that day, you know."

I looked up. "What?"

"That day at the park. The day you got Terry killed. I saw you looking over at us with that look in your eyes you always got around Shelley. You know, I waited a real long time for you to make your move, little brother. But you never did.

"You weren't the only one with a crush on her though. I tried to put my feelings aside, I really did. I waited years for you to say something to her, to ask her out, but you never did. But you weren't the only person on the planet that liked her, Johnny. If you weren't going to ask her out then I wasn't going to wait forever just on the off-chance you might finally man up and grow some balls."

I swallowed the lump building in my throat. Kyle never mentioned he had a crush on Shelley, nor that he was waiting for me to make a move. In my drug-fucked depression, I assumed he did it simply to spite me. That's what our family did, right? Stand on whoever was in the way of what we wanted. Now, ironically, I was the only one left. I should have been the first to die.

"I'm sorry." It was all I could say.

"Sorry doesn't bring me or my daughter back to life. Which is why we're really here, isn't it?"

I closed my eyes and shook my head. I jumped as the thing in the tunnels started scratching at the door again.

"Ah, he's back. The longer you draw this out, the closer he's gonna get, you know. The doors won't keep him out forever. They never do."

"W-who is he?"

"Still stammering like you're five years old and mommy just took out the soup ladle. Tsk tsk. But they call him the Wapiti. It's probably easier for you to think of him as the guardian of this cave."

"W-why—" I shook my head. I wasn't a five-year-old kid anymore. I had to get this under control. "Why is he chasing me?"

"Because you were naughty." It was Sarah's voice. "You were naughty and need to be punished."

It wasn't Sarah, it couldn't be, but the words still stung.

"Kyle. Please. You're my brother. How can I get away from it?"

"Oh, so now that it's convenient for you I'm your brother? I see how this works."

"Kyle, please."

"How about you tell Sarah why we're here in the first place, John. Maybe then we'll help."

The scratching at the door was getting more frantic.

"I don't know what you—"

"Yes, you do!" the voice boomed. "Tell her! Tell my daughter why she's dead! Tell her why she was ripped away from her mommy!"

It was the day that changed my life. I never spoke about it to anyone; I didn't even like to think about it myself. I'd never said the words out loud. I wasn't sure I could.

"He's not going to wait much longer, Johnny." The door handle jiggled a few more times and the scratching continued.

"How about I start? Just to get you going. We were in the car, correct?"

"Yes..." I closed my eyes. I could see the flickering lights of the torch through my closed lids, but I could also see that day as clearly as if I was there.

I was sitting in the backseat of Kyle's car with Sarah. They were on their way home from the hospital visiting Shelley, and Kyle had just picked me up to take me to my first job interview in years. I'd been sober from everything for months. I didn't have any suitable clothes though, so Kyle brought me one of his suits.

"Keep it, I have others," he said. I got changed in the back as Sarah slept. I threw my dirty clothes in the front seat and something fell out of my pocket. It was a tiny bag of white powder.

"Don't sugar coat it," Kyle's voice brought me back to the present. "It wasn't just powder. It was heroin."

"I didn't know it was—"

"That's not the point, John! You brought that shit into my car!

My baby girl was sleeping right next to you. I only agreed to meet you again after all those years—only let you see your niece again because you said you were clean! You weren't clean, John! Another lie!"

"But I was!"

There was a scratch at the door so deep it pierced my ears.

"More lies, Johnny."

I was sitting on a couch, a line of powder and a rolled up piece of paper before me. Over the years I'd tried so hard to justify my actions. I'd told myself so many lies that I didn't know what was true anymore.

"I could see it in your eyes, Johnny. You were high when you got in my car, and the only reason I didn't kick you out right then was because Sarah was so happy to see you. Well that was the biggest mistake of my life, wasn't it?"

I wasn't clean. I was never clean. That was the truth I'd tried to forget.

"So go on. Tell my baby what happened next."

"What happened, Uncle Johnny?"

Sarah's voice, so young and innocent, was a sword through my heart.

"I… I did something silly, sweetie." I jumped and there was a bang at the door. It started to crack. My heart pounds frantically in my chest.

"I lied to your daddy. I had something I shouldn't have. I-I tried to get it back."

Kyle picked up the bag from the seat and held it up while he was driving. 'What the hell is this? Did you bring fucking drugs into my car?'

"No, I—" I tried to snatch the bag away. I was ashamed, but I also didn't want him taking it away from me. I needed it. I spent a lot of money on it. It was mine.

"I'm going to take you to this interview," he said, his voice level and calm. "When you get out, you're never going to contact me again. Do you understand?"

I tried to grab the bag. "Kyle. Kyle please."

"If you try to contact me or Shelley or Sarah again, I will call the police."

I said nothing. I just stared at the bag of powder in his hand. It was singing to me a siren's song and it was all I could hear. I leaped forward and grabbed it, pulling it from Kyle's hand. The steering wheel veered hard to the right. We crashed. Everything went black. When I came to, there were sirens approaching in the distance and both Kyle and Sarah were dead.

"Because of you."

"Because of me." It was the first time I'd ever said it out loud. The first time I'd ever allowed myself to admit it. I wiped a tear away. Big boys didn't cry. Only nasty little weak boys did.

Planks in the door started to crack.

"Kyle, if that's really you, please! I know I don't have any right to ask you of all people, but I need to see Shelley. How do I find her?"

There was silence. Silence except for the banging at the door. I turned just as one of the panels went flying. Through the light of the torch, I saw claws grasping at either side of the newly created hole. Eyes peered through the gap, glowing like those of a cat in the firelight. Antlers protruded from just above its eyes, and as it rose to full height I saw the body of a man. At least, it looked like a man.

"Uncle Johnny. You should run now."

She didn't need to tell me twice. I threw the torch at the creature as it burst through the door and took off running in the dark. I had no idea where I was going but, it didn't matter. I just needed to get away from that thing. I ran until my lungs burned and my calves ached. Then I ran a little more. Images kept playing over in my head. Kyle getting that car set I wanted instead of me on my sixth birthday. My mother taking out the soup ladle when I came home with an F on my report card. That bully who gave me a bloody nose in the fifth grade before Kyle broke his right back. The art teacher in middle school who told me I should look for job alternatives because life as an artist was only for the truly talented. That first puff of marijuana at 13. My first hit of acid at 16. Running from dealers we had no money to pay. Shelley's smile. The way she looked at me when…

There was a door. Two torches were lit on either side of it. Unlike the others, this one was old, heavy, and deep red. There was a noise behind me. I turned to see the creature—the Wapiti—standing at the other end of the tunnel. I backed into the door, fumbling for the handle. It had to be at least two meters tall, even taller if you took its antlers into account. It was like a minotaur, broad and muscular with a long face like an elk. It stood there watching me, unmoving. It would be easy to mistake it for a statue if not for the rise and fall of its chest as it breathed.

I pushed the door handle and went inside.

The room was small and round. Two torches sat on opposing walls and steps carved into the cave led to another room above. With each step I could feel myself breaking down. All the lies I'd told over the years. All the pain I'd inflicted on others, and on myself. It washed over me, threatening to drown me. Only I kept moving. I didn't allow myself to break down into tears until I'd reached the top step.

"Hi."

It was Shelley.

She was sitting in the middle of the room, as beautiful as I remembered her. I stood up, dusting the dirt off my jeans but unable to stem the flow of tears.

"What's all that for?" she said. Another sob racked my body. I didn't trust my voice not to betray me. I took a step, and then another until finally I was standing before her. She held her hand out. "Here. Come on." I grabbed it. It was warm.

I fell into her lap and cried. She brushed my hair and waited, but when I looked up all I could say was: "I'm sorry."

"What do you have to be sorry for?"

"I... I lied to you. All this time I lied. I'm sorry."

She smiled. She didn't look angry or tell me off like everyone else always did. She just smiled and squeezed my hand. I missed that smile so much.

I took a deep breath. "There's something I need to tell you."

I was the only survivor of the crash. As I watched the ambulance take away the dead bodies of my brother and niece, I heard the officer asking for my name. Who was I? What was I doing in the car? How had the accident happened?

"Kyle," I replied, in a daze. "My name is Kyle."

"Can you tell us the names of the other occupants in the car?" they asked me. "My daughter, Sarah, and my brother, John."

All I could think about was Shelley. Shelley was sick and in the hospital. The loss of both her husband and her daughter would kill her. I couldn't do anything about Sarah, but Kyle and I were identical twins. I was high. I'd just been in a high-speed crash. I said the first thing that came to mind.

"My name is Kyle."

"Did you know?" I asked, searching her eyes. I didn't deserve such kindness, and I couldn't understand why she was giving it to me even now. "All that time we were together, did you know that I wasn't really Kyle?"

"I knew." She squeezed my hand again. "You might be a physical copy of your brother, but I knew. It was the little things. You sat on the left side of the couch instead of the right. You tapped with your feet when you were nervous and not with your fingers. And I saw you sitting up until the small hours of the morning trying to learn your brother's business so there would be enough money for my hospital care. I knew, Johnny. I knew."

It was the first time she'd ever said my name. My real name. Another tear ran down my cheek.

"Why... why didn't you ever say anything?"

She stood up and began to walk around the room, running her fingers along the cave walls. "For the first time in your life, you were trying to do something right. Kyle loved you, you know? He spoke about you a lot, but he just didn't know what to do to get through to you. You were the only family he had left. When I realized that you weren't him... I also realized you were working hard and turning your life around. I wasn't going to stop that. I was dying—we both knew it. But you still did all you could to make my final months on Earth as pain-free as possible." She stopped before me and held my face in her hands. "It's okay, Johnny. You can let go now. Thank you."

I closed my eyes as the tears flowed. When I opened them, she was gone.

I didn't run into the Wapiti on my way out. There were no more voices and no more doors. As I exited the cave, the moon was had emerged and the rain was gone. A wolf howled in the distance, but for the first time in my life, I felt relief.

I made my way back towards the car. Back towards the first day of the rest of my life.

SOMEBODY LOVES YOU

J. Speziale

As a social worker, I have heard terrible and heartbreaking things from the children that live in my foster care facility. Most of them have suffered in unimaginable ways. They are victims of abuse, neglect, and worse. A young girl named Sara has been living here for the past 6 months. Sara was placed into foster care after losing both of her parents. She has no other living relatives.

Today was Valentine's day, and each of the children left me a card on my desk. I didn't have time to read them during the day. I had to work late into the night, while all the children were asleep. While sorting through the brightly colored valentines, I also noticed a large stack of yellow notebook paper sticking out of the pile. After studying it for a few moments, I soon realized it was a story that Sara had written for me. As a form of therapy, I often have the children express themselves through art, whether it be painting or writing. Sara had locked herself away in her room the past few days. This must have been what she was so busy with. As I flipped through the paper, and read the words scribbled in black crayon, my stomach turned with unease. Upon correcting the jumbled mess of words, I was able to decipher her story:

There was a bad man that lived in our house. He loved mommy, even more than daddy did. His eyes were big and black, but his skin and clothes were very white, so I called him Mr. Chalk. Mommy and daddy couldn't see him. Mr. Chalk always stood behind mommy. When she turned around, Mr. Chalk disappeared. He was very good at hiding.

During the daytime, Mr. Chalk crawled really fast and went under the stairs. He liked to sleep there. When night time came, he wiggled out and followed mommy around. He always grabbed mommy's hair, and played with it. He loved mommy's hair the most. She looked confused when she felt him touch it.

Sometimes Mr. Chalk stood behind daddy, I told him to turn around and look. Daddy wouldn't believe me, and said that it was just my imagination. Mr. Chalk told me that he didn't like Daddy. He talked different than other people. I didn't like his voice. Mr. Chalk said that he was going to make daddy go away, so he could follow mommy around forever. That made me cry. When I told daddy what Mr. Chalk said, daddy got mad. He made me go to my room.

One night I was in the living room playing with my dolls. Daddy was at the top of the stairs. I looked up and started crying. Mr. Chalk was standing behind daddy. I told daddy to turn around, but Mr. Chalk pushed him. Daddy fell down the stairs. His head hit the floor with a big boom and blood was coming out. I heard mommy scream. I looked up and saw Mr. Chalk. He was clapping and smiling, but I couldn't hear the claps. When mommy tried to wake daddy up, Mr. Chalk stood behind her and played with her hair. She didn't see him. I told mommy that I saw Mr. Chalk push daddy, but she got mad and slapped me. It hurt. The ambulance came and took daddy away. Mr. Chalk followed mommy around more and more after daddy went to sleep.

Mommy and I wanted daddy to wake up and come home. I told

mommy to make breakfast because daddy always woke up for breakfast. Mommy was so sad and stayed in her room and cried all day.

Our neighbor, Mrs. Jones, drove me home after school every day. But one day, when I opened the front door, I saw mommy. She was swinging from a rope above the stairs. She didn't say anything when I screamed. I saw Mr. Chalk too. He was looking up at her, and he was angry. He started pulling all of mommy's hair out.

I ran outside and told Mrs. Jones to help mommy, and she called a policeman. They didn't see Mr. Chalk. The policeman told me that mommy was gone, and daddy was not going to wake up. I had to go live somewhere else.

Mr. Chalk followed me.

He lives at my new home now. I see him at night time. He talks to me. He told me he found someone he loves even more than mommy.

Now he stands behind her at nighttime.

That was the end of Sara's bizarre story. I looked around my empty office, and shivered from a chill that crept down my spine. Part of Sara's story matched up with the police report. Her mother's hair had been pulled out of her head when they found her.

I turned the last page and found a Valentine taped to the bottom of Sara's story. It was a big pink heart that had been cut out of construction paper. In black crayon it read: "SOMEBODY LOVES YOU." Drawn on the heart were two people, I could tell Sara had drawn them. The first was a woman with brown hair. The same woman Sara always drew to represent me, that I had seen in so many of her drawings. The second was of a man, with pale white skin and jet-black eyes. He was reaching towards the woman's head.

As I threw the valentine in my desk drawer, I caught a blurry flash of white out of the corner of my eye. I froze. Something was behind me, I could feel its presence. Icy air brushed against the back of my neck. Then... I felt it. My head jolted backwards as hair was pulled from my scalp. I screamed and whipped around in terror... only to find I was still alone.

BABY LOVE

Leo Bigio

Priiiiiing

My old doorbell rang for the first time in almost ten years. It was so loud that it should be punished by death. It's buzz vibrated the furniture, trembled my organs; I hated it. It was as sharp as a fishing blade, which forced my writing to violent, murderously stop.

I had a marvelous idea for a story an hour before about two children: brothers, running away together with nothing but toys and the air in their lungs. It got me so excited until the ringing echoed from this reality to the one I wished to craft, killing the latter. My fingers were rocks above the keyboard as my mind bended to the source of the damned ringing.

No, I thought. This makes no sense.

You see, only two people exist in my life.

First there's the landlord, Frank. I was sure he had already turned eighty when we first met a decade ago. You'd bet Frank is an ancient ogre if you saw him. Broad shouldered, huge jaw lines, tiny legs—one shorter than the other —he has the facial features of someone who was handsome once. Frank calls me every six months to check if I'm still among the living, even though I never delay with the rent. Sometimes I pick up his call, if I feel like it; inti-

macy shouldn't be given to people easily. Frank spills his life to the phone similar to a torture victim, doing so in exchange for nothing and without being asked. I know he lost a daughter to disease, two wives to divorce, and worked as a gun dealer in a war, although I couldn't say which one.

Priiiiiing

"Who is this?" I said to the unwelcome guest. No response.

Who is this? I thought to myself. No answer echoed back.

The second person in my life is my roommate Maddy. She's allowed to walk freely all around the apartment, but Maddy prefers to stay inside a big silver pan behind the counter in the kitchen. She produces big tasty eggs that are my main source of food, though we girls also eat some fruit, don't we Maddy? She is a secret in this building, for Maddy is a chicken. An adorable black chicken that was stressed out by the doorbell.

So was I.

I've been living alone on the top floor of a sad crooked building for nine years. I chose an 80 foot square apartment because there isn't money left in me for more space, nor is there need. The wood floor is fine for sleeping. I have two shirts, two pair of pants, one pair of shoes. I don't own a television. There's just a glass table in the middle of the single room and a plastic chair so I can work. The walls are black, scrawled with chalk in multiple tones of blue, green... mostly white. Sometimes I draw a flower here or there.

There's a single window facing the west that daily exhibits a corridor of gray walls from the other blocks of the building. There you can see drying underwear and towels and, at the very end, a small square of sky. There's a special hour each day, around a quarter past three, in which we're illuminated by sunlight for a few dozen minutes. It's greeted by great enthusiasm by the calamondin orange tree I garden by the window all year around. Besides this, the apartment is mostly casted in shadows. It took me a long time to nurture this disconnection from the world.

But this?

Priiiiiing

This was ruining it all.

I reluctantly got up, about to welcome this visitor for his persistence, but the peephole told me a secret first. There, lying in the corridor, was no ogre nor salesperson, but a curse. It was a baby. Embraced by a pink blanket, bathed by white light coming from the primitive elevator I dare not use. He had his hand lifted in the air, mesmerized by its shape.

I stepped back in confusion.

Maddy flew wild all around, giving me some insight about my distress. Is it one of the neighbors' children? I put an ear against the cold wood door. And yes. I could hear him crying in the background, muffed. It weeped as an abandoned baby weeps, knowing somehow it became an orphan moments before. I hesitated to look again. The sight of It would make it real—would make it mine.

Someone else will listen to it, I'm sure. Leave it to someone else.

A child. Here. He, Maddy and I, all extremely close and incredibly far.

I turned hot water on to flow heavy over the existence of the infant to no avail. Music met the same fate. My concentration became extinct, for I couldn't work, think, sleep nor feel anything else than this intrusion. There was no going back. The kid's presence dragged the clock, like a distortion in my sacred time, my time alone; it contaminated the orange's scent of the apartment. The pillows and the black walls and the sheets, the wood and plastic. Everything stank of it. Everything stank of the sons and daughters taken out of me a lifetime ago. Their hair and skin, muscles, bones and flesh. I had to be careful not to forget that the baby behind the door wasn't the same as any of the children that died inside of me.

I don't wanna be a mother again. I don't wanna be a mother again.

The orange tree bathed in the rare sunlight as I ran to the window. I wanted to watch the world go down. Whoever abandoned the kid either did it fast or hadn't left yet.

A dog barked in the distance. Cars flew around the horizon, the light hiding itself away. As the room dived in darkness once more, the sun stretched my shadow and my thoughts into a bridge to the child.

What if it's alone? Well, call the authorities then. Do not go out there.

The dispatcher sensed my distress. She instructed that I hold the baby until help came, though that was up to me. Maddy, swollen and frenetic, patrolled the house like a raptor. Side-to-side, she machine-walked moving her periscope of a neck everywhere. I reached for her and she embraced me in her wings; together we sat against the door's wooden surface.

"What to do, my baby love?" I whispered. My breath lifted Maddy's black feathers.

What to do?

If I gave this baby care, doesn't that always become dependency? He would suck me ever dry for more, I was sure. He would change reality with his appearance and smell, twist it to make me feel pity, compelling me to protect him and be his. Even so, my body doesn't allow me to be a mother, so any of that would be fake. It would be fake.

Is that too much paranoia?

Perhaps the dispatcher woman on the phone knew better. And whoever was in that corridor deserved more than a aged lady with nothing to give, nothing to take. Maybe he deserved kindness today.

It's funny how many songs you keep memorized even after a decade repressed in your brain. I made my belly listen to a lot of music in the past that would finally come in handy. Nervous, hesitant and low, the lyrics to "Baby Love," by The Supremes started sneaking out of my mouth, the last one I remember singing before my first miscarriage. It felt ridiculous and nostalgic in my voice.

Baby love, my baby love, I need you oh how I need you

But all you do is treat me bad

Break my heart and leave me sad

The child's whining faded as in the end of a track. It was completely gone when I hit the sixth verse.

I freed Maddy so I could peek out the peephole again. Maybe someone found him? No. He was in the same place with the same white light. But this time I noticed something that broke me. The blanket, his limbs, nothing moved. No particles of dust floated in the white light. The baby slept out of weariness, or worse. Suddenly his silence felt unbearable. Worried, I bent down to call the child through the crack of the door. I told him sweet things, lies. I said everything was gonna be alright. In return, warm, stinky air hit my nose, seeping in through the crack in waves. It was wet, almost unnotice-able, but It was there. Breathing.

"Finish it," whispered a deep voice from the crack.

An urge to scream contorted the muscles of my throat. With much effort, a deep animal growl came out of me in such a way that my face must have appeared melted. My bones barely kept my body glued together. In the confusion, I punched the door to back off; the wood punched me back harder. I fell.

"Finish the music."

Fingers reached under the door to spread across my floor. They moved around the door frame like white spiders, feeling each imperfection in every possible surface. The movement rumbled the door, detaching faster than a dream. Before I could step on them and force them back, Maddy blocked me to peck at the fingernails. They grabbed one of her claws, twisting it. I jumped to Maddy who tried to escape in vain.

"Stop!" I yelled. "Stop it! Stop it!"

The fingers twisted harder. Maddy choked with an impossible clucking. Her tiny claw was cracking softly. I couldn't pull her free or it would make it worse. I ran to the kitchen to get a knife, but the fingers had already pulled Maddy's leg into the crack, breaking it. The fingers sheltered themselves.

"What do you want?!" I yelled. "Wh-what do you want?"

"Finish it," the voice said.

"The police are already on the way!"

"Finish the music."

So I did. Without knowing when it would be enough, I kept singing.

Maddy cried alongside me when the lyrics ended the first time. I started over—then again once more. I sang until the words burned their meaning out. I sang until my dry lips cracked open. Until the music overpowered the crying. Reborn each verse.

Until I couldn't hide the love that lived inside of me. Born again and again, then abandoned years ago. Can expelled love be caught by someone else, like a disease in the air? Can it be recycled?

Resurrected?

I sang the music until I reconstructed the organs inside of me. Bones, muscles. A soul. Until I wondered what would be of the child out there, alone with whoever the fingers belonged to. Until I felt my belly full, my breasts full; until I wished the baby was my own.

Until the door opened.

It was Frank. Behind him, the police. Glued to the peephole, a picture of a baby in a pink blanket bathed in white static light.

ALWAYS CLEAN YOUR SEX DOLL

P.F. McGrail

It really is nothing like what you see in porn.

Well, almost nothing. I did walk into an orgy just once, and yes, they did ask me to join.

But they were old enough to be my parents, and fat enough to legitimately kill me, so I sprinted away from that place as fast as I could without waiting for 'just the tip'.

I never delivered pizzas to that neighborhood again.

But that was not the strangest thing. Not by a long shot.

Apartment 1913. The numbers are ingrained in my memory.

I came to hate that door.

The first time was pretty frickin' innocuous. Friday night, 8:00 PM, one large pepperoni and a two-liter of Coke. I figured it was a couple who had slowly lost their enthusiasm for going out at night, replacing it with the slow creep of apathy for two that's really just a euphemism for death.

The guy who opened the door was relatively young and had probably been pretty fit once. Fifty pounds and seven years after the glory days of high school football, however, he was now sharing his Friday night with me.

But not just me.

Sitting at the table was an anatomically-correct sex doll. I hadn't caught him mid-bang (his sweat pants would have been unable to conceal his state if he'd just pulled out), so he clearly had brought the doll to the table as a social occasion. He made no attempt to hide the thing.

It was awkward.

He asked me to come inside and place the pizza on the table.

That was even weirder. I had to delicately avoid the thing's hand as I gingerly placed the pizza onto the tabletop.

"Careful!" he shouted, pulling the pizza away. He picked up the doll's hand and gently started rubbing it. "That pizza's hot." He looked deeply into the sex doll's eyes, softly kissed her hand, and walked away to get his money. That left me alone at the table with the clearly-used doll.

Did I mention that I hate dolls?

It turns out that they're even creepier when I know they're getting laid more than I am.

I didn't want to look at her/it, but my eyes were glued to those blue ones. Her mouth, locked in a permanent, perfect "O," seemed to beg conversation.

"So," I offered, breaking the ice as he re-entered the room, "that's… a pretty doll… Do you collect them?"

The man turned around, the drawstring from his sweatpants flailing as he spun. "Doll?" he inquired, smiling blankly. "Uh, no, but my sister does."

He then looked over my shoulder at it. "You should put this on your blog, Charlene." He looked back at me, his smile growing. "She loves that blog," he explained, setting the money down on the table.

I could feel the presence of the doll's pseudo-flesh next to mine, which caused the hair on my own arms to rise. The moment that my hair made contact with the doll's arm, which was just an inch away

from the cash, sent a chill down my ass-crack. That was enough
for me.

He smiled and waved as I left.

The man loved his Friday night pizzas.

The following week, I delivered his large cheese and two-liter of
Coke right on time.

It really is a lot for just one person, I thought, as I heard footsteps
approach the door.

When he opened it up, it took me a second to realize what was
unusual.

It was the sex doll, of course.

This time she was leaning on her elbow against the far counter,
like she was lounging around to pass the time.

The thing is, there's no way he could have propped her up there
just before opening the door. I'd heard him walking from the other
side of the apartment. Besides, that thing was clearly heavy enough to
require a lot of effort for any movement.

So I guess she'd just been..... Standing there? Hanging out?

He smiled and waved as I left again.

I kept delivering to his building. What was I supposed to tell my boss?
That I was creeped out by a doll? No, the truth just wouldn't do. But it
got even weirder on the fifth week.

I rang the doorbell as usual, 3,000 calories of sadness in my hands,
and heard a scuffling on the other side.

It was slow scuffling.

Draaaag, flop. Draaaaag, flop. Draaaaaaaaag, flop.

It sounded like he was carrying a body bag across the room.

When the door finally opened, it just popped inwards a crack.
After an awkward silence, I realized that I was expected to enter.

I can't say exactly why I was so unnerved at this fact. It was just so unnatural to crack the door and expect the guest to invite himself in. I pressed my hand against the wood, slowly pushing it into the room.

The doll was leaning against the wall.

She was staring at me.

The man was nowhere in sight.

I looked anxiously around the room for him. I certainly felt like I was being watched. Where the hell was he? This was just... weird. Sick, even.

I realized two things at the same time.

The first was that it was the doll who was making me feel watched.

The second is that, with the flush of a toilet, the man established his presence in the bathroom. That room was tucked around a corner and out of sight.

I wanted out. I took three quick steps to the table and placed the pizza down. Each step further into the place made me feel worse, like I was going into an unholy shrine. I looked quickly around the table for evidence of money so I could justifiably bolt out of the place.

"Charlene has your cash," the man sang out cheerfully.

The fact that he'd known what I was thinking made me want to vomit each of the butterflies that had descended from my stomach to my balls.

I spun around to see Charlene's fingers tightly grasping some bills. Oh, no.

I knew that I'd have to touch the pseudo-skin before I could get out of there. The tears were already forming at the corners of my eyes as I reached out to delicately snatch the cash without touching its skin.

I shouldn't have closed my eyes. My fingertips brushed realistic-feeling skin during my blind fumble. I moved around wildly in the search for the money, feeling far more of her than I wanted to. She was uncomfortably warm.

I finally felt the tip of the bills sticking about two millimeters out from her fingers. It had appeared as though extracting it would be an ordeal, but it slid smoothly from her clutches.

I thought that was good news, until I looked down at my prize and saw it shine with fluid.

No wonder it had slid so nicely.

The urge to vomit kicked hard, but I barely held it in place. Holding the bills aloft, I ran out of the apartment and swore to myself that I'd never come back.

That was last Friday. Today is Friday. I didn't do a delivery route tonight.

My boss was pissed when I told him "no," because I'd never done that before. I didn't care though. I'd lose my job before I'd consent to hanging out with Charlene again.

"Fine, jackass," my boss spat back at me.

Classy guy, by the way.

"But you're closing tonight. By yourself."

Considering what I'd been through the past few Fridays, I figured that this wasn't much of a loss.

I was content with the idea of spending the evening alone in an empty pizza place. Really, I was.

That was before.

Before there was only one car in the parking lot.

Before I looked out and saw that my car was fucking gone.

Before my cell ran out of juice and died much earlier than it normally does.

Most importantly, that was before I looked into the two-passenger car now parked directly in front of the only door in or out of my pizza shop. Because everything changed when I looked into the driver's seat, and saw Charlene, all alone, staring back at me, mouth open wide like she was ready for a slice of piping hot, gooey cheese.

I CAN'T BE UNHAUNTED

P.F. McGrail

I didn't know exactly where I was going, to be completely honest.

I continued down the road with the empty street on my left and a sheer drop-off to my right. I walked in peace for several minutes.

Her voice broke the silence: "You know, you're being a brat."

These moments always frustrated me. Most men would never know how wrong they were until they stepped foot into the dating world. At that point, they could only hope to grasp the fact that they were far too wrong even to understand how incorrect they were.

As such, I didn't know what to say. Contradicting her would mean proving her right, and accepting her would mean proving her right.

I walked on in silence.

She slowed, pulling my arm to halt us and turn us toward each other. "Hi. I'm glad you came out here with me."

She smiled, and it was genuine. I couldn't help smiling back.

Damn it.

We continued walking; I pondered her tendency to pepper cordial greetings in the middle of the pre-established conversation. It was uniquely her.

I finally said what was really on my mind. "I don't understand. It's not fair."

"It's not fair because you don't understand, or you don't understand because it's not fair?"

I struggled for words. "Both," I finally conceded.

"Do you need to understand? Or do you just need to be with me for a stretch?" She stopped again. Holding me in place, she wrapped her arms around me and pulled her waist close to mine. She leaned her head back so she could still see me. "I didn't understand how you were beating me in chess, and that's why I lost. You didn't understand how I was beating you in Quattro, and that's why you lost. Sometimes the only way forward is accepting that we don't understand. Otherwise nothing great can ever happen, can it?"

I looked away in an attempt to unsuccessfully hide my smile.

"Hey," she said. "I like you." She turned and began walking away, dropping her hands from my waist so I would have to make an effort to follow.

I caught up. "You always had a way with words," I confessed.

She grinned again. "I am youth."

I frowned. "And you always will be, I think."

She turned away sadly. "Will that haunt you?"

I looked at her. "It already is."

I peered down at my feet and we continued for a stretch. When I glanced up, I saw a small stone edifice by the edge of the precipice.

"Look over there on the right," I pointed out.

She peered down at the thumb and index finger of both hands.

"Michelle, you're one of the smartest people I know. How can you not tell your left from your right?"

She smirked. "It's a real thing. I'm still extremely smart. I went to a school that was harder to get into than Harvard."

I rolled my eyes and pointed at the stone. "That's the Cathedral Oak Monument. Supposedly, the first Easter Mass ever celebrated in California was right there." I paused. "Is there something after —after?"

She walked on pensively. I could tell that the answer she was about to give wasn't what she would have said before.

"Immortality is measured in how we affect one another," she finally said.

I tried to come up with a response to that. I could not.

We walked past the monument, and it receded in the distance.

We passed by a house that was under construction. The address said 1913 Arroyo Drive, but no one lived there. It was still being built, but in my mind, it was already beautiful.

I continued to struggle. "It isn't fair," I finally said. "The last time I talked to you, it's—it isn't what I wanted to say."

"Well," she responded, "what would you say to me now?"

I fought for words. "But whatever you say back—it's not what you would have said before. Not really."

"So where do those words, the ones I'm so good with, come from now?"

I pulled on my hair. "They come from the effect you had on me, I guess, for better or worse."

"There is the answer to the last question you asked," she said with a final sort of tone.

I dropped my hands to my sides. "But that's not what I wanted. It isn't even the effect I wanted to have."

She turned to me and gave a sad sort of tight-lipped smile. "Nope."

I was exasperated. "So what do I do now?"

She laughed, just slightly, to herself. "What would you want from me, if our positions were reversed?"

I thought for a long while as I walked. I was surprised when I realized that I knew the truth.

"I'd want you to let me go."

She stopped walking, and, once again, she pulled my waist into hers. She was staring directly at me. "And why is that?"

I looked back at her sadly. "Because, if I were you, I would want to move on."

She leaned in and kissed me, gentle yet urgent, and then she was gone. I turned and continued toward home. I finished my walk alone, as I had started it. I traveled mostly unhaunted, and, lucky or unlucky, was disturbed only by the occasional companionship of ghosts.

Happy Birthday, Michelle.

TITS

P.F. McGrail

It had always come easy to me, if I'm being honest.

Honest, or arrogant.

At the time, I saw them as the same thing.

Take that for what it's worth.

Her tits were the first things I noticed. She did it on purpose, of course. They all did.

I always asked two questions: Age? How many minutes is she worth pursuing? She was a 19/13 on this scale, which made her quite an ambitious target, to be sure. But what's the point of the hunt if your quarry can't give chase? How do you feel powerful if there's not at least a little bit of squirming?

An accidental graze at first. I couldn't make it seem like I came across the room just for her. My perfect smile; she grins back and looks at her feet. Good. I walk away.

Lead with the smile when I return thirty minutes later. I've waited until she's next to a bottle of liquor, so I have to reach around her just a little bit. She sees my ass. I see hers. I rest one hand on her hips as the other reaches past. Offer to pour her a drink as well.

The third time I engage is when she's talking to a guy who's way out of his league. I butt in and make a crass joke about him. He's dumbfounded. She's smiling behind her hand. I tell him that 'Rick' is looking for him, and he awkwardly slinks away. This time I put my hand around her waist, and we walk out of the room.

When executed perfectly, the prey thinks it wants the snare.

∾

Something about foreplay reminds me of butter melting on a crispy waffle. The boundaries get blurred. Warm. Sweet. Decadent between the teeth.

She brushed the first feel away. The second was under her top, rather than over it. I kissed behind her ear when I undid the clasp on her bra (one-handed). That's the key: give her a rush, and it's undone before she knows it. When she brushed my hand away the second time, her bra started to slip. She smiled despite herself.

Her top came off shortly after that. And yes, her tits were worth the wait. Large, but grab-able. Firm enough to maintain their shape, yet soft enough to yield under a gentle caress. Nipples like chocolate candy, almost chewy. She liked the biting. She tried to hide it, but she couldn't.

That's when I got up to start the camera.

I told her it was to turn on some music, of course. Why is Barry White the soundtrack for fucking? I never did understand the desire to hear a velvet-voiced man when I was balls deep.

Whatever. It got the job done.

I flicked on the music. She didn't even see what else I was doing.

No time to waste. Breaking physical contact this late in the game is dicey.

Even when she's down to her panties, it's never a sure thing. I slid my fingers inside the cotton, but kept them along the edge of her hips.

When my hand is in her panties, but away from the fun parts, it's much more effective than going straight for the kill.

She breathed faster. It was working.

I kept my hand in place. It had the simultaneous effect of tantalizing her and disarming her.

That was the kill shot.

Nothing compares to the moment when she arches her hips for a pantie removal.

My pulse thundered in my ears.

Of course, the opposite scenario provides its own fun.

You see, for most guys, there's nothing to compare with the disappointment in the moment they realize they're not going to get laid.

I prefer to bypass that moment.

Because there's nothing to compare with the look on her face when she realizes that she is going to get laid, even if she doesn't want it. That's the best part of filming it. The dawning moments of realization are the parts I revisit the most.

I have at least three dozen of those moments recorded.

This time, however, she goes along with a smile and no fight.

Slut.

She pushes me onto my back and crawls forward, a hungry glint in her eye. She crawls to the head of my bed, legs spread with one of her knees by each of my elbows, and I check: shaved or unshaved?

She moves quickly. Pretty pushy skank, actually. She brings her hips to my lips and I see—

What.

Definitely unshaved, but there's more. Hairy spider legs, at least a foot long, reach out from her crotch. I squirm, but her knees hold me in place with surprising force. I open my mouth to scream.

Bad idea.

Eight hairy, bristly legs wrap themselves around my head and caress me, almost lovingly. Her crotch is pressed firmly against my mouth, my open mouth, and something goes inside.

It becomes immediately apparent that it's a stinger. Pain rips through my entire head as it pierces my tongue. I can feel the blood begin to flow down my throat.

Time to throw this bitch onto the ground.

But I don't. I don't move at all. I can't squirm, I can't scream, I can't do anything but watch. I realize in horror that the stinger must have had a paralytic, and it must have acted incredibly fast. I realize with equal horror that the paralytic has done absolutely nothing to diminish any sensory input. The pain in my mouth only gets more intense. I pray that I am going to pass out.

I don't pass out. I want to be away from her. I can't get away from her. Tears obscure my vision as I realize I'm going to experience every second of what's about to happen.

The legs work furiously. The bristly fur rakes my cheek. The arachnid exoskeleton is cold, but the rubbing sensation is unpleasantly warm.

She slides the legs up and down my neck, slowly. One leg reaches behind my ear, then slides inside of it. It has a pincer on the end. It's very sharp.

Two more legs slide through my hair. I want to moan in protest, but I can't.

My mouth is full anyway. The stinger slides in and out of my tongue. The lightning bolts of pain rocket back and forth through my entire head.

The legs pull tighter, like they're trying to crack a walnut. I had thought that the pain couldn't get any worse, but I was wrong.

I didn't want to die in that moment. But if I'm being honest, I would have been kind of okay with it.

The legs pull back and I have a moment of hope. That moment is summarily crushed when I feel eight pincers on my cheeks.

This. This pain is the worst imaginable. This time, when the pincers dig at my yielding flesh like a badger upturning fresh loam, I do want to die.

It's impossible to tell what pieces of me are being torn apart. The pain is too great. All I know is the hurt, and there is nothing else at all, nothing, nothing.

I don't know when she stopped. Time had gotten wobbly. I just know that there was an end to things.

You'd think I'd be overjoyed that it was over, but it stayed with me. Some experiences can't be left behind. Sometimes, the present can't become the past.

She pulled her panties back on, plucked my camera from its hiding place, and was gone.

I never saw her again, but the world saw me. That video had gone viral before I regained motor control. My face, of course, was prominent; I had been looking right into the camera when I turned it on.

I miss my face.

That was the last time I picked up a stranger and took her home. That was the last time I went to a party. That was the last time I had sex. That was the last time I kissed a girl.

No one wants to kiss the man with a hideous gummy-taffy mess where a face used to be. They want to look, but never touch.

Everything in my life is different now.

Some things never get left in the past. They tangle themselves into who we are, like musty cobwebs, and only get more intertwined when we try to pry them away.

It turns out that one of those things is unwanted sex.

THE WAGES OF SIN IS ETERNAL LIFE

P.F. McGrail

The first time I died was easily the scariest, but it was far from the most painful. One sensation comes from a lack of knowledge, and the other from an abundance of it.

After a certain point, pain and knowledge become inseparable.

The first death was simple. I was a pauper living on the outskirts of Rome. I had just lifted some denarii from a wealthy traveler, and was walking quickly away when he slid a knife between my ribs. I had lived a poor man's life, died a poor man's death, and was forgotten by the world the next day.

The pauper's grave was easy enough to rip apart. I tore through the dirt with surprising ease, emerging in the daylight to find the world had decided to keep me in mind after all.

I had no idea what made me able to rise up. Imagine my shock to find that five years had passed. I understood on an intellectual level that the world would persist after my own death, but I found myself horrified to find that people had continued to live on as though my passing had no effect on the world I'd left behind.

No one really accepts the fact that their own death will ultimately leave the universe unmarred.

Revenge consumed my mind in those early years. There was nothing left of my old life, so I was determined to find the man who had taken it away. After three years of fruitless searching, I came to the realization that he had tricked me. My thirst for vengeance had prevented me from being happy. Even after my resurrection, the man had managed to continue to steal my life. I hated myself for it, and so I began the slow process of letting the pain go.

It took me a year to make real progress. I understood that there must be some meaning to my life if my death wasn't permanent, so I searched for the purpose beyond my baser instincts. For the first time, I started to believe that there was one. I actually came to forgive my killer.

I encountered him by chance nine years after he'd first stabbed me. My inner peace did nothing to stop my desire to hurt him, and I was surprised to find myself attacking almost immediately. I didn't care if I got caught; I just wanted him dead.

After I pulled his own knife from his bag, he never had a chance. I stood over his bloody corpse, chest heaving, and assumed that someone would tackle me and drag me to a pauper's cell.

No one did. I was free to live my life as I saw fit.

I was horrified to find that I was none the happier. The man's last laugh was giving me exactly what I'd wanted.

All it did was prove that my pursuit had been a waste from the beginning.

And so I learned to be alone. I don't mean that I simply existed in solitude. I contoured my soul to accept the fact that the majority of the self is isolated so deeply in our own minds that no person will ever truly know us.

That knowledge helped me to face life and survive it.

It was always the same. I lived. I died. Five years later, I rose again. My body couldn't burn or rot. Wherever it had been left, it was reanimated with renewed vigor. Each new rising was accompanied by a short burst of strength that allowed me to escape my tomb. The strength always faded once I was free, and then I began life anew.

I embraced my solitude—which was occasionally physical and perpetually spiritual—as a talisman rather than a burden.

Everyone you've ever loved will die one day. You haven't accepted that. No one has. We need to deny death if we want to live life. I just haven't had that luxury.

That's my pain. That's my knowledge. And it was ripped away from me when I met Wendy.

∾

Attending lectures was a habit that I'd developed around the eighteenth century. I could be close enough to a large group of people to feel the humanity around me, but remained anonymous enough to prevent anyone from caring about me.

Loving someone means making yourself vulnerable. It's not that it comes with the territory; the two concepts are simply one and the same.

I had remained blissfully unloved, yet still able to feel the flow of humanity. The speaker at these lectures connected with each individual listening, but there was no reciprocation needed.

In 2003, Wendy was a college senior who was heading up a trip to Rwanda to dig wells for drinking. I listened to her lecture and thought I'd be ill.

Over the times and times, I had learned to pursue only prostitutes. They were the most honest people I'd ever met. They knew value and boundary like no other.

I didn't understand why Wendy made me ill. I just knew I had to talk to her. I searched centuries' worth of memory to find a way to introduce myself in a way that was charming but not pushy, intellectual without arrogance. I wanted to impress her without seeming like I needed to impress her.

I approached her after the lecture.

"Um. Hi."

Her smile made me feel sick again.

∾

I'll be honest. Most people would have called her a six, maybe a seven on a good day. She was extra curvy and rarely wore makeup. Her Midwestern twang made the occasional word hard to understand. If Wendy had an opin- ion, she made it known, and it was usually about remembering the forgotten people of the planet.

Maybe that's what got to me. I didn't think of myself as forgotten until she remembered everything about me. It scared me that she knew exactly what I was thinking when so little had to be said. Wendy had a light in her eyes that eluded written explanation. She gave me the things I was missing without having to say what she was doing.

There's a million bullshit sayings about "you know you're in love when..."

I'd dismissed every one with the casual flourish bred from several life- times of cynicism.

It petrified me to see how easily Wendy broke that shell. I had thought it impenetrable, but she overcame my defenses without even trying. I was flab- bergasted to find that the layers of solitude I'd thought so strong were in fact almost nothing, nothing at all.

Love is when you find someone you never knew you needed to survive.

This was an astounding lesson to learn after nearly two millennia of not knowing it.

It's terrifying. The blind man who gains sight will spend the rest of his years fearing for his eyes.

When she said "yes," the look on her face told me that she was even more vulnerable to me than I was to her.

~

In 2008, I was crossing the street. I looked left, the driver looked right, and I died at the scene.

As I lay gasping in the dirt, I already knew it was 2013. When I had regained my breath, I stood up, brushed the grime off the formal suit that had been selected for my burial, and quickly walked across the grass.

As I exited, I gave an awkward smile to the slack-jawed funeral attendees under the large tent.

~

I'd learned long ago that confronting people who had known me before I died was a bad idea. Eventually, I'd realized it was best to move on entirely with a clean slate.

Things were different this time. I was different. She had made me weak.

I first saw her in a coffee shop. She'd aged ten years in five, and that light was now dim.

I'm ashamed to say that made me feel good about myself.

I had planned a delayed re-introduction. But once I saw her, it was far too late. My legs worked of their own accord as I approached the front door.

She looked up, and the light grew. I nearly tripped over my own feet when I saw it. She stood, held out her arms, and embraced a stranger. She kissed him, and she meant it.

My legs, still acting independently of my mind, quickly carried me away from the carnage.

∾

I'm good at making connections. Sometimes those connections are, by necessity, dark.

We all need evil things at some point in our lives. We simply learn to adjust our perspectives until we're able to see in the shadows. Then they don't seem so dark. The cat is a monster to every mouse, and the farmer will cause more death than any army, but everyone finds a way to sleep at night.

I didn't know I needed Wendy before I'd met her. That was the only reason I had survived. But the thought of wanting her now, and not being able to have her, was perpetual pain. Death is the salve of the drowning man, but it's a cure I can never embrace.

I had to have her back.

Wendy would never know that her boyfriend had been murdered. There are people who are very, very good at what they do.

It's amazing how much of their souls they will sell for a little cash. In that way, at least, they're indistinguishable from the rest of humanity.

∾

I felt obligated to watch it happen. If you expect other people to live by the choices you make, but cannot face them yourself, rest assured that you made the wrong choice.

I got sick again as she stepped out of her apartment. The years and stress had signed their name in creases and bags on her face, yes. But the way her hair bobbed as she walked down the stairs, the current of wind catching in her sundress, the way I knew she smelled like grapefruit and lavender from across the street, served to turn my stomach and spin my head.

I had to be with her. If the solace of death was an option for me, I might have taken it. But that obligation would have to go to someone else.

Mindless rage coursed through my head when I saw him. Tall, semi-attractive, flecks of gray in his hair. I saw past all of her imperfections and right into his. He was an asshole. Don't ask me to explain why.

The white Mercedes turned down the corner. My fists clenched.

Life can turn on a dime, folks, and your bill is often paid on a stranger's fare.

The car was only going about forty, but that was enough. He closed the gap on them in a space of time that seemed both eternal and infinitesimally small.

She looked up at him for the last time.

And I saw the light on her face.

I was about to turn it off.

Wendy's light.

Me.

I had not wanted to believe that she could heal from me. But she had. She had.

She had.

We tend to assume that healing means we stop hurting, but they are often opposing ideas.

That's the dime. Here's the turn.

It was too late to call off the car. So I sprinted across the street, pulse racing, mouth screaming, tears streaming, snot spilling. I knew there was noise, but I couldn't hear a thing.

Mr. Asshole looked up at me in profound confusion.

I looked at him for the last time.

Our collision stopped me instantly, and I fell flat on my ass. He tumbled between two parked cars and landed harmlessly on the lawn. I looked stupidly behind me, vaguely realizing that the Mercedes logo was at eye level.

I woke up today, in 2018. Every part of me wants to see Wendy.

But I love her enough to give her a clean slate. I will never see Wendy again; it's my final gift.

I waited 1,913 years to find her. And it wasn't just her. I couldn't find me until she changed me. I didn't know how bitter coffee tasted or how soft linen could feel until I met her. Does that make sense?

Probably not.

Suffice to say that the price of four years with Wendy was two millennia without her.

I'm happy to pay that price again.

And it's time to start paying. One day at a time.

Just please don't judge the fact that I always carry two silly things in my pocket.

One is a tiny bottle of grapefruit shampoo. The other is a vial of lavender perfume.

Made in the USA
Middletown, DE
21 February 2020